The Greatest Sin

Illusive
Echoes

Published by Tangled Sky Press
www.tangledskypress.com

First printing, June 2016

ISBN: 978-1-944334-08-6

Illusive Echoes is a work of fiction. Names, places, and incidents are either products of the authors' imaginations or used fictitiously.

Map and cover copyright © 2016 by Alexandra Brandt

Illusive Echoes

The Greatest Sin #4

Lee French & Erik Kort

TANGLED
SKY
PRESS

This book is for all the Kariases of the world. May being trapped in a strange body never stop you from finding adventure, fulfillment, and that one person you can share your true self with. Hopefully, they won't be as cranky and ornery as Chavali.

Other Books by the Authors

The Greatest Sin Series
epic fantasy

The Fallen

Harbinger

Moon Shades

Illusive Echoes

Lee French
In the Ilauris setting
standalone fantasy tales

Damsel In Distress

Shadow & Spice (short story)

Al-Kabar

Spirit Knights
young adult urban fantasy

Girls Can't Be Knights

Backyard Dragons

Ethereal Entanglements

Ghost Is the New Normal (coming 2017)

Maze Beset Trilogy

superheroes in denim

Dragons In Pieces

Dragons In Chains

Dragons In Flight

Anthology Appearances

Into the Woods: a fantasy anthology

Merely This and Nothing More: Poe Goes Punk

Unnatural Dragons: a science fiction anthology

Missing Pieces VIII: short stories from GenCon's Authors Avenue

(coming August 2016)

Non-fiction

with Jeffrey Cook

Working the Table: An Indie Author's Guide to Conventions

Erik Kort

(as Erik Marshall)

Wards of the Thicket

adventure fantasy

Children Without Faces

Children Without Voices (coming 2017)

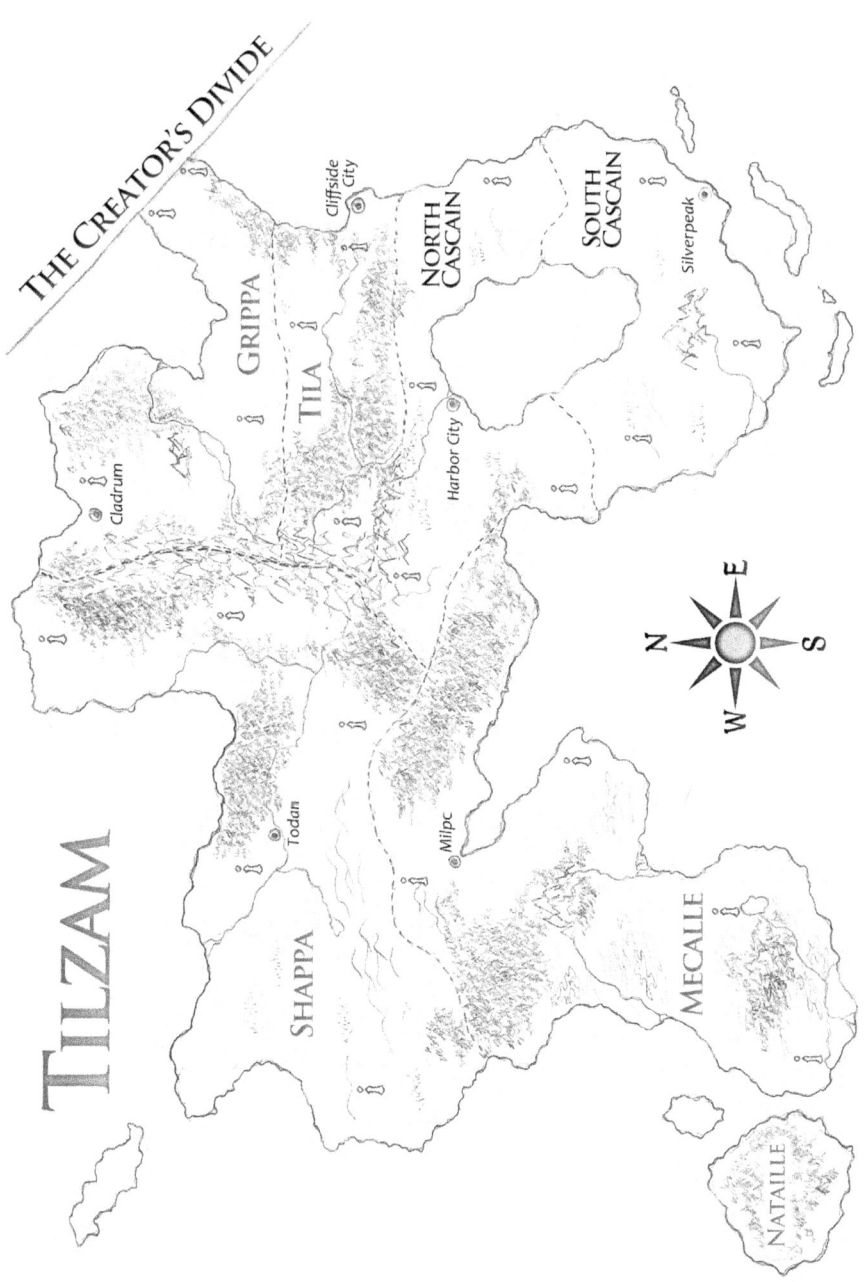

Prologue

Harris took a deep breath of the fine spring air, reveling in the cheerful sunshine and citrusy scent of flowers. At the Fallen tower, small piles of snow still lurked in the shadows while the crocuses pushed up through the mud. Out here in the Shappan countryside, birds chirped, crickets sang, and the hooves of his horse thumped soundly on the packed earth road. The creaking and jangling of the wagon caravan he traveled with blended in his mind, creating pleasant music to accompany the forested scenery.

The delightful weather made up for having to leave. He'd finally figured out Chavali's knife training schedule and had planned to lurk in the shadows of the practice room to watch Eliot teach her. When they finished, he'd intended to intercept her for a chat. Though he couldn't be sure and didn't know why, he suspected she'd been avoiding him since the battle at Eagle Falls. Then again, so far as he could tell, she'd been avoiding everyone but Eliot, Colby, and maybe her healer.

Only now, when he had nothing better to do, did it occur to him to wonder why he hadn't been assigned a healer. Every Fallen he'd met so far seemed to have one at their beck and call. Dozens of those white-robed women roamed the underground corridors of the inverted Fallen tower, so he assumed they had enough to cover all the Fallen agents. If he could get Chavali's healer assigned to him, then he could "accidentally" run into her at the end of her sessions.

He patted the bag slung on the pommel of his saddle, pride surging in his breast for the thirtieth time since Eldrack handed him this assignment. Harris didn't know what was inside the bag, only that it needed to reach the king. With such a notable intended recipient, it had to be important. His soul had been bound to the Fallen, like every other agent, but he hadn't felt completely trusted until Eldrack placed this bag into his care.

Someone in the front shouted and the wagon Harris followed slowed to a stop. The two rear caravan guards trotted their horses past him, heading for the front of the line. Harris's horse stamped and whickered, its ears flicking back and forth. He patted the horse to calm it. Reflexively, he reached for the most valuable thing in his possession and made sure the bag remained secure.

As he rubbed his hand over the bag, he noticed a difference in the noises around him. Other horses seemed as restive as his own. No birds chattered. The crickets had gone silent. A light breeze carried vague murmurs from the front of the caravan.

Growing uneasy, Harris twisted the Fallen ring on his left hand. Every Fallen agent had one. Chavali wore hers on the same finger Harris had chosen for his own. He wished he could use it to hear her mock him for letting himself get rattled by nothing. She'd sneer and roll her eyes, then call him a coward and a fool.

He took a deep breath, picturing her perfect lips as she scowled at him in annoyance. The thought calmed him. Someday, he'd kiss her. She'd slap him. He'd ignore it to crush her against his body and she'd melt into his arms.

Harris rubbed his eyes, wondering if he'd ever reach that point with her. Moments later, he screamed. Black feathers decorated the arrow shaft sticking out of his thigh. His horse reared. He grabbed the bag as he fell. Hitting shoulder first, he groaned and focused on protecting his head.

When he stopped rolling, he stared up at the cobalt sky, wondering what had happened. In the distance, a woman shrieked a battle cry. Harris rolled, sending sparks of pain shooting through his leg. His horse had bolted, bodies lay on the ground, and the clang of metal against metal filled the air. Through the wheels of the wagon in front of him, he saw unfamiliar boots tromping toward him.

Half running and half crawling, Harris scrambled off the road. He headed for a nearby copse, hoping it would give him enough cover to wait out the attack. There, he could bind his wound. As soon as the attackers moved on, he could shamble to the next town and use his ring to commandeer a horse. Eldrack trusted him and he intended to live up to that.

The shrubs and low pines welcomed him with thorns. He tripped over a rock and landed face first on a bed of stiff pinecones. Fresh pain from the arrow snapping in half made him cry out. Though he couldn't stop hyperventilating, he knew someone had heard him and would come looking.

With a gulp, he realized he might not survive this. Whether he did or not, the bag had to be delivered to the king. He dragged it into view, wincing as he pushed against his injured leg for leverage. A glint of sunshine flashed off his silver ring and he remembered Eldrack saying it allowed each agent to be tracked so long as they wore it.

He glanced back and saw an unfamiliar man striding toward him in tight-fitting clothes matching the green of the grasses along the side of the road. Blood covered his sword. Harris blanched and wrenched the ring off his finger. He yanked the bag open and pried off the lid of the metal box inside. Heart racing, he shoved the ring into the box and slapped the cover back into place.

Blood rushed in his ears as he cinched the bag shut and tossed it deeper into the thicket. Then he drew his dagger and rolled onto his back. His pursuer saw him and slowed. Raising his sword, the man stalked closer.

Harris braced against the nearest tree and lurched to his feet. Brandishing his small blade, he clenched his jaws together to keep his teeth from chattering. His hands shook anyway. With a glance down, he saw blood along the entire length of his pants leg and thought the injury must be more severe than he imagined.

"Hand over the box and I'll let you live," the bandit called out. His clothes showed no signs of wear beyond recent blood spatter. This man had been recently outfitted for this particular job.

"I don't know what you're talking about." Harris wiped a sleeve across his brow. It came away slick with sweat.

"Sure you don't." The bandit darted in and lunged, his sword pointed at Harris's belly.

Harris lashed out with his dagger, managing to swat the blade aside. It missed him and skipped off the bark of the tree trunk. He gripped his thigh, hoping to stop the bleeding, and held his dagger up again.

"I'm not your enemy." Harris panted, trying not to sound as pathetic as he felt. Desperate to live, he spewed the first lie that came to mind. "I was only with these people to steal what I could before leaving in the middle of the night."

The bandit threw his head back and laughed. He feinted to the left. Harris, too winded to see the trick, dodged into the real blow. The bandit's sword sank into his belly and out through his back to hit the tree.

"Thanks for making it clear I shouldn't trust you," the bandit growled. He grabbed Harris's dark mop of hair and forced the blade in deeper.

Eyes wide and mouth hanging open, Harris couldn't breathe. The dagger fell out of his hand. He dropped to his knees and fell to the ground when the bandit planted a boot on his chest and shoved him off the sword.

The bandit stared down at Harris, blood dripping off the end of his sword. Harris gasped, trying to suck in air. His hands jerked, refusing to comply with his wish to hold his gut. The taste of copper filled his mouth.

Crouching beside him, the bandit peered at the wound. "That's got to hurt. You'll linger for a while, you know. Pure agony while you bleed to death. I've seen it before." His voice sounded less sinister than Harris thought it should. "Tell me where the box is and I'll end your pain swiftly."

Harris closed his eyes and imagined Chavali smirking. She'd approve of him using his last breaths to lie for her. "W-wagon. Th-third wa-wagon b-b-back."

The bandit patted him on the shoulder. Harris heard pine cones crunch and the bandit's leathers creak as the bastard walked away.

Chapter 1

Two rocks thunked against a board nailed to a log, then clattered into the wooden wheelbarrow it rested inside. Another rock hit the side of the wheelbarrow with a clunk and dropped to the ground. The fourth rock fell short and rolled to a stop two feet away.

Chavali reached down and ruffled Haizea's dark hair, wishing she could see the red-brown color she knew matched her own. Instead, her eyes let her see nothing but shades of gray. Regardless, she breathed in the crisp, fresh air, reveling in the sunshine on her face. The winter had seemed determined to last forever until it suddenly warmed last week. With the snow melted, Marcus had asked her for help clearing stones from the field they used for a selection of crops. Chavali elected to make it a game.

"That was closer than before. Keep trying."

The little girl picked up another rock from the damp, muddy ground and hurled it as far as her small arm could manage. Once again, it fell short. Nearby, Biholtz hefted a rock almost as big as Haizea's head and heaved it at the wheelbarrow. The thirteen-year-old's stone landed inside with a heavy thunk.

Haizea flopped on the ground. "I can't do it!" she wailed.

Hiding a smirk, Chavali crouched beside the four-year-old girl. "You've heard enough stories of the four goats to know better. You've never done this before. Move closer until you can get it into the bin, then practice until you can take a step back."

Danel tossed another rock plucked from the sheep meadow. This time, his stone bounced from the side to the handle and finally inside the bin. The six-year-old boy threw his hands in the air and shrieked with glee.

"You see? Danel tried plenty of times before he succeeded. Come, find another rock and move closer." Chavali offered her hand to Haizea and raised an eyebrow when the girl sighed dramatically instead of taking it. "If you're tired of this, you can go inside and help Penny wash clothes."

"I want to play with my doll!"

Chavali sighed. That doll had been rescued from the fire set by the man who murdered their clan. Only the four of them had escaped his brutal attack with only a precious few possessions, the doll among them. She hated to deny time with it. "You can go play as soon as you get your first rock into the bin."

Haizea sighed again, but she also sat up. Her lower lip trembled.

Unwilling to be moved by pouting, Chavali snatched up a rock and stood. She lobbed it at the wheelbarrow and hit the board again. She saw the little girl scramble to her feet and had to cover her mouth to avoid laughing at the mud smeared all over Haizea's hair and back. Biholtz would have to wrestle Haizea into the bathtub, not Chavali.

Moving away, Chavali scanned for more stones worth picking up. She found and tossed one, missing the target. Her rock sailed over the top to land beyond the wheelbarrow. Three weeks practicing knife throwing with Eliot had done wonders for her aim, but she still had a long way to go.

"I'll get it!" Danel scampered to her rock and pounced on it.

Chavali searched for another rock. Danel carried the stone to the wheelbarrow and dropped it in. He gripped the side and leaned in, his lips moving as he counted the stones inside. Chavali saw the wheelbarrow wobble under his weight. A sudden surge of panic exploded through her, flinging sharp jolts through her arms and legs. She reached the wheelbarrow and snatched up the boy.

Heart racing, Chavali ran several yards further. She slowed and looked back to see nothing had happened. Biholtz stared at her. Haizea had curled into a ball, holding her knees. The wheelbarrow stood sturdy and straight. Panic still clutched her heart, but she couldn't say why.

"What happened?" Danel asked, his voice small and breathy.

"I..." Chavali squeezed him tightly. She had no explanation. Danel couldn't have overturned the wheelbarrow. The rocks inside it weighed more than he did and the barrow's struts rested on flat ground. In that moment, she'd been convinced beyond doubt he would be buried under an avalanche of stones.

She took a deep breath. "Please be careful with yourself."

Danel buried his face in her neck. "I will."

Fierce desire to surround herself with clan flared in Chavali's heart. "We should take a break. Haizea, let's sit and have a snack. Biholtz, get water and biscuits."

Biholtz tossed her last rock into the wheelbarrow and grabbed Haizea from behind. The little girl shrieked with laughter as she was lifted into the air. They trooped together to the back stoop of the farmhouse where the children lived with their adopted clan elders, Marcus and Penny. Chavali sat with Danel and Haizea in her lap while Biholtz disappeared inside.

"Tell us a story, Chavali," Danel begged.

"We're only taking a short break." Both children stared up at her with wide, pleading eyes. She sighed. "Yes, fine. A small story." The spirits of their dead ancestors, eager to provide whatever story she wished to know, flooded her mind with lore and tales. She twined her fingers through the air, coaxing them to accompany the story with images. "When I was young, our clan got stuck in the mountains of south Tila during the winter. Our flock of sheep numbered thirty-five when we entered those mountains, but sixteen when we finally were able to leave."

Biholtz returned with stacked wooden cups and a pitcher of water. Penny followed her with a plate of biscuits. Behind her, Marcus carried a blanket. Everyone stood so he could lay the blanket on the ground, then they sat for a small picnic. Biholtz reached for Haizea.

Chavali wanted to have clan around her, even adopted clan. She beckoned for them to cluster, moving the clan's illusory sheep and wagons to accommodate. Marcus groaned as he shuffled his old bones so his wife could help him shelter Biholtz while Chavali snuggled into the group with the two small children. A warm smile lit up Penny's wrinkled face as she handed out the biscuits.

The loss of her family several months ago struck Chavali keenly now, for reasons she couldn't explain. Having everyone close helped.

Clan bound them all, the connection running deep even for Marcus and Penny, who'd been brought into it recently.

"What happened to the sheep?" Danel asked.

His question forced Chavali to realize she'd trailed off and fallen into woolgathering. Danel wouldn't interrupt her otherwise. "We followed a path to a mountain pass, one the clan had taken before. Often, the clan went around the mountains instead of through, but not this time. The weather was clear and pleasant, and frost hadn't hit in the foothills yet."

Racing hoofbeats interrupted her. Though the farmhouse sat along the main road out of Cloverdale, riders seldom raced past. Most Fallen urged their horses to nothing more than a canter. This poor beast galloped across mud. Chavali craned her neck to watch the horse and rider pass the house. To her surprise, four riders raced along the road, headed for the Creator's Tower. From there, they could teleport to any of the twenty-two other Creator's Towers.

Chavali frowned, wondering what could send four Fallen speeding away at top speed. No mission she'd been sent on so far had required such haste at the outset. Perhaps she'd hear about it later. For now, she shook her head and returned to basking in the warmth of her clan.

Chapter 2

Inside the Fallen tower, an underground hive of activity housing several hundred Fallen, healers, and servants, Chavali sat in her room three days later, struggling through a book with her nascent reading skills. The story told of a Shappan follower of the Order of the Feminine Divine who suffered trial after trial on the path to recovering a powerless artifact of her family.

Though Chavali could relate to the desire for a lost link to her past, she found the tale ridiculous. This woman did things Chavali would never do for something as minor as an object. To recover a member of her clan, she'd do all this and more. To rescue Biholtz, Haizea, and Danel four months ago, she'd stormed a stronghold full of telepaths. But for an object with no magical power, she would have turned away from the task early in the story.

Someone knocking on her door provided a welcome interruption from the tedious chore of churning through this book Colby had gifted her. She tossed the thin tome on her small table and opened her door to the chime of beads hung on the outside clacking against the wood. A servant stood there, which usually meant a summons from Eldrack or her healer.

"You're to report to the third conference room on the left as soon as possible," the servant said with a shallow curtsy. When Chavali nodded and thanked her, the woman left her alone.

Conference room meetings always meant a mission. Chavali tugged her cloak off its hook and draped it over her chair. Her backpack sat on her dresser, already repacked after her last mission. She set her heavy boots with her cloak, knowing they could be sent to the mountains where snow still covered the ground. If the mission took her to the beaches of Mecalle or South Cascain, she'd leave them and her cloak behind.

Outside her room, she followed the stone hallway to the wide spiral stair plunging deep into the earth. With her room on the tenth floor, she had to descend three quarters of a full turn around the massive central column to reach the thirteenth floor and its conference rooms. On her way down, she greeted several Fallen while making an effort not to tarry. Though missions seldom required hurrying, Eldrack appreciated promptness.

At the thirteenth floor, she stepped through the archway and saw a large man walking into the door she'd been directed to. Only Colby's broad, seven-foot-tall frame filled a space so completely, and she struggled to decide whether his presence on the same mission pleased or annoyed her. Though he'd proven himself valuable and trustworthy, and she appreciated his skills with the giant sword he carried on his back, he'd pester her about her progress with reading the entire time. Worse, he held honesty as the most important value a person could have.

She sighed and pushed it all aside. When Eldrack called, his Fallen did his bidding regardless of their personal opinions and relationships. The Administrator commanded their loyalty for many reasons, not the least of which being he'd had every last one of them revived from death. Chavali remembered her own death with a shudder and took a deep breath to also set that aside.

Inside the conference room, she found the expected space normally used to assign missions. The round table in the center, large enough to comfortably seat eight, had five sitting around it already. Colby looked up with a smile and pulled a chair out for her. Portia nodded to acknowledge her. Eldrack and Railan sat opposite them. Another Fallen woman Chavali didn't know occupied the other chair and touched her temple with two fingers in an informal salute.

The unknown woman intrigued Chavali. She'd met elves before, but never one with hair so short it didn't reach her long, pointed ears. Dark metal wires spiraled through the lobes of her ears and snaked into her skin at her jawline. As someone with a feather grafted into her skull, Chavali could appreciate unusual adornment and longed to know the purpose of the wires.

"Thank you for coming right away." Eldrack, a middle-aged man with the bearing of a harmless clerk, gestured to the empty chair for her. He flipped open a folder lying on the table in front of him and frowned.

Chavali slipped into the chair and flashed Colby her thanks for his gallantry. Without waiting for any response from him, she focused on Eldrack, who'd likely held any explanation until she arrived.

"A week ago, I sent a Fallen agent to the capital with several important packages." Eldrack's gaze fell to the papers in the folder, but

Chavali got the feeling he didn't read anything there while he spoke. "He took a longer route than necessary to meet up with an artists' caravan en route to Todan, which was supposed to allow him to travel without attracting attention. Three days ago, the caravan was attacked and he was killed, along with everyone else. The caravan was ransacked and little was left behind.

"His body was recovered, and the team discovered he'd lost his Fallen ring. In light of that, we tracked it and found it's been moved to North Cascain. As far as we can tell—" Eldrack's voice caught and a shadow passed over his face. Whichever agent they'd lost, he clearly felt responsible for the death. Something else also tugged on him, something darker and sharper. After clearing his throat, he continued. "We think he suspected the attackers were after the most important of the packages and also guessed he might not survive. It's likely he slipped the ring inside the package."

Chavali blinked, surprised by such a tactic. She doubted she'd have thought to do such a thing while facing imminent death. "Who was this agent?"

When Eldrack failed to answer, Railan said, "Harris."

The blood drained from Chavali's face. As irritating as she found the former bandit, she hadn't wished him true ill will since he became an agent. He'd earned her trust and proven both tolerable and manageable, two traits she prized in men. With his clever thinking in the face of death, her estimation of him raised by several degrees. "How did he die?" she whispered. "Was it swift?"

The jagged scars cutting across Railan's face painted her scowl dark enough Chavali didn't need to hear the answer. "It was...

unpleasant."

Colby growled in the back of his throat. Portia dropped her gaze to her lap, her lips pursed so tight they went white. The unknown woman touched her fingers to her brow in a gesture Chavali recognized as an elven wish for the dead to rest peacefully.

Chavali narrowed her eyes and clenched her jaw, wishing she had someone to curse for this evil. "Then we have someone to repay for their kindness."

"This is not a mission about revenge." Eldrack schooled his face to grave neutrality, but not before Chavali caught uncharacteristic anxiety in his expression. "It's about recovering the cat statue the three of you and Harris endured so much to obtain from the Lady of Ket. That was the package. If you can find the party responsible for his death, deal with them as usual. The ring is now in Harbor City."

Chavali's mind reeled. They'd suffered so much in Ket. All four of them had nearly died there. They'd walked away with that stupid statue and more questions than answers. The Lady of Ket hadn't known what the box contained when she handed them the statue, and only a handful of Fallen knew about it, all in this room. Eldrack had to know more than he said. As usual.

"Who can we contact in Harbor City?" The elf had a soft, breathy voice and an accent marking her as hailing from North Cascain.

"No one," Railan said. "We have two agents in the entire country, and neither is in Harbor City. The Watch there is impossible to slip spies past. They're beyond paranoid."

"I've never been to Harbor City," the elf said, "so I can't help navigate it. Why send me?"

"You have the right accent, Sivry. No one will question your presence," Railan said.

"My real accent is close enough," Portia said. "I'll be fine. Them on the other hand..." She gestured to Chavali and Colby.

Eldrack rubbed his eyes. "The three of you are familiar with the statue. That's what matters. Go there, blend in, and—"

"Blend in?" Chavali scoffed. Her accent, unique to her clan, had already faded a slight amount, but still marked her as foreign everywhere she went. "I do not blend in." She tapped the swirling tattoo on her forehead, designed to make the curled, pink feather sprouting from her skull appear to be part of an exotic plant. "Neither does Colby."

"It's true," Colby said. "A big guy on a big white horse stands out no matter where I go, whether I wear armor or not."

"Especially given he won't go along with faked backgrounds and purposes," Portia said.

Colby frowned but said nothing. Chavali longed to snatch Eldrack's hand and force him to think about everything he hid from her. One day, she'd send the spirits crawling through his mind to devour all his secrets.

Eldrack clenched his jaw. "You're the agents best suited to this mission. Time is of the essence and Harris's killer is out there. Dismissed." He remained seated and let a flicker of a scowl show before saying. "Chavali, I need you to stay behind for a minute, please."

Railan stood with Colby, Portia, and Sivry. "I have a little information about Harbor City," Railan said as they filed out. "It's not much, but it's better than nothing." The four of them left the room.

When Railan shut the door behind them, Chavali laid a hand on the table and drummed her painted fingernails on the surface.

She watched Eldrack sit and fail to meet her gaze long enough to know he wouldn't reveal anything else without prodding. "I know Harris well and sending me to apprehend his killer is foolish. You are not a fool, Eldrack. Which means there is another reason."

"I thought I was clear. You're familiar with the cat statue. You're also one of my best investigators. That makes you the right choice." Eldrack held something back and Chavali wanted to know it. "I've assigned you to this mission and that's the end of that. I asked you to stay behind for another reason."

Chavali crossed her arms. "I see." The discussion, she could see plainly, was closed. Only time would allow her to re-open it.

"As I said, we recovered Harris's body. He's already bound to the Fallen and he proved a valuable agent, so I've opened a file for consideration of his continued service."

Not expecting to be privy to such a discussion, Chavali raised her brow. "Oh?"

Finally, he met her gaze. She saw nothing more than grim determination. "You recommended him in the first place, and as you said, you know him well. I'd like your input on that consideration. A healer will have to be convinced to bring him back, and she'll want to interview you."

The idea of dredging up every thought she had about Harris hurt. Chavali shied away from tackling those emotions, not sure she wanted to examine them closely. "I have little to say that I have not already said."

"You've known him far longer now than you did when you brought him to me."

"We've discussed him before."

Eldrack laced his fingers together on the table and leaned toward her. "You delved into his memories."

"What of it? Most of what I saw is meaningless, too rushed and tangled to decipher."

Something in Eldrack's eyes changed. A sense of satisfaction, or maybe victory, seemed to have hardened them. "Then you need to deal with that before it infects your mind. Kelly will assist you."

Chavali's lip curled. "Is this an order?"

"Does it need to be?"

Staring him down, Chavali wanted to leap over the table and wring his neck. He'd maneuvered her into a corner. Agree or be forced to agree—the lack of options galled her. Then he let his eyes soften into sympathy. She hated that more.

"Fine," she snapped. Rising with a swish of her wool dress, she wished she dared to slap him. Someday, when her five years among the Fallen ended, she would. "I will deal with it when I get back." She stormed out.

Chapter 3

Fists clenched at her sides, Chavali fumed up the stairs to her room. When she first woke after her death, Eldrack had promised he wouldn't lie to her. As far as she knew, he hadn't yet. The questions he refused to answer grated on her nerves, though. What difference did those stupid memories make? None had ever bled over into her dreams or thoughts.

Granted, her dreams had changed drastically here. The nightmares she'd lived with for ten years since she's assumed the mantle of Seer of the Blaukenev clan had been horrific and bizarre, but they'd become familiar. Here, they'd changed and now she never knew what to expect anymore. Perhaps the memories she'd ripped from others *had* tainted some part of her mind.

She flung her door open, more irritated for thinking Eldrack might be right. Muttering a stream of insults in her clan's native tongue, she tore off her shoes and tossed them aside.

"You seem lively today." Healer Kelly stood in the doorway, radiant as always in her white robes and with her light hair in a messy bun. She wore a brave smile, one acknowledging the potential danger of addressing Chavali in her current mood.

Chavali scowled and jammed her foot into a knee-high leather boot. "I am in a hurry."

"You're also forgetting to use contractions."

Ignoring her, Chavali yanked the leather laces of her boot and tied it. She picked up the other boot and repeated the process, taking out her frustration on the footwear.

"I'll be overseeing the interview for Harris."

Chavali froze in the act of tying the second knot. "I do not wish to speak of this now."

"Are you upset he's dead?"

Glancing up, Chavali saw Kelly offering her sympathy. "Of course I am upset he is dead," she snapped. "I knew him. I do not appreciate it when people murder my..." She groped for the right word, not sure how to categorize him. "...acquaintances."

Kelly drifted inside the room and shut the door. "Is that all he was to you?"

"This is not important." Chavali tied off the knot and stood, smoothing her dress down. She curled her fingers around the strap of her pack and wondered how much she'd have to divulge before Kelly would let her leave. The healer couldn't physically stop her from walking away, but this was Chavali's room. She wouldn't be chased out of her own room by anything, especially not something as frivolous as uncomfortable questions.

"Grief is a process, Chavali. You have to let yourself work through it."

"Do not tell me how to mourn my friends and family," Chavali growled. "I have lost more than enough for two lifetimes."

"Which was Harris? Friend or family?" Kelly leaned against the small table and offered Chavali more sympathy.

Chavali bared her teeth, angry at herself for saying too much. Her knuckles went white on her pack's strap. "I have told you not to invade my room to interrogate me. When I wish to speak to you, I will come to see you."

Hurt drained the sympathy away from Kelly's face. The infernal healer never did bother to hide her feelings. "That only works if you actually come to see me. You haven't been to my office in at least a month. I thought we made a lot of progress together, then you stopped coming."

She returned to the door and turned her back on Chavali, her hand on the knob. "I just didn't want you to be blindsided by the interview when you get back. It's important. If you care at all about Harris and want him to have the same second chance you were granted, you need to take it seriously. I'll have to find a healer for him, and if you can't convince her that he's worth it, he'll stay dead."

When Kelly didn't breeze out to go do whatever healers did in their free time, Chavali took a deep breath and tried to calm down. Harris's death had taken her off-guard. If only to herself, she could admit she cared about him. No matter how much he annoyed her, she trusted him with her back. "And what is this mysterious 'it' I must convince her he is worth?"

Kelly's shoulders tightened. "That's a complicated matter, and you need to leave for your mission. We'll discuss it later. Just know it's not a price to be paid lightly." She opened the door and slipped out.

"Wonderful." Chavali watched the door swing shut. The moment the latch clicked into place, she regretted spewing so much venom at her healer. Kelly had one job: maintaining Chavali's mental health. Chavali had to wonder what mad devil's bargain had thrust her into such a position. No one in her clan would have willingly shouldered such a chore.

She hefted her pack and chided herself. Her little sister had fulfilled the role without question or complaint. Pasha's voice rang in her memories, goading her to dance. She had always found ways to lift Chavali's mood. Sorrow settled in her heart as she remembered Pasha laughing and waggling her rear at the clan's men.

She covered her face and willed tears to stop. Harris didn't deserve to die. Like three days ago, she longed to hold close what little she had left of her clan. Instead, she had to go find a cat and a killer. Colby and Portia wouldn't object to her stopping at the farm on the way out to say goodbye, at least.

Wiping her cheeks, she gripped the doorknob and took a deep breath. For Harris, a true friend, she would delve into those wretched memories of his. For Eldrack, she would find the damnable statue. For herself, she'd slit the throat of Harris's murderer, no matter who they turned out to be. Whether Colby wanted her to or not.

Chapter 4

Two hours later, Chavali accepted Colby's help to step onto a small, flat-bottomed boat. They'd teleported from the Creator's Tower near Cloverdale to the one near Harbor City and now stood on the banks of a small river that joined the larger Silvein, which flowed into Lake Hardrun. Chavali's clan had circled the lake several times in her lifetime. Her predecessor, Seer Marika, had claimed the name meant "the doom that sleeps fitfully" in some ancient, forgotten tongue.

Portia leaned against the side, covering her mouth despite the boat not leaving its dock yet. Sivry stood at the bow, breathing deeply of the fresh, warm air and damp earth. Colby let Chavali go once he saw she had no problem on the slick deck and sat with the boat's captain, engaging him in idle chatter. Colby's giant white horse, Karias, stood in the center, his white tail twitching.

Chavali stepped beside the beast and patted his neck with her bare hand. The spirits surged across the link formed by contact, revealing Karias's surface thoughts to her.

"I hope the fine weather will hold," Chavali said. In such mixed company, she would honor the horse's desire to keep his true nature as secret as possible. Not even Colby, his bound companion and partner, knew how intelligent his mount truly was.

The skies to the west seem clear enough and this sunshine is divine. I imagine boat travel feels similar enough to wagon travel that you'll have no difficulties. Karias nodded toward Portia.

Chavali smirked, though she wished she could dispel her friend's discomfort. "Portia, you should move to the front. It may help to feel the wind on your face, and you have less chance of upsetting the boat's balance there."

Portia nodded and shuffled to stand beside Sivry. The captain pushed off and the boat floated down the narrow stream.

Colby is sleeping well lately. I think you've finally untangled all the damage done to him in Ket.

Chavali nodded, sharing the same opinion. After spending time three days a week for nearly two months delving into his memories and pulling out artificial triggers, she felt confident no more remained. She glanced back at Colby, wondering if the horse knew him even half as well as she did now.

Colby caught her eye and smiled. Before she turned away, he patted the captain and appeared to wrap up their conversation.

Karias stared at Chavali with one big, light-colored eye. *We should talk later, when you can speak freely.*

Having no such desire, Chavali shrugged.

"Poor Portia." Colby stood on the other side of his horse.

"It was her choice to hire a boat." Chavali pushed on the horse's neck, wanting him to either raise or lower it so she could see Colby. "Do you have any thoughts about our mission?"

Karias refused to move his head. *You two should wear bright colors and juggle strange objects. Then Portia and Sivry can slip in undetected while the Watch focuses on you.*

"I don't see how we can possibly keep from being noticed," Colby said, oblivious to Karias's comment.

Chavali smirked. "It's probably best if we enter the city separately and plan to meet a few blocks in. That will give everyone a chance to evade notice. You and I together will be impossible to miss."

You'd be better off making a spectacle of yourselves. See if you can talk him into pretending to be your husband. I'd enjoy that.

Grateful she had no drink in hand, Chavali coughed. "Or the two of us could admit defeat from the start on this point and remain together while Portia and Sivry slip through."

Sivry shifted until she faced them, leaning against the prow. "That sounds like a good plan to me. When Railan said they were paranoid, she wasn't kidding. They'll swarm you. Portia and I can meet you later, when you've gotten through."

Portia held up a hand to interject, then she threw up over side. Chavali waited patiently through the retching sounds while the boat glided past tree-lined shores. They spooked a tree full of small birds into the sky and she caught sight of a deer herd leaping away.

I guess we'll have to stop and find her a meal when we get there.

Chavali covered her mouth to hold back a laugh. To avoid any more of that, she patted Karias and pulled her hand away.

Portia wiped her mouth and sagged against the boat. "Splitting up is best. Once we're inside the city, on solid ground, I can set up a trace on the ring. I could do it now if I could focus on anything. That should get us to the right building or pair of buildings. It's not perfect, but it's close."

"They may have separated the ring from the statue," Colby said.

"They may also think the ring is part of the statue." Chavali twisted her own Fallen ring on her finger and wondered if the killer would recognize it. Colby, Portia, and Sivry also wore one, like every other Fallen. In Shappa and at Creator's Towers, it allowed them to claim certain powers granted by Shappa's King Martef. Elsewhere, such as here, it seemed a liability.

She unhooked the necklace holding her etched Seer's pendant and slipped her ring onto the chain. The chain went back under her dress, both pendants now hidden from view.

Portia whirled and heaved over the side again. Sivry tapped her long, thin fingers on the ledge and stared into the distance.

Chavali considered a number of other suggestions and warnings, but said nothing. Colby and Portia had earned enough respect from her to not need to hear any of it. They'd be careful, avoid saying more than necessary, and keep close what secrets they had. Colby already knew he represented the greatest threat to their mission under direct questioning.

The rest of the journey down the river passed swiftly. They joined the Silvein where the land to the west changed to rolling hills covered with the furrowed rows of farming fields. In Cloverdale, no one had begun planting yet. Here, many miles south and east, horses pulled wagons and plows with people hard at work sowing seeds.

Their boat rushed through the river delta. Gulls circled overhead and vessels dotted the surface of the lake. The captain steered through a thicket of fishing boats until they saw the whitewashed walls of warehouses and gleaming ceramic rooftops beyond them. Trade barges churned the waters in both directions.

As their boat slipped into a berth on a long wooden dock, Chavali noted rows of boats with furled sails mingling with squatter, squarer specimens. Larger ships docked farther west where the water probably ran deeper. Stepping off the boat with Colby's help, she looked down and saw the sandy floor several feet underwater with dark shapes waving in the current.

Colby saluted the captain once Karias had hopped off without incident. "The captain warned me not to pay any tolls or fees. Entering the city, regardless of how it's done, is free."

Chavali nodded and let Sivry and Portia lead them up the dock. The narrow wooden bridge over the water connected to a larger, walled walkway. The four-foot, blinding-white concrete walls wouldn't prevent anyone from jumping over the side and walking into the city, but they'd be obvious to the guards manning the thirty-foot towers spaced along the docks.

As they walked, people on docked boats watched them. Some seemed to regard them with nothing more sinister than curiosity, while others shielded children or glared. If this treatment kept up inside the city, their job would be a greater challenge than Chavali thought. She lifted her hood and tucked her feather inside it.

Two guards in chain armor and dark livery stood at attention when they approached an iron gate preventing easy access to the city. One guard gripped his sword while the other crossed his arms. Both broad-shouldered men stood a head taller than Chavali but at least a foot shorter than Colby.

"Halt," the crossed arms guard ordered. "Declare your business in Harbor City!"

"Visiting relatives," Portia said, her voice hoarse and accented the same as the guard's. "My aunt and uncle live on Merceride Avenue."

Both guards, faces stern and forbidding, flicked their gazes over each member of the group. "You're not with them?"

Portia glanced back and Chavali saw her sigh. All that time spent planning to split up and they'd walked together to the gate. Along with Portia's seasickness, this mission already had all the signs of a disaster.

"They're just my servants," Portia said.

"You brought a horse that big on a small boat? Where's the rest of your mounts?"

Portia smirked. "Only have the one. I mean, would *you* tell that man he can't bring his favorite pet?"

Both guards looked Colby over. He obliged by planting his fists on his hips, which allowed him to flex his arm muscles. Chavali watched the three men engage in a short, silent battle of posturing and peacocking. Each clenched fists, hardened stares, and flexed muscles. She had to stifle a roll of her eyes.

Portia coughed and spat a gob of bile to the side. "May we enter the city, please?"

The crossed arms guard shifted to rest a hand on the hilt of his sword. "There's a ten gold fee for bringing an animal in this way."

"If you want to try to take ten of my gold pieces, you're going to have to face your boss and explain how your boot got shoved so far up your ass it came out through your mouth." Portia leaned in and said something else that made the guard's eyes pop wide.

Waving away the stench of Portia's breath, the guard stepped back and pushed the gate open. "Fine," he grumbled, "be on your way. Your entry has been noted and approved."

Chavali followed on Sivry's heels, glad to be through such a ridiculous entry checkpoint. Anyone could get through that questioning process, insuring nothing more than delays and annoyance for all parties entering the city. She wondered how they managed the entry for merchants and trade goods. Cursory inspections of randomly selected crates and sacks struck her as their style. Unless some process magically eliminated bribery, this place had no better security than anywhere else.

Chapter 5

The packed dirt road before them, thick with wagons, horses, and sweaty workmen, led past warehouses. Chavali noticed one man robbing another at knifepoint less than fifty feet away from the gate in broad daylight. The mugger's ragged beard and dark robes covered wiry strength, visible in his movements.

She turned away from the incident, knowing interceding would attract more attention than they could afford, but she'd remember both attacker and victim. Thankfully, Colby missed it or they'd be in a fight already.

"I've seen it!"

The group turned a corner to find a man clinging to a bar's facade, his dark hair and beard wild and unkempt. Under a layer of grime, his clothes seemed of good quality. He locked gazes with Chavali and his entire expression blossomed with awe. After a moment of stunned staring, he leaped from his perch, landed in a clumsy roll, and ran to kneel at her feet with his hands—soft and unmarked by toil—held inches from her skirt.

"Dark butterflies," he gasped. "The Guide!"

Chavali stepped back, aghast. No one had ever seen the spirits of the dead clinging to her before. It should be impossible. Even she couldn't see them—she felt their influence on her mind and heard their incessant whispers.

Sivry jumped into the way as the strange man lunged after Chavali. "Back away," the elf said, her hand on her sword.

"Please, my Lady, let me touch you." The man grabbed Sivry's thighs as if she were nothing more than a wall barring his passage and peered around her, eyes hungry for another glimpse of Chavali. "I am a humble servant of your will. The dark butterflies have shown me the truth! He is coming. You are my Queen and I will do your bidding to oppose him."

Recovering from her shock, Chavali took a moment to draw the mantle of clan Seer about her. She could hope only madness touched him, and not some true gift of otherworldly sight. "If you wish to be granted the boon of my favor, you must perform a quest for me."

The man sat back on his feet and wrung his hands in supplication. "Anything, my Queen! My life is yours to command."

As a fortune teller for her clan, Chavali had made a career of telling people what they wanted to hear. This man needed to be sent to do some noble task, and she scrambled to think of one. She scanned him, seeing no sign of a love token on him. In his current condition, she guessed he might be twenty years old.

"I have lost my scepter to vile creatures of darkness. Though it cannot be recovered, it can be recreated. Find pieces to craft a new one and make it with your own hands. You may not steal anything or harm anyone to make it or the magic will be tainted. Do you understand?"

He nodded and fell to his hands and knees. "I will craft you a new scepter, my Queen."

"Go. When you finish, the scepter will lead you to me."

The man backed away from her, offering pledges and promises, then scrambled to his feet and ran up the street. Chavali noticed they'd attracted an audience and heard a whisper ripple through the crowd. They spoke of something blue and a death, neither of which made sense to her.

Portia gripped her arm and pulled her across the street. "You're masterful, as always," Portia murmured. "That was a spectacle, though. We need to get away from here. Now."

Agreeing, Chavali hurried in Portia's wake. They stopped several blocks away, at the mouth of a narrow alley. Chavali leaned against the wall to catch her breath. Colby rode past on Karias's back, flashing a hand signal to let them know he saw them.

"What was that about?" Portia crouched next to her, fishing inside a small pouch with one hand. "Dark butterflies?"

Sivry slipped into the alley and stood opposite them, staring at Chavali. "Eldrack said you have unusual skills, but I didn't think he meant acting."

Chavali gave the elf a sour smirk. "I don't know what he wanted. I merely wished to send him away without anyone coming to blows or harm." Her clan knew about the spirits, but Chavali had held that information back from Eldrack and had no intention of divulging anything to other Fallen. "He took me by surprise or I wouldn't have needed your rescue."

"You're welcome." Sivry regarded her with a mixture of amusement and suspicion.

"Yes, thank you for your help."

"Since we're stopped anyway," Portia said, "I'm going to cast the spell to find the ring. Make sure no one can see what I'm doing."

As Portia set her ring on the ground, Sivry stepped into the mouth of the alley, blocking the view with her body. Chavali crouched and spread her cloak to help shield the working. She'd seen few true spells of this type. Most magic required nothing more than force of will and perhaps a gesture.

"May I ask how this works? It seems involved."

"Sure." Portia set four translucent stones on the ground around the ring, spaced equally to form the corners of a square. "My particular form of magic use is best suited to fighting. To put it in simplistic terms, I can make weapons and shields out of nothing and control them with my mind. When doing something that isn't my forte, I need focus objects. These stones serve that purpose. They're...calibrated, you might say, for the purpose of seeking an affinity connection. In a sense, I'm going to make four tiny daggers of my will and stab the stones. The stones help me focus that power into seeking all the rings exactly like mine nearby."

"Fascinating." Chavali touched her necklace through her shirt. "You will find all of ours, yes?"

"Yes, but also the missing one." Portia sighed. "He was a pain in the ass, but I miss him anyway."

"This is also how I feel."

"I don't intend to let his killer live."

"Neither do I."

The two women nodded with firm conviction.

"Whichever of us needs privacy to handle this, the other should distract Colby," Chavali said.

"Agreed." Portia held out her hand.

Chavali gripped her forearm, carefully avoiding skin contact. The pact sealed, she let Portia work.

Chapter 6

Portia led the group through the streets, gripping her ring tightly. At intersections, she paused with her eyes shut for several seconds before continuing. As they left the docks behind, the city reminded Chavali of a larger, wealthier version of Ket. The cobblestone streets had little filth and no missing stones. Buildings had been whitewashed recently enough not to show wear or grime. Strange, dark arrows painted on the walls pointed in different directions at the corners of several streets, but Chavali had no idea what to make of them.

The sidewalks surprised Chavali. She'd never seen raised platforms on the sides of streets before. Only the widest, busiest streets had these walkways. Pedestrians—none showing signs of poverty—used them in streams to avoid the horses, carriages, and wagons trundling along the streets. Where streets crossed, mysterious, unspoken etiquette forced everyone into turn-taking for right of way.

Their walk took them in a tightening spiral past shops selling goods with gradually increasing quality and amounts of frivolous ornament. Interspersed among them, inscrutable, hulking stone buildings blocked the sun's rays. Chavali strained to collect rumors along the way, wishing she could spare the time to pause and hear more of several private conversations. Later, if they needed to, they'd find an inn and she'd have a chance to catch up on local gossip.

When Portia stopped, they stood before an impressive, whitewashed building with five-foot-high, stylized letters carved over the huge stone double doors. Chavali struggled to make out the words, finding the unusual letter forms challenging to decode.

Portia slipped her ring onto her finger. "It's in there. Before you ask, yes, I'm sure."

"Either the Watch is behind the attack on the caravan or they apprehended the attackers for other reasons," Colby said.

Karias stamped a hoof and snorted. Chavali glanced around and noticed four different uniformed men and women watching them. One rode a dark horse, another patrolled on the other side of the street, and the other two stood near the front doors of the building, openly staring with suspicion etched in their features.

It appeared to be a staging location for the Watch, the one kind of place they needed to avoid. Chavali gathered her cloak closer. "We should not tarry here." They needed to know more about the inside of this building, though, which meant someone needed to get inside it. As the others resumed walking up the street, she noted several ordinary people using the front doors.

Chavali touched Colby's arm. "I have an idea. Don't go far."

He nodded. "Be careful." His gaze flicked to her forehead, reminding her why she might not be the best choice to go inside.

"I will." Breaking away from the group, she joined a stream of people crossing the road and hurried to the front door of the Watch building. Despite its size, the door swung open easily and she scanned the room beyond it.

The large, airy stone room held two dozen people, half in uniform. Four sat behind a half-wall of the same light-colored stone as the floor and walls. The rest bustled about behind the protective divider, consulting filing cabinets, using the door in the back wall, filling out forms with quill pens, and rolling carts full of papers and envelopes. The other people sat on flat benches lining the walls, waited in four lines to speak to the clerks, or milled about.

Twelve feet overhead, dark beams supported the wood ceiling. Corkboards covered with paper notices lined the side walls. Two more uniformed men flanked the doors. Chavali couldn't see how people moved from this side of the low wall to the other side. She supposed the Watch employees used a different entrance, or it had some door mechanism she couldn't discern. Otherwise, the place seemed logically laid out for the purpose of interacting with citizens not accused of crimes.

Not sure what story to approach the clerks with, Chavali pretended to gawk at her surroundings like any farmhand would on her first visit to the city. This act carried her past a small group of people in the center of the room slowly enough to overhear them discussing their quest to recover stolen items. The conversation suggested a path forward and she stepped into the shortest of the four lines.

The clerks handled their duties with polite efficiency, taking information and handing over forms to be filled out. Chavali waited while the person in front of her reported his missing horse. Their clerk handed him a thin stack of forms and wished him well in an apathetic monotone then shooed him away to fill them out elsewhere and return them. He leaned around the man to pointedly fix Chavali with a dull, incurious look of impersonal concern.

"Can I help you, ma'am?"

Intrigued by the challenge of cutting through his weary boredom without arousing suspicion, Chavali smiled sadly and leaned against the wall. "I hope so." She held his gaze, then looked away with a bashful glance aside. "I've had a difficult time trying to recover an object taken from me."

Impervious to her efforts, he opened a drawer next to his legs. "Is it from the art raid?"

Surprised by both his manner and the conclusion he drew, Chavali let her brow raise. "Yes, actually. How did you know?"

He cracked a small, fake smile. "You're not the first person to come by today." He retrieved several pieces of paper covered with ink and blank lines. "You'll need to fill these out. A complete description of the missing piece is required, and you'll have to sign it. That's an affidavit and you can be prosecuted for dishonesty on the form." Flipping through a file, he selected another four pages and set them on top of the stack. "These extra pages are because you're a foreigner making a claim."

Chavali took the pages and gave him a brave smile. "How long should I expect to have to wait?"

"The pieces will be released after the trial this afternoon. As a non-citizen, you'll have to be processed before anything can be released to you, and that will take three to five days after you submit the papers."

"Oh?" She ignored the non-citizen issue in favor of the trial. In her experience, nobles or town leaders handed down judgments of guilt or innocence with little deliberation. The way he spoke made her think this trial encompassed much more. "Where will this trial be? Is it open to watching?"

The clerk blinked at her and she caught a flicker of curiosity in him. Now that she had his genuine attention, she wondered if she'd done the right thing in trying to get it. This man would remember her. "Yes, trials are a chance for the Inspectors to show off. It'll be in the Courthouse." He pointed behind her, directing her attention to a large map on the back wall. "It's near the center of the city. When you come back afterward, you'll need to file that paperwork."

"Which part of this map am I in now?"

"The lower-middle left."

She thanked him and hurried to the map on the wall. Thick lines crossed thin ones with labels in neat printing she had to puzzle over to decipher. The symbols made no sense to her even after she found the legend in the corner. Each dot seemed to represent one of three different things and each type of line had several explanations. None of the labels used words she recognized, making them difficult to sound out.

When she thought she'd found the Watch building and the Courthouse, she traced the route between them and did her best to memorize the labels along the way. This frustrating task took long enough to cause the guardsman nearby to glance at her several times. When she felt confident she'd remember the directions, she flashed him a bright smile with her head held high and breezed out.

Chapter 7

"I don't understand. We should be there by now. It didn't seem so far on the map." Chavali stood on a corner, certain she'd gone the right way, though she saw no sign of the Courthouse. This part of the city had none of the gleam they'd seen around the Watch building. Tall apartments crowded the narrow road, leaning far enough to touch overhead. Metal bars protected shop windows. Dogs and children ran freely, and refuse packed the corners everywhere.

If they wanted to escape the Watch at some point, this neighborhood would fulfill their needs. Karias and Colby seemed enough of a presence to keep pickpockets and muggers at bay, at least.

"I'm certain I remembered the letters properly."

"I thought we were following the blue path," Sivry said, "then we turned off it a few blocks back. you seemed so sure that I didn't say anything."

"Blue path?" Portia asked.

"All the important municipal routes are color coded," Sivry said. "They do that in every city in North Cascain. That's why they whitewash so many buildings. So you can see the markings."

Portia, Colby, and Karias all looked to Chavali, who sighed heavily and rubbed her eyes. "Had I known, I would have sent someone else inside to check the map."

"She's colorblind," Portia explained with a poorly stifled grin.

"Oh." Sivry looked away. "I see. I can probably get us back to the blue route, but there's no way to know which one we were supposed to be following."

Colby coughed to cover his amusement. "Which part of the city is it in?"

Chavali pursed her lips, annoyed such a minor thing had tripped her up. Government officials should, in her opinion, know better than to use colors instead of patterns. The fact she had yet to convince Eldrack certain changes still needed to be made in the Fallen tower to accommodate her didn't relate to this matter. "The center."

Sivry glanced up and down the street and sniffed the air. "I believe that leads to the water, so we should head this way." She led the group to the next side street, an alley barely wide enough for Karias. At the other end of the alley, Chavali spotted a Watch wagon slowing to a stop on the other side of a wide street. She opened her mouth to suggest asking for directions.

Flames engulfed the front half of the wagon and its driver. The rushing, crackling boom shattered nearby windows.

Colby wrapped his body around Chavali, shielding her from flying debris. When shouting and the tinkling of glass rushed in to fill the eerie silence in the wake of the explosion, he set her aside like a fragile doll and leaped onto Karias's back. They charged. Sivry ran behind them.

Portia tugged on Chavali's hand, urging her to the mouth of the alley at a more cautious pace.

Smoke covered the wagon with a thick haze. Ash and smoldering cloth drifted to the ground. Uniformed members of the Watch lay on the street, injured or dead. The wagon's horses bolted up the street, thrashing to flee through confused riders and tangled carriages. The Watch driver's body burned along with his seat, spewing more smoke into the air.

Chavali recognized Colby and Karias through the haze, battling dark shapes. Crossbow bolts rained down from above, pinning a fallen Watchman to the street and thunking into wood. Metal clanged. Horses shrieked. Portia raced into the smoke, heading for a guard rising to his hands and knees. More crossbow bolts clattered on the street. Screams and wails echoed off the walls.

Covering her mouth with the edge of her cloak, Chavali peered up. Those shooting had concealed themselves well and she saw nothing. Her attention snapped back to the street at the stomping of boots. Watchmen poured into the area as if they'd been nearby, waiting for disaster to strike.

A cloaked figure ran at Chavali, his dagger catching firelight. Though he seemed intent on the alley more than her, she braced herself for the impact. Silver burst through his chest before he reached her, and he stopped running. Blood spattered Chavali's face. She blinked and had to wipe her eyes. He met her gaze as he realized he breathed his last.

The man's body crumpled and Chavali saw Sivry behind him, withdrawing her sword from his body and whirling to block a crossbow bolt with the blade. Watchmen swarmed her from behind. After parrying a blow aimed at her leg, she raised her hands and dropped her sword in surrender.

The crossbow bolts stopped. Fresh, clean air blew through, pushing the smoke away. Colby stood near the back of the wagon, a cloaked body at his feet and five Watchmen holding him at sword point. Karias shifted and whickered, performing his impression of a normal horse. Portia knelt at the front of the wagon, her hands on her head, while a Watchman retrieved shackles for her from his belt.

"Ma'am, are you all right?" A Watchman approached Chavali, looking her over critically. He couldn't have realized her connection to the others.

Chavali scanned the aftermath, seeing other Watch officers approaching other parts of the gathered crowd. She wiped her face with two fingers and stared at the blood, wondering what quality she lacked that made her stay behind when Colby, Sivry, and Portia charged in. Stupidity, perhaps, or foolishness.

"Ma'am? Did you hear me?" The Watchman touched her shoulder, genuine concern on his face.

Already disoriented by the swift, brutally efficient attack, she held up her fingers. "It's not my blood," she told him, keeping her voice breathy and confused.

With more delicate deference than she expected, the Watchman flipped her cloak open and let his gaze trail down her dress. "Have a seat until the dizziness passes. You'll be fine." He helped her to the ground and moved to the next person with blood on their clothes.

Chavali watched while Colby and Sivry were forced to their knees with Portia, the three of them lined up with their hands on their heads. Beside them, a local woman knelt in the same pose, her shabby, unadorned clothes marking her as likely to be a prisoner already. Chavali's mind whirled. They had no Crown authority here. If those three were arrested, she had no idea how to free them, let alone how to get the cat statue. Eldrack might be the only one capable of interceding on their behalf in such a case. Before contacting him, though, she would make certain to exhaust all other possibilities, including blatant fraud and whatever cooperation she could elicit from the criminal elements already here.

The crowd parted on one side and a tall woman strode into sight. Mid-tone hair pulled into a bun at the nape of her neck framed a round face with sharp eyes and an aquiline nose. She wore a simple, high-necked shirt with a vest and pants tapering into knee-high boots. A gleaming metal chain fastened a flared cloak around her shoulders with the opening over her right arm. Metal bracers on both forearms bore a stylized image of a long-legged, long-necked bird. She wore a thin sword on her belt.

As she moved briskly into the scene, everyone treated her with deference. Many in the crowd offered her open adoration. The nearby Watchman, Chavali noticed, tightened his jaw when he noticed this woman's arrival. At least one member of the Watch didn't like her, yet the crowd jostled to worship her.

"It's the Princess," a breathless woman near Chavali said.

"She's so wonderful," gushed another member of the crowd.

"She'll find the monsters responsible."

"Thank the Creator she's here. Everything will be fine."

The princess touched her finger to her lips and silence rippled over the scene. Everyone watched as she circled the wagon and four prisoners, eyes sweeping from side to side. Though Chavali didn't understand the spell this woman had cast over the crowd, she had no desire to be singled out for scrutiny. She mimicked the locals.

Once the princess completed her circuit, she walked it again in the opposite direction. She stopped in front of Colby with her back to Chavali and remained there for several long beats. Finally, she spoke, her alto voice rich as velvet.

"A coordinated assault freed the prisoners from this transport. An incendiary device triggered by a mage nearby murdered one man and injured several others, as well as throwing enough smoke into the air to disguise the arrival of their ground force. A separate group of no more than four bearing crossbows provided support for the operation. It required no more than twelve individuals to carry out, but more likely had ten. The horses were intentionally run off rather than burned to create extra chaos. Nevertheless, one prisoner did not escape. Officers, take her to the east side Watch facility for questioning."

She spun on her heel and scanned the crowd where Chavali sat. Peering among the dozen people standing around Chavali, the Princess stalked toward her. Two members of the Watch hauled the unknown woman away.

"Ladies and gentlemen," the princess announced, "the danger here is passed and those who caused it will be apprehended shortly. Despite one prisoner remaining, there will be no trial this afternoon. It will, most likely, not happen until after the Queen's birthday celebration. If you were injured or believe you saw something helpful, please stay where you are. Otherwise, we must begin the work of removing the dead and clearing the street. Officer," the princess said as she laid a hand on the nearby Watchman's shoulder, "make sure someone sends backup to the west side Watch facility. I suspect Evidence Storage will be attacked shortly, if it hasn't already been."

The crowd broke into applause and dispersed, though many lingered to watch. The princess stared directly at Chavali, offering polite recognition to the citizens trying to catch her attention. "You." She pointed to Chavali. "Come with me."

Chapter 8

Trapped by the princess, and intrigued by her orders to the Watchman, Chavali wondered if this attack had anything to do with their statue. She stood with the aid of the wall, feigning mild dizziness. That the Princess fingered her for questioning came as no shock. Her hood had fallen during the chaos and everything about her appearance announced her as a foreigner.

"How may I be of service?" Chavali asked.

"What a fascinating accent you have." The princess smiled, a pleasantry masking steel. "Let's dispense with the pretense of weakness, though. These are your people, aren't they?" She waved at Portia, Colby, and Sivry.

Brow raised in surprise, Chavali stepped beside the intriguing princess. Colby had probably given away their connection with a glance, making him more of a liability than usual around the princess. The matter of her physical condition, though, she couldn't explain away so easily. If the princess's skills at reading people rose to the same or a higher level than Chavali's own, they all had to be careful here.

"They are, yes."

"Why did you order them to attack the wagon?"

The curious phrasing proved the princess had a great deal of intelligence. Such a question had been crafted with the intent to draw wordy explanations and denials. Chavali sneered inwardly at the bait. "I ordered them to defend it."

"And why would you do that?"

Chavali saw Colby open his mouth. She tried to wave him off behind the princess's back, but couldn't be sure if the woman saw it or not. At least Colby stayed quiet. "To prevent loss of life among the bystanders."

The princess nudged the dead attacker with her boot. "Or perhaps to cover your tracks by murdering the only two people who could identify you as involved in the plot."

"It would be quite stupid for me to remain behind in that case."

"Mmm." The princess stepped in front of Colby and bent to take a close look at him. She brushed her fingertips across a dark spray on his light-colored shirt. Chavali assumed it must be blood from the dead man. "Carrying lethal weapons is courting disaster."

"As you well know," Chavali said.

"Indeed I do." Rubbing her blood-smeared fingers together, the princess gave Colby a final once-over. "Where are you staying?"

Again Chavali gestured for Colby not to answer. "We are without accommodations at this time."

The princess snapped her fingers, which brought a Watchman to her side. "Conduct these three and their horse to Eidel's Landing. See to it they secure rooms and stabling."

Escort to an inn sounded better than an arrest. However, Chavali noticed she hadn't been included in the order. "Will they be allowed to leave?"

"Yes, but not immediately." The princess waved off her concerns while the Watchman gestured for the trio to stand and go with him. "Why do you think this attack happened?"

Chavali clasped her hands in front of herself, considering how to handle this woman. She could become a valuable ally, one who could take skills or other expertise in trade for the statue. Revealing the goal now, though, would be foolish. Chavali needed to wait for an opportune moment when no suspicion remained against her.

"Am I under arrest?"

"You're being detained."

"For what reason?"

The princess squatted beside the scorched wagon and swiped a finger across the front wheel. She retrieved a kerchief from a pocket and wiped her hand. "Suspicion of espionage."

"An intriguing charge. Is this common for those who do not sound or look like you?"

"Yes." She stood and beckoned for Chavali to follow as she left the scene. "These prisoners were on their way to the trial this afternoon. Have you heard about it?"

Chavali had to jog to keep up with the princess's longer-legged, ground-eating pace. It left her little concentration to work with. "I recall some mention of it."

They turned a corner and the West Watch building loomed in the distance. "They were art smugglers. I cracked the ring a few days ago and staged a sting operation yesterday. We discovered a cache of stolen paintings and other artworks, as well as arresting six members of the ring. The prisoners in that wagon were being transported from a secure holding facility to the Courthouse for the trial this afternoon. It's a high profile case."

Not sure why the princess would explain this to her, Chavali considered the information. If she only cracked the ring a few days ago, Harris's attackers must have been sloppy on their return. Because this had to be about those people. Otherwise, she'd stumbled across a grand coincidence of time, place, and art.

"They certainly went to a great deal of effort to recover those prisoners, didn't they?" the princess asked.

"They did."

"They had enough members to risk ten to recover six, and no fear of murdering Watchmen."

"A formidable group."

They reached the Watch building and Chavali saw nothing out of place. Uniformed officers still stood at their posts and people entered and exited through the front doors. As she'd suspected, the princess led her around the building to the back. Watchmen stood sentinel at a wrought iron gate, barring passage to anyone not in uniform. They nodded to her and watched Chavali.

Beyond the gate, they followed a short, straight flagstone path to another set of guards watching a plain metal door. The princess waved, and one guard opened the door for her. Both men looked Chavali over as she followed in the princess's wake. She suspected they wanted to remember her in case she did anything untoward inside.

The door let them into a stone room with several uniformed officers busy with papers at desks. One glanced up and acknowledged the princess with a nod, then turned again to her work. They strode up a tidy, clean hallway lit by small glowing globes on the ceiling. Paired doors lined it on both sides with crossing hallways after every fourth pair. Though each door had a label, they passed too quickly for Chavali to puzzle the letters out.

One door opened as they passed it, and the woman stepping out caught Chavali's attention. Like the princess, she wore close-fitting clothes different from the utilitarian Watch uniforms. Embroidery decorated the collar, cuffs and hems of this woman's coat and pants, though the shapes and tones matched the princess's. They also had similar facial features and severe hairstyles.

"Kalei," the princess said with a perfunctory nod of her head.

"Ambrye," Kalei said with her own nod. Her gaze fell on Chavali. She saw the feather and twitched so fast Chavali couldn't decode it. "Who's this?"

Intrigued by both Kalei's assertion of equal status and what Ambrye would say, Chavali smiled pleasantly.

"A foreigner I suspect of espionage," Ambrye said.

Chavali laughed, playing the statement off as a joke. "Well met, Kalei. I am Chastity." She offered Kalei her hand to shake.

Kalei shook Chavali's hand, allowing the spirits to swarm her. Her thoughts swirled around intense curiosity about Chavali's purpose here. *Is this how Ambrye does it? Bring in strangers and take credit for their work?* "What brings you here?"

Though Chavali longed to know more about what appeared to

57

be a rivalry, she let go when Kalei did. Since the question hadn't been directed to her, she left it for Ambrye to answer.

Ambrye let one corner of her mouth curl in a smirk. "I'm sure you'll hear about it soon enough. Come, Chastity, we have work to do."

Chavali nodded. "Good day to you, Kalei."

Kalei clenched her jaw. The moment Ambrye turned her back, Chavali caught an irritated grimace. Her shoulders tight, Kalei stalked away.

Amused by the exchange, Chavali hurried to catch up with Ambrye. They took a flight of stairs down to a small room with a middle-aged clerk working at a desk. Three corridors led from this room. Ambrye offered the clerk a greeting too fast for him to respond before she plunged down a hallway. After passing four open doorways, they reached the end of the corridor, a fifth open doorway into a vast, cavernous room filled with shelves that Chavali assumed must be Evidence Storage.

Floor-to-ceiling metal fencing protected most of the room. Outside the fence, a small area held benches and two more desks with metal filing cabinets. The fence gate stood open and two women guarded the entry. The two women nodded and let Ambrye through. At her gesture, they also permitted Chavali inside.

"Report?" Ambrye snapped.

"There was a break-in, Inspector." The guard gestured for Ambrye to investigate for herself. "No one knew until we got a message a few minutes ago to come check."

Chavali raised her brow. She'd heard Ambrye order a message sent but hadn't realized they'd have magical communication across the Watch. That Ambrye hadn't sent the message herself intrigued her.

Perhaps only the Watch routinely needed such a capability. Curious about the gate's mechanism, she bent to examine it while Ambrye clearly pretended to sort through papers on the desk and not watch her.

The simple latch and lock surprised Chavali. "Did magic secure this?"

"Why do you ask?" Ambrye said, still faking interest in the papers.

"Because an ordinary street thief could likely open this. Securing important items with such a flimsy barrier seems foolish and I have heard you are not a fool."

Ambrye quirked her brow and set aside the papers. "The entire room is warded and the physical lock is mostly for show. Opening this gate requires a specific key, of which there are two copies. The clerk stationed here keeps one and Watch Captain-General Crayton has the other. Which would you like to accuse of treachery?"

Chavali shrugged. "Neither. It's just as likely one of them is among the dead bodies I can smell within."

At Ambrye's glance, one guard said, "When we found the gate open, we secured the room so nothing would be disturbed before you could investigate."

Waving Chavali aside, Ambrye paced through the gate and kept going. She moved with purpose, headed down the aisles to someplace specific. Chavali caught up with her in a conspicuously empty section with three bloody corpses littering the ground. Though she'd seen many more dead bodies than she ever wanted to, bile rose in Chavali's throat.

Ambrye crouched beside the nearest, her boots on the edge of a still-wet pool of blood. The man's gray hair and thin frame suggested he must be the clerk. He'd either helped them and been rewarded for it or been overpowered and eliminated as a witness. Chavali could picture a group of men taking the key and dragging him along to keep him quiet. The clerk made a noise or somehow called attention to himself, or perhaps tried to escape. The leader ordered him killed rather than dealing with him.

When she shifted to get a better look at anything other than the corpses, Chavali noticed a thin circle of some grainy substance on the floor, catching the light around the edge of the bare shelves. All three bodies lay outside the circle. Chavali guessed the substance to be some kind of metallic dust, but without knowing what color it was, she had no guess for what type. If she could swipe some, the other Fallen could look it over. Doing so under Ambrye's nose would be a challenge.

"What was in this space?" Chavali asked.

"Everything we recovered in the art raid."

"A striking coincidence."

Ambrye snorted and plucked a thick wooden key from the clerk's body, still hanging from a leather cord attached to his belt loop. "What do you think happened here?"

Chavali stepped around Ambrye and the clerk to get a closer look at the two uniformed corpses. Both also had slashes across their throats and lay in puddles of blood. Colby or Eliot would probably have more useful insights to offer here, as both had experience examining such situations. From Colby's memories, she knew the guards had both died swiftly, though from the two boxes lying on their sides next to a shelf, she suspected a brief struggle.

"Someone escaped with your evidence, and no one noticed."

Ambrye's mouth went thin. "Have you ever seen that silver-blue dust before?"

"No." With the Inspector calling attention to it, Chavali felt safe stooping to examine the dust more closely. "May I touch it?" At Ambrye's nod, Chavali ran a finger through the dust and rubbed it with her thumb. Though it looked grainy, the dust felt smooth and fine. "Intriguing." Under the guise of examining its properties further, she swirled her finger in the dust more. The shapes she drew held their form. That meant nothing to her, but might matter to Portia.

She stood and slipped her hand into her pocket to deposit a pinch of the dust. Did the thieves steal everything to conceal a specific theft, such as the statue, or did they genuinely want all the artwork? Several other questions and thoughts danced in her head, but she had no intention of discussing them with Ambrye.

The princess stood and picked her way to the ring of dust, where she squatted and poked at it herself. Chavali turned away from the whole scene, wondering again why she'd been brought here. Most suspected spies probably weren't taken to crime scenes and asked to assist with the investigation. The espionage accusation seemed likely to be an excuse for something, perhaps keeping an eye on Chavali or gauging her reactions.

Wiping her finger on a kerchief, Ambrye stood. "I've seen enough. Let's go."

Chapter 9

After requesting personnel files for everyone working Evidence Storage, including the deceased, Ambrye led Chavali out of the Watch building again. They used a different door, this one taking them to a fenced area full of carriages. Ambrye selected one with the same bird symbol as her bracers and had Chavali climb in with her.

"To my office," she told the driver. The carriage set off with Ambrye making no attempt to hide her stern stare at Chavali. "So, Chastity, what occupation is it that gives you such familiarity with the smell of dead bodies?"

Chavali watched the city roll by. The ride proved smoother than she expected, with little noise from the horses. "I am a fortune teller. An entertainer."

Ambrye waited. She gave Chavali the impression of a snake, coiled and ready to strike at the first sign of weakness. After several beats without Chavali elaborating, she asked, "What brought you to Harbor City?"

"A boat."

"Of course." Ambrye crossed her arms. With the gesture, her face smoothed into a mask of neutrality. "How long before you leave?"

"My friends have business here. I expect it will take a few days, perhaps as long as a week."

"What business is that?"

Chavali waved the question off, using the gesture to buy time to think. She recalled the story Portia had given at the docks. "Something to do with an aunt. It's mundane and boring."

"Yet they charged into a conflict between thieves and city guards. Your friends seem anything but mundane and boring."

Wishing to deflect the subject, Chavali laughed. "They fall closer to 'stupid' and 'foolish.'"

Several beats passed with only the muffled clopping of hooves intruding on the thick, stifling silence. Ambrye glanced out the window, then leaned forward, fixing Chavali with an intense glare.

"I know you aren't as stupid as you pretend. Whatever foreign interest you represent, it's not welcome here. Conduct your business and be on your way out of North Cascain."

The carriage stopped and Ambrye stepped out, not waiting for a response. Chavali mulled over the unspoken warning that she and the other Fallen would be watched. They'd have to step carefully, especially given their interests overlapped with Ambrye's. On the bright side, if they could find the thieves first, no one would have to know they wanted the statue.

She stepped out of the carriage in front of another impressive stone building. These people had a fondness for such structures. Ambrye leaving her here smacked of the princess being annoyed with her, as she had to know Chavali would never find that inn on her own.

Surveying the area to pick out someone to pester for directions, she noticed a man lurking near the entrance to the building, deep in conflicted thought. His tight, closed body language spoke of someone dreading his duty. He otherwise seemed average, matching the mid-tone coloring of the locals and wearing the same cut of clothes.

Intrigued by him, she approached. As she got closer, she saw the worn spots on his shirt, the interesting stain—old blood, most likely—on his pants, and the scuffs on his leather boots. Combined with his deceptive muscle, she suspected he lived a rough-and-tumble life. Though she had a place to be and a statue to find, she saw an opportunity to ply her trade. Her clan would approve of seizing it.

"Excuse me," she said as she reached him. "I saw you from a distance and noticed your aura. It's strange and curious. May I examine it?"

The man blinked at her. "What?"

"Your aura. It called to me." She reached for his hand. "I mean you no harm."

He snatched her wrist and glanced around. "Are you trying to pickpocket me?" *This has to be a distraction. But I don't see anything. Maybe she's crazy.*

"No. I swear you have nothing to fear from me."

No reason to trust her, just like no reason to trust Gina. Except maybe there is. I hate this. "Sure, lady. Keep moving." He tossed her hand away.

Now curious and interested, Chavali stood her ground. "I can help you with Gina."

He froze. "What? How do you know—" He grabbed her arm and hauled her around the corner. Thumping her against the wall, he leaned in close enough for passersby to mistake them for lovers.

Though his treatment annoyed her, Chavali played her part in the fiction by taking his hand and smiling at him. "You don't know if she has betrayed you, yes?"

Velsin told me to kill her. He thought of Gina, a woman with bright green eyes and short brown hair. His mind painted her as beautiful and talented. The poor man had fallen in love with her but hadn't yet admitted it to himself. Much to Chavali's surprise, she recognized this woman.

He sighed. "Yes. I have no idea."

"If she has, you must do something unpleasant?"

"Yes." *She wouldn't betray us. Or would she? To save her own skin, maybe she would. But she's been in there two days. Long enough to tell them everything about the Broken Ring.*

"And she is inside. I can find out for you."

His brow furrowed. "Why would you do that?" *Who are you and what do you want?*

"I told you. I saw your aura. It called to me. The Creator has put us together for Her own purposes. I want no money from you. Tell me what I must do to see her and I will find out what you need to know."

I should do this myself, but I can't. Maybe the Creator really did send you to help me. He hung his head. "Claim to be her sister. They should let you talk to her. It'll be monitored, so tell her...tell her Rylen sent you."

She squeezed his hand and let go. "Wait here. Succeed or fail, I won't be long." When he stood aside, she slipped away. Glancing back, she saw him lean against the wall, cover his face, and slide to the ground. Whatever this Broken Ring did, Rylen seemed a decent man. Though his distress came more from his feelings for Gina than murder itself, he did seem to find killing generally unpleasant and distasteful. He definitely wasn't an assassin.

Colby would be pleased with her for choosing to help him. He'd also berate her for the approach she took to the problem. Chavali smirked as she imagined his response to her tale of what happened after they parted. She'd already lied, cheated, and stolen, three acts he found abhorrent above all others. The day was still young.

Chapter 10

Chavali waited inside a small stone room. It held one metal table with two matching chairs, and two iron rings set in the floor. As Rylen had suggested, she claimed to be Gina's sister and found herself searched, then escorted to this room. In place of the dagger normally sheathed at the small of her back, she had a claim chit.

She'd been sitting for a few short minutes when the door opened and a uniformed guard hauled the woman from Rylen's mind in. Gina, the female prisoner left behind in the transport attack this morning, frowned at her, but said nothing as the guard clipped her leg and waist shackles to the rings. Both women stayed silent until the guard left them.

Gina set her hands on the table, her iron bracelets clunking against it. "So, Sis," she said, her words slow and careful, as if she had to think about them. "I wasn't expecting to see you here. I thought you'd forgotten all about me."

Chavali covered Gina's hands, offering small comfort. "Rylen convinced me to come."

Why did he send you? That dolt doesn't have the balls to face me? Gina pictured him in her mind and Chavali saw how the two of them often butted heads. The woman had no idea he cared as much as he did because he was too stupid and cowardly to tell her.

"Really? What's he want?"

"He is chiefly concerned that you might be suffering here. More than just for being jailed, I mean."

"What?" *Why? That numbskull would rob a grandma before he'd show "concern" for anyone rotting in jail. Especially someone picked up for something so stupid and now suspected of fourteen kinds of conspiracy.* She agonized over her initial capture, an incident when she'd been negotiating with a black market art dealer she'd fenced through a few times. It turned out he'd been a Watch plant all along and had been waiting for her to bring him a big score. She knew she should've gone to the Ring's usual contact, Clara.

Chavali had to stop herself from sitting up straighter. This act of largesse on her part had stumbled her into someone associated with the art theft. The timing added up, and an expensive piece had to have come from that collection. Once again, she had to admit Colby had a point about helping strangers: it often paid her back in unexpected ways. "I don't know him well, but it's plain as day that he's in love with you."

Gina stared at her, thoughts frozen in shock. Then a thought popped into her mind, of Rylen offering her a hand when he didn't need to. She remembered him punching a woman in the face for insulting her. Fifty other moments filled her head, crashing in a wave of sudden understanding.

"Yes, I imagine it's surprising," Chavali murmured.

The nudge of her words pulled Gina out of her memories. *Now I find out. Rylen, you're such an idiot.* She looked at their hands. "I guess I never noticed."

"Men are like this. I doubt he's fully realized it for himself yet. He wanted to come in to see you himself, and was goaded to do so by a mutual friend, but worried about what he might have to do to protect the house. Would you like me to deliver a message for you?"

Gina puzzled over Chavali's statement until she realized Velsin must have sent him. *Of course it'd be Rylen. The man could sneak in and out of the jail if he put his mind to it. He'd hate using that skill to kill instead of steal, but he'd do it if it meant keeping the whole Ring safe from discovery. I'll bet he would've come sooner if only he'd had time.*

"Tell him..." A lone tear slid down Gina's cheek. "Tell him I wish I'd known before. And I'll be in here forever because I'll never tell them what they want to know." *I'll never betray Velsin, and I'll never betray you either, Rylen. I wish—*

Not wanting to eavesdrop on Gina's anguish, Chavali pulled her hands away and stood. "So long as you live, there is hope. He is, after all, a man of a great many talents, is he not? Take care of yourself, Gina. I may not be able to return."

She left Gina behind, pleased with herself for discovering so much in such a short time. These two would-be lovers were resourceful enough to find a way to overcome their separation and she needed to do nothing more than prod Rylen to make an effort.

He sat where she'd left him, miserable and dejected. When she crouched beside him and laid a hand on his knee, he searched her eyes. His face crumpled in despair. "That didn't take very long."

"Did it have to?" Chavali smirked. "She is true, Rylen. You don't need to kill her. Her loyalty to you and your employer is strong enough to overcome all but the worst torture."

For a moment, he stared, then he brightened enough to burn away storm clouds. "Really?"

"Yes. She was quite clear. Her own arrogance caused her arrest, and she holds no one else responsible for it. You and yours are safe from her."

He seized her hand and kissed it. "I can't imagine how to repay you." His mind helpfully supplied a few physical options, though he had no real interest in her.

Uninterested in his idea of what either she or Gina looked like naked, she tugged her hand away. "Let's call this a debt to be paid. A favor for a favor."

"Of course. If I can do it, it'll be done."

She smiled, pleased to come to such a favorable agreement for so little work. "I need nothing now. Where can I find you later?"

"The Ringer. It's a tavern near the docks. Ask for me there. If I'm not around, leave a message." He took her hand again and squeezed it, letting her see he hadn't lied about the location.

Chavali squeezed his hand back and stood. "It's worth saying that a clever man might be able to find a way to get in to see a prisoner for pleasant reasons." With that, she knew she sent his thoughts churning by the look on his face. "Good luck, Rylen. I hope to find you in good health and spirits when next we meet."

Chapter 11

Eidel's Landing showed Chavali that Ambrye had good taste in accommodations. Warm wood and bright lights greeted her when she stepped inside the large inn. Cushioned booths lined the walls of the spacious common room, tall stools provided seating at the polished bar, and round tables filled the otherwise empty space in the middle.

The aroma of roasting garlic filled the air, making Chavali's stomach growl. She hadn't eaten since a paltry few bites of bread and cheese on the boat. Few customers populated the room, and she avoided them as she wove her way to the bar. As she sat, intending to discover where to find the others and order food to be sent there, a man at the far end of the bar jumped out of his seat.

"Crumbling!" he cried. "I see it, plain as the jewels on a frog's behind!"

Chavali leaned to see the lunatic and found a man with nothing more strange about him than a wild look in his eyes. The cut of his clothes matched what she'd seen on the streets and showed no unusual signs of wear or soil. His hair was combed, his face clean-shaven. Aside from his mad raving, he fit in here.

"Watchers, watchers, everywhere! Pillars crumbling in despair."

The rhyme made Chavali give him a second look. Earlier, the dark butterfly man had given an uncanny description of her spirit connection. This man used a cadence and rhyme that reminded her of her own prophecies. Though the spirits hadn't forced one on her since Ket, she remembered every single incident, and this man's words sounded like the type of thing they'd make her say.

He focused on her and asked her, "Can't you see it?"

The bartender snapped his fingers at the waitress setting dishes of steaming food on a table. "Minnie! Go fetch the Watch to pick this guy up. Sorry, folks." He threw a towel over his shoulder and hurried around the bar to hustle the madman outside.

The waitress set the last plate down and sprinted out the door.

"Purple! Purple! He is coming in purple! The foundations are dying. Purple!"

With a grunt, the bartender shoved him outside and slammed the door in his face. "Sorry about that, folks," he announced to the silent room. "He seemed fine when he walked in."

Chavali stared at the door, dumbstruck. When the spirits swarmed her for a prophecy, she saw purple. How could two men, so different in so many ways, say such precisely disturbing things to her? She'd traveled the entire continent several times over with her clan since she became the Seer and never before encountered a single person with any curse like hers. No one had ever seen anything special about her until Robin came for her and murdered her clan. She shuddered and turned away.

Behind the bar again, the bartender gave her a kindly smile. "I'm sorry about that, miss. Third one this month. Can't stop idiots from being idiots, you know?"

While she agreed with the sentiment, Chavali had no idea what he meant. "The third what this month?"

"Blue Death user." He said it so offhanded that she chose not to ask for more information. "Would you like something to eat or drink?"

Several minutes later, Chavali sat on the bed in the room Portia had rented for both of them, eating thick, creamy soup in a bread bowl. Of all the food choices, it had seemed the quickest.

Portia and Sivry sat opposite her on the other bed. Colby opened the door and walked in, relief emanating from him in palpable waves.

"I'm so glad she let you go. We didn't have any good ideas for what to do if they decided to jail you. What happened?" He made several awkward half-gestures, as if he couldn't figure out how to behave in this situation. They'd held a similar meeting in Ket, so Chavali had no idea what bothered him. Finally, he sat on the floor between both beds and crossed both arms and legs.

"That was Princess Ambrye, who apparently serves the city as an inspector. The people here adore her and are in awe of her powers of observation. In fairness, I found her quite sharp. Sharp enough to guess when I lied to her."

"Nothing good can come of that," Colby said with a sigh.

"Hush." Portia waved him off. "Let her tell us everything she magically managed to deduce while walking around."

Chavali snorted. "Very well. A gang called the Broken Ring was involved in fencing the goods stolen when Harris's caravan was attacked.

Their black market contact is named Clara, and I know what she looks like. I have my own contact within that group, but am certain he played no part in the attack itself. It's unclear who currently has our statue, because it was stolen along with everything else from the Watch building, which happened at the same time as the attack on that prisoner transport."

She stood and had Portia cup her hands, then turned her pocket out onto them. "This dust was found at the scene of the evidence room art theft. It surrounded the area with the missing evidence."

"See? She's brilliant." Portia turned her attention to the dust.

Chavali smirked and sat again. "While the people love Ambrye, and are quite excited about the queen's birthday celebration a week from now, the Watch is more conflicted. Some members seem neutral, others actively dislike her. I can't say with certainty why, but given her pronouncements at the scene, I suspect she steals the spotlight. Additionally, she has a rival inspector, Kalei, who feels Ambrye must cheat somehow, though I fail to understand how anyone could cheat at such a thing, other than by causing the crime in the first place and pretending to solve it.

"What I cannot explain is this Blue Death matter. For a second time, I was targeted for interest by an apparent user of this substance." Since Sivry had no knowledge of Chavali's peculiar abilities and neither Portia nor Colby knew the full truth, she refrained from explaining more than this.

"While you were out," Sivry said, "I did some scouting. The guards made sure we got rooms, then left. There's a regular patrol on this street, which is probably why the princess suggested it. I discovered this

Blue Death is a drug of some kind. It's being distributed by a gang in the dockside area, called the Drowned Ones. People are afraid of them, especially since the Watch hasn't been able to nab any of them. Rumors say the leader can see the future and uses that to evade capture."

Chavali glanced at Colby, who met her gaze with a frown. "It can't be connected," he said.

"It can be," Chavali said, echoing his frown, "but we would prefer if it were not." Too many threads connected this mission to what happened in Ket. Half the trouble there involved a woman who'd drowned and been animated by...*something.*

Colby nodded. "We'll have to watch out for them. I stayed here in case the Watch needed to see someone being a good boy. It sounds like we have avenues to follow. Portia?"

"This dust? I don't know. I'm not sure if it's silver mixed with some blue substance or some material that grinds up both silver and blue. I'll have to try magic on it to get anything useful. It'd be best to wait until morning."

Unsurprised after Portia's explanation of her magic earlier, Chavali set her empty bread bowl aside. "I think this black market contact is the best option to proceed. It isn't too late to go now, but I worry about venturing into what I think might be an unsavory area so soon after Ambrye warned me to leave the city." Once they contacted Clara, it should be a simple matter of paying whatever price the statue demanded.

They could be home in a day or two without having to scour the city or solve other people's problems. It would be a refreshing change of pace. Of course, going home so soon meant dealing with Kelly and delving into Harris's memories. Karias also wanted to talk to her.

She stifled a sigh.

Sivry flicked her gaze from Chavali to Colby and back. "Are you sure you don't want to share the room with Colby? Portia arranged things this way, but I thought I'd ask."

"What?" Chavali and Colby asked at the same time.

"You two are involved, aren't you?" Sivry shrank from Chavali's withering glare. "That's what I heard in the tower. And you kind of...act like..."

Chavali rolled her eyes.

"Good friends?" Colby supplied.

"That place is worse than a wagon full of old women," Chavali spat.

Portia stood without a word and dumped the small pile of dust onto the nightstand. She hid her face and pawed through her pack.

"If you're uncomfortable sharing a room with Colby, I'll switch with you. Because I trust him."

"Thank you," Colby said.

"You're welcome." Chavali fixed Sivry with a pointed stare. "Do I need to move my things?"

Sivry shrugged. "No, you don't need to. I just thought you'd want to. I was trying to be accommodating."

Nothing in the world could stop gossip. Chavali knew rumors floated around about the two of them. She didn't care. Rather, she only cared enough to be irritated by them. No one needed to know what she did with Colby in his room. Bleating goats would bleat even if they knew she spent that time searching his mind for manipulations and undoing them.

She looked to Colby and scoffed at the idea of them together. Aside from embodying everything Colby most disapproved of, her heart still belonged to Keino, that bastard. A man who'd irritated her in life shouldn't have so much sway over her in death. But he invaded her dreams. He'd never done that before he died.

"No harm is done." Chavali hefted her pack. "Perhaps we should switch anyway. Portia needs her rest to prepare for the spell working. My nightmares won't help that."

Chapter 12

Chavali sat on the bed in Colby's room, staring out the window and nibbling on her cold, soup-soaked bread in the light of a single candle. Stars dotted the sky outside, half-hidden by nearby buildings. Harris and Keino both weighed on her mind. Neither would leave her alone, even in death.

Colby returned from the washroom and climbed into bed. Even with his head touching the wall, his feet hung off the end. "I'm sorry about the rumors."

Chavali waved him off. "People talk. This is what they do. I apologize in advance if I wake you. Lately, my nightmares are strange and I sometimes wake screaming."

"I'll try not to overreact."

She wished she felt tired enough to sleep. Then she wouldn't have to bear the sympathy Colby offered. "So long as it's shadows you insist upon beheading in my defense, you should be fine."

He took a breath like he had something else to say, but held it. A few long seconds later, he said, "Good night, Chavali."

"Good night." She leaned against the wall and couldn't suppress a memory of Harris bumping into her last week after knife practice with Eliot. He'd offered to run down to the cafeteria on the nineteenth floor and fetch her lunch. She'd turned him down in favor of bathing. The next day, he stopped by to tell her he'd been sent on a mission by himself, and to ask about pointers for what Eldrack expected on his return. Then he was gone.

Perhaps he deserved more from her than reluctance to face the memories she'd pulled from him. Though she blamed him for attacking her in an ambush in the first place, she could have let him go or handed him over to authorities. Instead, she brought him to the Fallen. Once he'd stepped inside the Fallen tower, his choices narrowed to join or die.

She'd never tried to mine others' memories before. Her work with Colby had expanded her understanding of the limited telepathy granted by the spirits, but she had yet to explore it fully. Beyond that, everything she did with Colby's memories happened in *his* mind, not her own. She'd snagged Harris's memories and locked them away to avoid dealing with them. As soon as she got home, Kelly would force her to pry the lock open.

Dealing with this on her own terms appealed a great deal. Determined to try, she snuffed the candle, slid under the covers, and closed her eyes. As she did when she delved into Colby's mind, she took a deep breath and focused on her goal. With him, she needed little effort now. He'd learned to accept her intrusion as she'd learned to force it with increasing deftness. This time, however, she had no other mind to dive into.

Goading herself to think of Harris, she recalled the moment they met. At the time, she didn't realize how lucky she'd gotten in fighting back against him. He and his band chose to attack her and her mission partner on their way to a small village. The way she'd held a knife to his throat while her partner finished up the rest of the bandits reminded her of a man holding her at knifepoint. Keino charged to her rescue. He heard her cry for help and came for her. Like he always did.

This was no time to think about Keino. He had nothing to do with Harris. The two men had never met. By the time she met Harris, Keino had been dead for months. Chavali clenched her jaw and pushed Keino and all his baggage aside. She needed to learn more about Harris.

She recalled Harris picking a lock for a wine merchant's shop in Ket. His deft fingers made short work of the task and he moved with the grace of a cat. Unlike Keino, who moved like the hulking brute he was. His strength showed most clearly when he snatched her wrist to make her pay attention to him.

Mindful of Colby's need to sleep, Chavali kept her frustrated growl quiet. She forced herself to remember sitting in bathrobes with Harris, waiting for their clothes to dry in front of a roaring fire. He impressed her with his pragmatism and practicality. Were she interested in sharing her life with someone, Harris would be a reasonable choice. The idea of enduring his thoughts, though, made her lip curl.

Keino's thoughts had been the one thing she couldn't handle about him. When he kissed her, he thought about her as a prize to be won and a possession to be protected. He knew she could read his mind and showed her those ideas on purpose, believing it would please her. Why did she always attract such idiotic, frustratingly—

Chavali scowled. If everything turned to memories of Keino,

she'd never get anywhere with this. Perhaps the afternoon spent sparring with the princess had tired her more than she thought. Tomorrow night, she'd try again. For now, she indulged in one of her favorite memories of Keino.

She sat in her family's wagon, lacing beads onto a lock of hair. Keino stood behind her, holding the rest of her hair out of the way. Pasha would do this for her, but her little sister had other duties that morning. As her bodyguard, Keino's entire job revolved around doing whatever she needed, whenever she needed it.

In the mirror, she watched him trace the line of her neck and shoulder with his eyes. His hand hovered inches from her skin, his desire to touch her plain. For the third time, he shifted closer to her, his body heat warming her back.

"Keino," she chided. "If you can't hold my hair properly, get out."

He breathed in her scent. "I just want to touch you."

She glared at him in the mirror. "I have to deal with strangers today. Don't push me."

For once, he did as she asked. He stepped back and withdrew his hand with a heavy, melodramatic sigh. "I could protect you easier if you took over your own wagon. If you ask, no one in the clan will deny you. Having to work around your family gets in the way."

"You only want me to get my own wagon so you can keep me to yourself as often as possible."

"Is that wrong?" He met her gaze in the mirror, his eyes filled with longing.

Chavali turned her attention to fastening the last bead. She wished she could fall into his arms and hated that she couldn't. Fear kept them apart more than anything else—her fear of his thoughts and of the consequences were she to give in. "Yes. Your services are no longer needed here. Go."

He let her hair fall and crossed his arms. When he opened his mouth, she held up a hand to forestall him. "Out," she snapped and flicked her hand toward the door.

Without further argument, he stalked out. The satisfaction of seeing him do what she told him made her smile. She adjusted the off-the-shoulder neckline of her dress and brushed her dark eyebrows with a finger, then turned away from the mirror.

Dipping her hand into the pouch at her belt, she grasped a handful of the bones and crystals she used as divining props. She tossed them on the floor and watched them bounce and roll. This memory suddenly felt off. Chavali never threw more than five of her bones and baubles at once. Fifteen lay on the floor now, in a strange pattern.

She crouched and traced the lines they formed with her finger. Her brow furrowed as she puzzled out the letters and fitted them together. "He...is...coming. He is coming." She tapped the final bone, marked with a symbol for disaster. When she checked the other symbols, they were all the same. Stranger still, she saw them all in full color. This bone's purple ink wash stood out against that tiger-eye cylinder.

None of this made sense. Each of her bones, crystals, and other oddments had a different symbol carved and inked on one side. She used them as prompts to help her fake readings for customers. Seer Marika had taught her that trick and what the symbols meant. Someday, she would teach the girl chosen as her own successor.

The wagon rocked as someone pounded on the door. Chavali fell to the floor and noticed a strange chest in the corner with a heavy lock holding it shut. The door slammed open and Keino filled the doorway. His brown eyes pleaded for her regard. He set one foot into the wagon and it groaned under his weight. The floor tipped toward him.

Chavali scrambled for anything to keep her from sliding to him. Her hands and feet scraped across the wood floor to no avail.

"Why do you always push me away?" Keino took another step into the wagon, forcing it steeper.

Patting the floor in a panic, Chavali found a loose board and clung to it. "I can't give you what you want."

Keino slammed the door shut and held out a hand for her. "Don't fight me, Chavali. I can't protect you if you won't let me."

"Protect me from what?" Chavali dangled from the board, her feet too close to Keino's hand for comfort. The chest, anchored against the wall, thumped and bounced. The wagon rocked in a strong wind, sending Chavali swinging and threatening to drop her on Keino. "Is this about Harris?"

"I promised I'd protect you, Chavali! Let me. You never let me do what's best for you."

Light spilled through cracks in the trunk. Something thumped against the lid, trying to break through.

"Harris is there, isn't he?" When the wagon swung her toward the trunk, she flung herself at it. She landed on the edge and reached for the lock.

Keino stepped toward her. "Stop fighting me! I've only ever wanted to keep you safe. Why can't you accept that?"

She hung her head and let her arm fall limp. "You've never understood. Never." The wagon bucked and the window shattered. Shards of glass flew through the air, wicked and sharp. Keino leaped to shield her. The top of the wagon ripped away, revealing darkness.

Chapter 13

Chavali sat up, gasping for breath. "Claws," she rasped, her throat raw. She barely saw them, but knew the thing tearing off the top of the wagon used huge, thick claws to do it.

It was just a dream. You're stronger than it. I know you are. Anything you put your mind to, you can conquer. Whatever you saw, it's over.

She recognized the voice in her mind, and the steady rock of Karias's presence. Colby sat on the edge of her bed, his hand holding hers. In the darkness, she saw nothing of him but an outline against the faint moonlight outside.

I wish I could do something to help you with this the way you've helped me with mine. Here's a cup of water. Drink.

Colby pressed a cup into her hand and let go of her. She sipped the water, not sure what to make of her nightmare. The vision had changed from memory to dream, but Keino behaved too close to the truth for it to mean nothing. Was his spirit vying for dominance over the others? How could that even happen? Seer Marika had never hinted about any such thing being possible.

"Do you think you can get back to sleep?" Colby's voice, rough and weary, stabbed her with guilt. "If you need to talk about it, we can talk about it."

"No, I am fine. Thank you. I am sorry you must suffer through this."

"It's what friends do." He squeezed her shoulder and shifted to his own bed. "If you ever want to talk, you know I'm here for you."

Too many people want to be her confidant. Chavali took a deep breath. "Yes. I know." She listened to his bed creak and his covers rustle. He deserved at least to know what disturbed his sleep. "I dreamed of my clan. And Harris. The dead. Always the dead, never the living."

He left a heavy silence for several long seconds. "None of those deaths were your fault, Chavali. Not a single one. Every one of those people was murdered, and the fault lies squarely on the shoulders of their killers. Nothing you did or didn't do forced them to be depraved."

She stared out the window, not sure how to respond. By the time she thought to thank him again, she noticed his breathing had become deep and even. Lying down, she worried Keino's spirit might be growing in power somehow. She had no idea what to do about that or why he wanted her to stay away from Harris's memories.

Resisting him seemed her best option. Anything else would require explaining everything to Eldrack or Railan, a prospect she found unpalatable. When Eldrack stopped keeping secrets from her, she'd consider doing the same. Even so, she had no intention of revealing clan secrets to either of them.

Eventually, she fell asleep. She woke before sunlight hit her face and drew the curtains over the window for Colby's benefit. He deserved to sleep as late as he wanted. Making as little noise as possible, she dressed and slipped out to the common room. Sivry joined her as the waitress delivered her breakfast.

"Portia is still asleep," Sivry said after greeting her.

"The same for Colby. He can stay behind with Portia and assist her. I doubt he would be especially helpful on our errand anyway."

"You know him, so I trust your judgment on that."

Chavali arched an eyebrow as she cut her egg-topped biscuit. She could tell the woman meant nothing by the statement beyond the obvious, but felt inclined toward making a point. "I do know him rather well, yes. He's generally an impediment to anything requiring subterfuge. Handy in a fight."

Sivry grinned. "I got the point, Chavali—"

"Chastity, please. My name is too exotic to be used on missions. Portia and Colby already know, so it slipped my mind."

"Chastity, then. Are we good?"

"Yes, quite." Chavali had nothing further to say until they finished breakfast and set off for the bleaker parts of the city. When she explained where to find Clara, Sivry thankfully recognized it from her explorations. They passed the city center, where the wealthy lived, and kept going.

On the fringes of the north side, Chavali felt like they breached an invisible barrier holding back despair and desperation. In the span of one block, the streets became rough, the people's clothing threadbare and grimy, and the thug-like denizens plentiful.

Two musclebound, scarred men loitered near the entrance to

Step'n Stein, a tavern of questionable virtue that fit in with its surroundings. Steel bars criss-crossed over blacked-out windows, and a layer of grime darkened the door. When Chavali touched the dingy knob, she found it sticky. Refusing to think about what might be on it, she pushed the door in and entered a smoky, dingy room too small to cover the entire first floor of the building. She grimaced at the stench of old fish, burnt lemon, and dried sweat.

Chavali's boots stuck to the floor enough to make a slurping noise when she picked up her feet. She peered through the murk and picked out Clara from Gina's memory of her. The middle-aged woman sat in a booth next to the back door, sipping from a small, flowery teacup and reading a stack of papers in a folder. Wire-frame reading glasses perched on the end of her rounded nose. Opposite her, a man in a hooded cloak picked up a cup and stood. He walked away like a man who'd concluded his business without satisfaction. Chavali saw little of him—a strong, clean-shaven chin and a fit body—before he disappeared through the back door.

Having never interacted with any kind of black market before, Chavali could only guess at the etiquette of approaching one of its major merchants. She glanced at Sivry, thinking the elf might have some experience, but had no idea how to explain the problem without alerting every large, sketchy man present to their purpose. Seeing no other option, she threaded through the tables to the booth in back and stopped beside the table.

Clara looked up and covered the top papers with her arm. The loose linen of her blouse obscured the entire stack. "Can I help you with something?" She had a warm, earthy voice perked with suspicion.

"Rylen sent me."

"Did he?" Clara raised her brow. "Why would he do that?"

"May I sit?"

Clara looked Chavali up and down, then did the same to Sivry. She closed her folder and moved it to the bench beside her. "You may, yes. Both of you."

"Thank you." Chavali slid into the booth, leaving enough space for Sivry to sit. As she'd hoped, the elf sat and directed her attention outward, watching the room for trouble. "My name is Chastity. I'm looking for a particular object he thought you might be able to assist me in locating. It recently passed through the hands of the Watch. Briefly."

Clasping her hands in her lap, Clara regarded Chavali with matronly curiosity. "I meet a lot of people, Chastity, but I've never heard your accent before. Where are you from?"

Chavali smirked. "Not North Cascain. Beyond that is none of your business."

Clara laughed. "I see. You have secrets to keep, just as I do. Very well, then. What is the object?"

"A statue depicting a cat, about this big." Chavali held her hands to indicate a shape roughly one foot long and half as wide. "It was last seen inside a polished metal box. The piece was part of a collection confiscated by the Watch a few days ago, and then liberated from the Watch yesterday."

All traces of amusement fled Clara's expression. She went still and pressed her lips together hard enough to turn white. Chavali wished she had a good excuse to touch the woman, because she also caught a flicker of recognition at the description of the statue in Clara's eyes. "From the

West Watch building?"

"Yes, just so. Is this a problem?"

Clara glanced over her shoulder and scanned the room. She leaned in and lowered her voice. "Walk away. Leave it be."

"I cannot." Chavali cast for a reason other than the truth and grasped at the first thing she thought of. "It's an heirloom of my husband's family, taken while en route to his brother for safekeeping. Neither is yet aware of the theft, and I wish to keep this true."

Pulling her glasses off her nose, Clara sighed. "If you'd come to me before the Watch raided the Ring, I could have gotten it for you."

Chavali hid her surprise. She'd expected to hear the Ring had sold it to Clara. The statue had been hidden in a vault for decades, or maybe centuries. Who else could find it as valuable as Eldrack?

"You know who broke into the Watch's Evidence Storage."

"Of course I do." Clara sipped her tea, not quite hiding a grimace. "The Bloodflies don't keep their work quiet."

"I haven't heard of these people before."

Clara barked a mirthless laugh. "Where've you been?" She shook her head. "The point is, I don't deal with them."

Annoyed at the complication, Chavali took a moment to think. They'd have to learn more about these Bloodflies. The group terrified someone handling business through an underground marketplace in a city with paranoid, observant authorities. She supposed they must have been the ones who attacked the prisoner transport also. Based upon that experience, she knew they weren't to be underestimated or trifled with.

"On the chance you come across it, will you contact me to purchase it?"

"Yes. But don't expect much. If you want to commission a replica to fool your husband and his family, I can connect you with an excellent artist."

Chavali tapped Sivry on the shoulder, and the elf stood. "Thank you for your time. I appreciate it."

"Good luck," Clara said. She then muttered something as Chavali and Sivry walked away. It sounded suspiciously like, "You'll need it."

Chapter 14

"I heard a little about the Bloodflies while I was out yesterday," Sivry said, once they'd put the bar behind them. "Mostly, people talked about how scary they are. Didn't think to connect them with the attacks, but now it makes sense. It's some sort of gang."

"A gang with enough members to risk many to retrieve prisoners." Chavali agreed. "And one with knowledge of the route the transport would take. I wonder how secret this information is kept?"

"Ambrye would know."

"Ambrye dislikes me a great deal."

Sivry smirked. "She knows your name. That's a step in the right direction."

Chavali snorted. As they left the slums behind, she saw a carriage for hire trundling down the street with its vacant card hanging in view and hailed it. They rode back to the inn, Chavali pondered the situation in silence. Hopes for a swift mission remained, though it now seemed unlikely. Portia could still trace the ring, but if these Bloodflies didn't want to sell it, they'd have to pursue other options.

Because Clara wouldn't even consider approaching them and people generally found them frightening, Chavali had no expectation the gang would deal fairly. These Bloodflies had chosen a dire name. She doubted that had been accidental. After seeing their handiwork, she knew they'd earned it.

Calling on Rylen to explain about the Bloodflies seemed a waste of the boon she'd earned. Conversely, asking him to help her infiltrate their headquarters stretched the meaning of "favor" too far to be reasonable. If they could find no other options, she'd consider it.

When they returned to the inn, Chavali had a mind to get a cup of tea. Few patrons sat in the common room, and she had her choice of seats at the bar. As she turned to ask Sivry to go up and let Portia and Colby know they'd returned, she noticed the bartender hurriedly averting his gaze. Her attention piqued, she scanned the room.

Two men in the back shared drinks, one watching Chavali discreetly. On the other side of the room, a woman sat by herself with a steaming mug. Her gaze flicked up and her shoulders tensed. Recognition and anticipation painted her features. A man near the front door paid them no attention, but his clothing stuck out as odd compared to what Chavali had seen here so far.

She followed Sivry to the stairs. "Something is going on," she murmured to the elf.

"The air is tense," Sivry agreed.

"Hurry. I worry for Portia and Colby."

Sivry nodded and quickened her steps. She unlocked their room door as Chavali checked inside hers and Colby's. Finding no sign of the big man or his whereabouts, Chavali hurried into Portia's room to find the elf on one knee beside four stones and a smear of silver dust in the center. Portia's pack sat open on the floor.

The stones had been scattered, Chavali thought, as had the dust. She could almost see Portia crouched beside the proper square arrangement, weaving her magic over the construct to focus it. Something had happened to disturb the working. Colby knew better than to interrupt.

Chavali shut and locked the door, then leaned against it. Sivry met her gaze, echoing her unease.

"Should we—" Before Sivry could finish, something thumped into the door hard enough to shove Chavali forward and make the wood crack. The next thump smashed the lock and threw the door open. Two uniformed guards rushed in, swords drawn, while more blocked escape through the doorway.

Chavali knew futility when she saw it. She stood her ground and held her hands up. Sivry remained on the floor, but also raised her hands. With neither resisting, the guards sheathed their swords. One grabbed Chavali's wrist with a gauntlet and the other hauled Sivry to her feet.

"Chastity," Chavali's guard said, "you and your companion are under arrest."

"For what?" Chavali could think of three things she'd done since leaving Ambrye's presence that the princess might have objected to. She had no idea how the woman knew about any of it. While she might have noticed Chavali speaking with Gina, that happened yesterday. If the interview peeved Ambrye, she would have done something about it then.

"Our orders are to detain you, not have a conversation." The guard dragged her out of the room and threw her at the wall, though she didn't resist. These men could cut her down with little effort and she knew it.

Looking over her shoulder, she kept her hands up. "I wear a dagger at the small of my back."

The Watchman groped her roughly from behind. Chavali twisted and slapped him. Even as her arm flew, she knew he'd treat her worse for it, but she refused to accept his unnecessarily harsh manhandling. She hadn't resisted or tried to hide a weapon from him.

As expected, he reacted. She grunted in pain and surprise when he punched her in the side, then squealed as he twisted her arm behind her back and shoved her into the wall again. Crowding her from behind, he growled into her ear, "Try that again and you'll be carried out."

Scowling, Chavali glared at him. Though she hated backing down from such an ass, she said nothing else. He patted her down from head to toe, then forced her ahead of him with both hands behind her back. Outside, he tossed her into an enclosed wagon. Another guard shoved Sivry in hard enough to knock her off her feet. As the wagon bounced over the road, they helped each other sit up.

"I'd like to say slapping him made things worse," Sivry said, "but these men seemed primed for violence. I think they wanted to provoke us."

Chavali rubbed her side and found it tender. "This thought has also crossed my mind. I cannot imagine why we've been arrested, but it's clearly something they find upsetting."

"Let's hope they explain before they pummel us into unconsciousness."

Chapter 15

Chavali sat in a small room similar to the one she'd met Gina in. This one had no table and one chair bolted to the floor. Her wrists and ankles had been shackled to it, and she now waited for someone to come and fail to get information from her. Sivry had been led elsewhere, and Chavali hadn't seen any sign of Portia or Colby.

The cramped confines set her teeth on edge. She'd grown used to her room in the Fallen tower, but she still remembered her family's wagons with longing. Though small on the inside, they'd moved. Every day, they'd bounced along roads and paths, sometimes even forging through wilderness. Every night, they'd stopped someplace new and different. In the tower, she had to cope with the stagnation of stationary life. The people, always wild and intriguing, made up for it, even when she wanted to strangle them. Including Eldrack.

She wracked her brain, trying to come up with a reason for the manner of her arrest. Nothing made sense. Lying to the Watch to get access to Gina should only have prompted Ambrye to question her again, and the princess seemed the type to come to the inn herself and get to the point. Stealing the dust likely wouldn't trigger this either. At the worst, that would prompt Ambrye to have them watched, to see what they came up with. Though the timing suggested correlation to the visit with Clara, logic again refused to cooperate.

Chavali wondered if she'd read Ambrye wrong. In that case, she had no basis to guess from. Yet, in her years of reading minds and selling fortunes, she'd grown quite adept at judging the nuances of behavior. Ambrye's precision and neatness pointed to an ordered, logical mindset. Her escort of Chavali to Evidence Storage spoke of guarded suspicion, the kind that kept friends close and enemies closer. She made grand, showy displays yet wore little to announce her station, suggesting confidence and competence with no need for false humility and only a trifling amount of arrogance.

All this combined to tell Chavali she'd missed something.

The door opened, sparing her from further contemplation. A uniformed woman strode in, head high, and long, light-colored hair tied in a loose tail. Stripes on her shoulders spoke of rank and the calm in her composure attested to experience. She stopped in front of Chavali, close enough to force her to crane her neck to meet the woman's steely gaze.

"Your name is Chastity?" Her voice reminded Chavali of Penny's dry wit and high intellect.

"Yes."

"What are you doing in Harbor City?"

"At the moment, I'm sitting. May I have your name?"

The woman gave her a withering stare. "Captain Denton. Why did you come to Harbor City?"

Without knowing the structure of the Watch, Chavali had no way to evaluate the woman's rank. She could, however, assume the woman had more authority than an average Watchman. "For the delightful conversation and ambiance."

"Do you have any idea how much trouble you're in?"

"Yes, it's quite clear that being foreign is a horrible crime in this city. If you don't mind, I would appreciate having my possessions dumped outside the city with me when I am removed. I can acquire new clothing, but it's a hassle."

Denton leaned down, putting her face close to Chavali's. Her breath smelled of stale coffee. "Do you think this is a joke?"

"No, I think this is a strange tactic to use against someone Ambrye decided to allow to run loose in her city. But perhaps you're unaware of this. Do the Inspectors tell the Watch what they're doing?"

The tiny lines around Denton's eyes tightened and her mouth went thin. Chavali had struck a chord and wondered how deep she could make it reverberate. With enough pressure, she could learn a great many things. Some might even help her escape this infernal room.

Denton straightened and crossed her arms. "How do you know the princess?"

"We met by chance." Chavali watched Denton pace with the patience of a caged animal. "She found my accent offensive. If you bring her here, I'm sure she'd corroborate."

"Yes, I'm sure," Denton sneered. "What did you do with her?"

The wording of the question made Chavali pause. It was a curious way to ask about their meeting. "Why do you not ask her? I suspect her word is more trusted than mine."

"Answer the question."

"We shared a conversation. We examined Evidence Storage. We rode in her carriage. She asked me questions, I was helpful."

"Helpful." Denton snorted. "Like now?"

"Quite." Chavali grinned. "I am not your enemy, Captain. My interests here do not run counter to yours."

"Oh? And what are your interests here?"

"My business does not require me to break any of your laws. It is, therefore, my own."

"Are you sure about that?"

Growing weary of this, Chavali rolled her eyes. "Go speak to Ambrye. I have nothing further to say until she is consulted."

"I'd love to, but she's gone missing."

"Missing?" Too surprised to hide it, Chavali blinked stupidly. "That woman does not tie her boot laces without checking it off her to-do list."

Denton smirked. "That may be, but she left a note behind saying that if anything happens to her, you and your friends should be the first suspects. You won't explain your business, your friend had more of that mysterious silver dust from Evidence Storage and she's a mage, and I know you were out and about this morning. Where did you go?"

"You think I was out abducting her?" Chavali's mind raced, trying to guess what the others might have blurted out in their clumsy attempts to deal with such an accusation.

"I have no reason to believe otherwise."

Though she hated to do it, Chavali saw no other option than speaking plainly. If she continued to be difficult, she could wind up sitting here for a very long time, and who knew what would happen to the statue. "We are here to retrieve an item stolen from our employer. It was part of the art collection raided from the Broken Ring, then stolen by the Bloodflies from Evidence Storage. I took some of the dust when I visited there so the mage could study it. We have no interest in your politics, princess, or anything else aside from that cat statue."

Denton blinked at her. "A statue."

"Yes. Small enough to carry in a saddlebag."

"All this with you is about a small statue. A piece of art."

"Yes. I believe the Bloodflies have it, and it is our intention to take it from them, one way or another."

Waving her off, Denton said, "They couldn't have pulled the Evidence heist off. They're nuisance level thugs. Who's your employer?"

"A private individual. I am not at liberty to reveal his identity." Chavali puzzled over Denton's dismissal of the Bloodflies. They seemed more than a nuisance to her. Several men had been killed, and Clara seemed certain they were responsible. Chavali trusted Clara's fear. Perhaps the situation had changed since Denton last heard. New members or a new leader could send a gang in a new direction. She knew that from Harris.

"Regardless," Chavali said, "I assure you he wants only the statue. Once we determined the Watch no longer possessed it, we ceased to be interested in either the Watch or the Inspectors."

"Agents of a wealthy foreigner are crawling around in my city and you expect me to believe it's all about something as meaningless as stolen property?" Denton threw up her hands in exasperation and stalked to the door. "We'll see what your friends have to say about that," she snapped, then she left the room and slammed the door shut.

Chapter 16

An hour later, Chavali still sat in the chair. She shifted every few minutes, growing increasingly disturbed by her forced position. Every part of her body grumbled at her imprisonment. She rattled her chains and tried to stand, over and over. At this point, she thought delving into Harris's memories would be preferable to remaining chained to this uncomfortable chair.

Nothing made sense here. Denton had no reason to hold her. Colby should be pounding on the door. Portia ought to have burned a hole through the wall. Sivry...she didn't know Sivry well enough yet to determine what the woman could do, but she had some useful skills or she wouldn't be Fallen. Those skills should have been plied by now. Chavali should not be in this chair anymore.

She rattled the chains again and growled at the empty room. The spirits gave her no power over ordinary objects. She could craft illusions, she could read minds, she could tell the future, she could lie, cheat, and manipulate, but she couldn't escape chains holding her in a chair. If only a guard would check on her, she could talk them into at least unlocking the chains. Pacing the room sounded superior to her current predicament.

Worse, she knew Denton left her alone to taunt her into giving up information. The woman probably didn't believe a word Chavali said because of the words left unsaid. She hated not being believed when she told the truth. When she lied, it annoyed her, but when she chose honesty, it truly rankled.

She pulled on one wrist, wishing with all her might the chain would break. Instead, it cut into her skin. Beads of blood formed on her wrist. If she kept doing this, she'd cause enough damage to bleed out. Denton would win. Chavali wouldn't allow that to happen.

Gritting her teeth, she shut her eyes. Bile rose in the back of her throat and she forced herself to swallow. The incredible need to get away gnawed on her sanity and she forced herself to sit still. Frustration goaded her to scream for Denton and she forced herself to stay quiet.

With her eyes closed, she could almost believe the chains had been removed. To distract herself more, she tried to think about Harris. Her mind scrambled to recall his appearance and failed. He had dark hair. His eyes...he definitely had eyes. Their shape and shade eluded her. She pictured a collection of scars, yet couldn't remember where he'd had them. Had she seen his bare back? Was that instead Colby's back she recalled, or maybe Eliot's, Keino's, or another Blaukenev?

Pushing yet another train of thought aside, she caught on her dream last night. Keino had been so clear and coherent. As one of the many spirits of their clan's dead, he should never be able to shoulder his way to the front. They jostled for position, none able to step to the forefront over any other. Aside from the prophecies they forced on her, they remained in the background, whispering unintelligibly or passing on the thoughts of those she touched.

Yet Keino had pushed his way forward. He'd invaded her dreams. If she understood last night's, he barred her from Harris's memories. That made no sense, of course. The spirits couldn't affect her like that. At least, she didn't think they could. They certainly never had before.

Finally, the door opened. Chavali opened her eyes to see Denton. Before either woman could say or do anything, Colby stepped in. He took in the sight and rushed to Chavali's side, then lifted her hand and scowled at the blood on her chafed wrist.

"Release her or I'll break her free," Colby growled. *I can't believe they did this to you. None of the rest of us were chained down like an animal.*

"I'd like to see you try." Denton crossed her arms and smirked.

The degree of Colby's anger surprised Chavali. Nothing in his mind had ever shown her he had the capacity for such rage. It roiled inside, priming him for violence.

Despite her discomfort, Chavali sneered at the captain. "If your goal is to make us hate you and this city enough to do things you could actually be justified in arresting us for, you are succeeding admirably."

Showing no fear of Colby, Denton stepped behind Chavali and triggered the bindings to release. The cuffs holding Chavali's wrists and ankles popped open. Now that she could get up, Chavali restrained the urge to jump out of the chair. She crossed her legs and let Colby examine her arm.

I'd like to put her in chains for a while. See how she likes it. This should heal without scarring. Colby retrieved a handkerchief from a pocket and wrapped it tenderly around the abrasions. *If I'd known you were chained up like this, I would've...I don't know, but I would've done something.* Thoughts of punching Denton filled his mind. He stopped touching her and tied the makeshift bandage off.

Chavali clasped her hands in her lap and glared at Denton. "What do you want?"

"She doesn't want anything. I do." A new woman stepped into the room, escorted by a younger man. The woman had the same sharp angles as Ambrye, but tempered with age. Her dark velvet skirt and blouse marked her as wealthy. That same long-legged bird Ambrye wore as a decoration adorned her sleeves and a brooch on a metal chain around her neck.

The escort bore the same bird device on his own dark, rich clothes. Something about him seemed oddly familiar, though she couldn't guess what. His features held little resemblance to this woman or Ambrye, making him appear no closer a relation than anyone else on the streets here. Still, with only a few paces to judge, Chavali guessed him to be her son or nephew over a paramour. He offered her deference, and his touch and proximity spoke more of duty than interest. She might have suspected an advisor but for his age, which seemed to be near Ambrye's.

Behind them, a second woman, this one also near Ambrye's age, followed inside, then Portia and Sivry. The younger woman also reminded Chavali of Ambrye, but less so. Her features were softer. Where Ambrye projected cool, intelligent competence, this young woman flounced and swished with youthful indiscretion and foolishness.

Portia made a furtive rude gesture behind the newcomers' backs. Sivry's mouth went thin when she saw Chavali's condition.

"Your Majesty," Denton said with an incline of her head.

"Ah." Chavali stood and smoothed her skirts, refusing to offer deference or respect to the Queen of North Cascain and what must be a prince and another princess. "It's been interesting to visit your city, but the welcome has been rather tiresome. I mean no personal offense, your majesty, but you can take what you want and put it in...indelicate places."

The queen sighed and gave Denton a flat look. Denton shrugged and looked away. When Chavali moved to leave, the queen side-stepped to block her exit.

"Please, hear me out." The queen held up her hands in entreaty.

Chavali glanced at Colby. The man's glare could have burned sheet rock. She also checked Portia and Sivry and found both uninterested in anything but leaving. "Give me a good reason why I should listen to anything you have to say."

"My daughter sent me this note." The queen offered her a folded piece of paper.

Unless the note consisted of pictures, Chavali knew she'd take too long puzzling over it. She nodded to Colby, who took the paper and read it aloud, his frown deepening with every word.

"Mother, if you're reading this, something has happened to me. There's a group of foreigners staying at Eidel's Landing, led by an exotic woman named Chastity. These four individuals are either responsible or the best chance of discovering the truth. At the moment, I can't tell which. Ambrye."

Chavali raised her brow. "I see. I gather her opinion holds much weight here."

"She's a brilliant investigator," the queen said, "and no one has ever been steered wrong by her observations before."

While the man nodded in grave agreement, the younger princess failed to repress grinding her teeth at this pronouncement. Jealousy seemed the most likely cause. Chavali wished she had an excuse to touch the girl and find out how deep it ran.

"Can you think of a reason we should wish to become involved in this matter?" Chavali asked Colby.

Colby crossed his arms and crumpled the note. "Nothing comes to mind, no."

"I have a reason," Denton growled. "Help with this or you're all under arrest for Ambrye's abduction. Her suspicion is enough to allow me hold you here for a very long time."

"Please," the queen begged. She touched her brooch. "Do you have children?"

Chavali scowled at the blatant attempt to manipulate her, but as she studied the queen's face, she saw honest fear for a child. The manipulation likely came as a matter of habit. One didn't succeed as a ruler without it.

"This isn't about princesses and art thefts and abductions," the queen continued. "She's my daughter and she's missing. The other Inspectors...I think she suggested you could help because you're outsiders. You have no stake in this and no preconceptions. And if you find her, you can take that statue you want, no questions asked."

"Mother—"

"No," the queen sliced her hand through the air to cut her escort off. "I don't care if it's the key to the Creator Herself. If that's what it takes to find my daughter, it's yours."

Though she preferred the idea of buying the statue from Clara, Chavali sighed and ignored Portia, Sivry, and Colby all emoting their different desires. She instead considered how to approach the problem. In Shappa, this was easy—they flashed their Fallen ring and assumed the mantle of Agent of the King.

"We will need enough authority to question suspects regardless of who they are, access to Ambrye's office and quarters, and the ability to move around the city without being trailed by spies or reported on by the Watch. In addition, we request our stay at the inn to be paid for."

"Done. Denton, take care of all that. Is there anything else?"

"If we need to speak with you or anyone in your household, we expect to be granted an audience in a timely fashion." Because the queen offered her cooperation, Chavali waffled over asking for permission to read her. Explaining her ability would require delicate wording and could provoke a rejection. No, better to be circumspect. She offered her hand to shake with the queen, to affirm their deal.

The queen gave her a tense smile and slipped her hand into Chavali's. "Whatever I can do to help find my daughter, I will, though I would ask that you practice discretion with whatever you discover."

As the words left the queen's lips, Chavali's vision misted over with purple. The timing, as usual, made her want to curse. She didn't bother trying to let go of the queen or flee. Nothing would stop the spirits from shoving a prophecy out.

"Heron's blood divided, lust misguided—he is coming—passion derided. Tainted memories—he is coming! Feathers on the ground. Protect. Let me. Bound. Promise." For a moment, Chavali thought it ended on a very strange note. She raised her hand to her forehead, expecting the resulting migraine to hit any moment. Instead, she felt the spirits pressing as if they might burst through her flesh and devour her. "Water creeps and rushes, fire leaps and flushes. He is coming."

Finally, it let her go, and she staggered. Colby scooped her into his arms without hesitation, adjusting his grip to avoid touching her skin without needing to be told.

"She needs someplace to rest." His voice rumbled against her ear.

"What in the name of the Creator just happened?" Denton demanded. "Is this some kind of joke?"

"Shut up and get a cup of hot water," Portia snarled.

"I don't understand," said the queen. "Heron's blood is my family. Was that about Ambrye?"

Colby hurried away from the voices. Chavali groaned and wished someone would cut her head off so she didn't have to suffer through the agony. Secure in the knowledge Colby and Portia knew what to do, she let coherent thought stop.

Chapter 17

Someone pressed a steaming cup against Chavali's lips. The foul stench of her medicinal concoction never stopped her from drinking it. She wrinkled her nose and choked the tea down.

The thundering herd of horses crashing through broken glass inside her head subsided within minutes of swallowing the last gulp. Chavali opened her eyes to see Colby in dim light, using his substantial girth to barricade the door of the small room he'd commandeered for her. She lay on a couch with a pillow under her head.

As always, the vile brew made her feel fuzzy and detached. This sensation, far superior to the pain it wiped away, would pass. She sat up slowly, rubbing her eyes.

"Your timing never fails to be dramatic," Colby murmured.

Chavali smirked. "I no longer require quiet."

"Do you want to talk over the prophecy before submitting to interrogation about it?"

"I suppose so." She regarded Colby, noting he seemed more protective than usual. He reminded her of Keino. "Why did you lock

Portia and Sivry out?"

"Portia delivered your tea and left to run diplomatic interference. Sivry is on the other side of the door by choice, providing a second obstacle."

"Ah. I think I heard the queen say 'Heron's blood' meant her family?"

"That's the bird on her family's crest."

Chavali nodded, willing to accept the correlation. Other prophecies had used similar methods to define the people they referred to. "At a guess, there's strife in her household she is unaware of. Someone using sex or the promise of it to get what they want. I'm not sure what to think of 'he is coming,' as I keep hearing it."

Saying it out loud gave her a sinking feeling she knew what man the spirits wanted to warn her about. Only one had ever done anything to affect the spirits enough to cry out such a warning. They could be telling her of some other man, but she thought it must mean Robin: the man who'd murdered her clan, trained the woman behind the disaster in Ket, and probably had some hand in the unpleasant business that befell Eagle Falls.

She shivered. Everywhere she went, his tentacles touched something. His blue eyes, staring at her through someone else's memories, made her want to crawl under a rock and hide forever. He wanted to control the spirits and use her at his whim. She'd killed herself to deny him.

The other out of place section also worried her. Death hadn't stopped Keino from insisting he needed to protect her. Again, he seemed to have pushed his way to the forefront of all the clan's spirits, and she didn't understand. Interfering with a prophecy struck her as a flexing of his power. If he kept charging forward, what could he accomplish? Could he appoint himself as a mediator between her and the rest of the spirits, demanding a toll or other favors in return for access to them?

"Are you all right?" Colby's gentle words helped her shove her fear aside.

"Yes." The lie fell from her lips without effort. "Discounting some as a message for me, I can make guesses about this prophecy. You can let them in."

Colby nodded. "We don't have to work with them, you know. We can find the statue on our own."

"You surprise me. I expect you to want to charge to the rescue of a princess, especially one dedicated to justice."

"Sometimes, priorities don't make sense." With this, he opened the door and tapped Sivry on the shoulder. "She's recovered, but keep your voices down. No shouting."

The queen, her daughter, her son, Portia, Denton, and Sivry all trooped inside the room, filling the small space with too many people. Colby sat beside Chavali. Portia took the last spot on the couch and Sivry sat beside her, perched on the arm. The queen sat in the only other chair, her back straight and bearing regal. The prince crouched beside her on one side while the princess crossed her arms and kept her head up on the other. Denton leaned against the wall, also with her arms crossed, and didn't bother trying to hide her annoyance.

"The first thing I will say is my prophecies always are true. If we can decode them soon enough, we can prevent things from happening. So, this is what I think it means. Ambrye is obviously already in danger.

There is someone in your household who stands against you and is responsible for her abduction. It could be a family member, a servant, a close friend, a secret lover, or anyone else closely associated.

"This person is likely against Ambrye because of some event in the past. This event probably seemed unimportant to everyone but her abductor. To them, it is a driving force, a thing that shaped them. I think they will kill Ambrye if we do not find her first, but there are no hints offered to how long we have."

Silence hung in the room for several seconds. The princess broke it with a snort, fiddling with a small jeweled ring on her pinky finger and shaking her head. "This is ridiculous. There's no such thing as accurate prophecy. She's playing you, mother. Royal houses always have traitors. And this nonsense about fire and flood? That's the usual garbage doomsayers spout."

"Bricene," the queen said, her voice full of quiet intensity, "this is about your sister."

"Or maybe it's about a bird."

Chavali shrugged. "There are many ways to interpret such things. I have spent many years dealing with this curse, and studying symbols and their meaning. This is all I offer to bolster my interpretation. I might suggest, however, that the ones who decry them loudest often turn out to be the ones implicated by them."

Bricene paled and held her hands up in surrender. "I-I didn't mean that. I just— Mother, I don't want you to be fleeced by some foreign shyster."

"I appreciate your concern. We should go home. With Ambrye missing, your safety is of even greater concern than before." The queen stood and gave Chavali a strained smile. "Please find my daughter."

The prince, who had so far done nothing more than seem distressed, stood with her. "If my sister thinks you can help, I know you can."

Chavali nodded, unwilling to promise anything. She watched the queen and her children walk out, then the queen stopped at the door and waved for Chavali to approach. When she did, the queen whispered in her ear.

"You'll eventually discover I have a discreet gentleman companion. He's been away for a few weeks and won't be back until my birthday celebration, so he's unlikely to be involved."

Surprised by the volunteering of this information, Chavali had nothing to say in return. Without him present, she doubted he would turn out to be the villain. Any whispers about him, though, would now be explained, making their jobs a tiny bit easier. "I understand."

The queen left and Chavali wished Denton would follow her. Unfortunately, the captain showed no intention of doing so. Denton took the chair previously occupied by the queen. Leaning back, she crossed her legs, mouth set in a displeased line.

"You can go too," Colby said.

"I don't think so. If you don't tell me what you're up to, I'm going to assume it's no good. I don't care what that note said, I don't trust any of you. Bricene is right—you could be an impressive con artist."

Chavali laughed. "Of course I am a con artist. This is what I do. You don't trust me because you can sense I am skilled at lying without being able to tell when I do it. The prophecy, though, is very real. We have gained a vested interest in locating your princess, partly because we have a healthy appreciation for the value of life, and partly because it will win us the statue we seek. Given that, I would appreciate if we could dispense with the hostility and verbal fencing. It's tiresome in allies."

Denton studied her, then turned her measuring gaze on the rest of the group, one by one. "On one condition—you work with the inspectors."

Chavali's lip curled.

Sivry spat, "No deal."

"Absolutely not," Portia said.

Colby crossed his arms and frowned.

Denton arched an eyebrow. "Either you involve the inspectors, or I put a leash on you."

"A leash or a leash," Chavali scoffed, "how generous you are with choices. Perhaps you'd like us to walk around with chains on our ankles as well." She took in the stubborn set of Denton's chin and the tension in her shoulders and realized two things. First, Denton had no reason to trust them. Second, an inspector could be behind Ambrye's disappearance. If one was, the easiest way to find out would be to have them close at hand.

She heaved a long-suffering sigh and waved for Denton to leave. "Fine, collect your inspectors and introduce us. We will need a guide for the city anyway."

Denton nodded and stood. "Wait here."

Though she disliked the commanding tone Denton used, Chavali waved her off again and watched her leave.

Chapter 18

"Great," Portia grumbled.

"Chavali picked the better of two bad choices," Colby said.

"Agreed," Sivry said. "Did you have a chance to run either of your rituals while we were out?"

"Yes," Portia said with a nod. "Both. The silver isn't particularly unusual in itself, but someone grated and chopped it, which is a strange method of making silver dust. The blue component appears to be plant material, but I didn't get more than that. The dust as a whole has a strange magical signature. I've never seen anything like it before."

Chavali pondered the color. Something tugged at her memory about blue and... "Teleportation. In Eagle Falls, that unusual flower we found was blue."

"And the color we saw when that one man teleported was also blue," said Colby. "It has some connection to the Creator's Towers. If they found out about the flowers somehow, they could have ground some up and used it."

Chavali scowled. "The Continental Trade Syndicate is tied up in this somehow, then, or the Order of the Creator's Path." She had no desire to tangle with either. The former cared about money more than people and the latter controlled access to the Creator's Towers. "This seemed so simple when we arrived."

"Let's not worry about that so much. The silver thing is interesting, so we can maybe follow that up. As far as the statue goes, the ring is still in the city, but I can't get any more specific than that. It's muffled somehow. It could be underground or under a magical shield. That's beyond my skill to deal with. But, so long as they don't realize the ring is a separate piece and remove it, we'll be able to keep trying to track the statue."

Denton pushed the cracked door open, now trailed by a man and a woman. "This is Inspector Nasha and Inspector Reynolds."

Nasha had a different look than the locals. Her darker hair and lighter skin marked her as hailing from someplace farther north. She had the same tall, broad build as Colby, leading Chavali to guess Grippan ancestry. Her clothes, dark and loose-fitting, probably made her stand out even more among the citizens.

Reynolds, on the other hand, could blend in on the streets here with no trouble. He had a very average look to him, with all the same features as the locals. His clothes mimicked the Watch uniforms with minor differences in the buttons, cut, and fit. He'd added a knee-length cape fastened at his neck with a jeweled tie.

"Chastity, Colby, Portia, and Sivry."

Denton gestured at the door. "I assume you'd like to visit the silver shop attacked last night, as it's probably connected to the silver dust found in Evidence Storage."

Reynolds stepped back. "I'd like to join you, but I'm actually busy with two other cases. Murders don't suddenly solve themselves because inspectors go missing." Though he said it with a jaunty grin, Chavali caught unease beneath it. He probably thought Inspectors immune to crime and found Ambrye's abduction personally distressing.

"I can go," Nasha said, her voice soft and silky. "I've just wrapped a robbery and there are no leads to follow in my other case right now."

"Then we should go." Chavali led the way out.

"Excuse me for saying so," Colby said to Nasha as they navigated through the building, "but I can tell you're from Grippa. I am too."

"Oh, yes." Nasha smiled, making dimples in her cheeks, though it seemed strained. "I'm originally from Itreon."

"Oh. Huh. I've...been there. Nice place." Colby's distress came through too loud and clear for Chavali's taste.

"What brought you to North Cascain?" Chavali asked. She wondered about Colby's full connection to Itreon and decided she'd ask later, preferably when he'd forgotten about the exchange. Taking him off-guard would make the conversation more entertaining.

Nasha turned her pleasant, fake smile on Chavali. Worry frayed the corners of her mouth and eyes, but was it worry for Ambrye or for being discovered? "My studies. There are people here with more open minds about a variety of subjects than in Grippa. The weather is also quite nice. It doesn't snow here, and the fish is excellent. Before you leave, you need to try Hardrun perch. Ocean fishes don't compare."

"I will keep that in mind, thank you." Since Nasha clearly had no interest in discussing the subject of her study, Chavali let it go. She didn't need to know everything about this inspector now. There would be time to delve her secrets as they searched for Ambrye.

They stepped into a cool spring rain shower to commandeer a carriage. Though Chavali felt cramped inside it with five people, two of them large, it bothered her much less than being chained to a chair.

"How well do you know Inspector Ambrye?" Sivry asked as the carriage creaked down the street.

"Not very." Nasha shrugged and looked away. "She's five years younger than me. We have nothing in common aside from the job. I couldn't tell you if she has a lover, for example. She's sharp-witted, though. It's surprising someone managed to take her off-guard long enough to abduct her. My guess is they used overwhelming force, which works against anyone."

The lies ran so thick Chavali thought she might choke. Nasha knew Ambrye much better than she said. Wanting to hide that intrigued Chavali, and she needed to prod. But not now. For now, they needed to get basic information.

"Do you think she might have arranged her own disappearance so she could rescue herself and gain even more popularity?"

Roused from plotting her own tactics, Chavali blinked at Sivry. The possibility hadn't occurred to her. Checking the other faces in the carriage, no one else thought of it either. The question raised Sivry in her estimation, and she studied Nasha's reaction.

"I...suppose that's possible, but I'd be very surprised." Nasha frowned. "She was born and raised in the spotlight. She's never been anything other than beloved by the people of this city and country. Manufacturing reasons for people to celebrate her...it's unnecessary. At this point, she could step down as an Inspector to focus on supporting her mother and the people would still be enchanted by her."

Finding the logic sound, especially for not relying on knowing Ambrye well, Chavali nodded. "Excuse me for asking, but where were you last night and this morning?"

"At home." Nasha shifted uncomfortably. "It's not a very good alibi. I spent most of yesterday filing paperwork and just wanted to relax and sleep." The lilt in Nasha's voice gave her away. Her lie, though, meant nothing to Chavali until they had a reason to accuse her of some crime. She could easily have a lover she wished to keep private, or some questionable hobby. They cared about neither.

"If it makes you feel better," Portia said with a smirk, "we all stayed at our inn, which is as bad an alibi."

Nasha chuckled. "We're all suspects."

Chavali wondered if Nasha realized the truth of that statement.

Chapter 19

The rest of the ride passed in quiet. They reached a smooth street lined with craftswomen's shops. Two uniformed members of the Watch stood outside the silversmithy they'd come for. Other stores on the row offered ceramics, blown glass, and steel goods.

An empty window frame and soot marred the well-maintained facade of the silversmith's shop. Shards of glass littered the sidewalk and street, pointing to force from within pushing it out. Through the hole, Chavali saw broken shelves and overturned tables. More broken glass mingled with goblets, candlesticks, tea service items, and silverware.

No spectators lingered nearby, which Chavali thought odd. She scanned the other stores and saw figures moving behind windows without paying attention to the scene outside. Perhaps they'd already seen everything they cared to and now busied themselves about their work.

Nasha approached the Watchmen first. They stepped aside to let her pass.

"Inspector," one Watchman said with a deferential nod. "The

shop owner is dead. No other casualties or injured. We've already canvassed the area and found no witnesses. It doesn't appear to have been a robbery."

"Good work," Nasha said. "These people are working for the Queen. Let them through."

Chavali nodded to the guards and followed Nasha inside the building with the others trailing her. Her boots crunched over broken glass and wood splinters. The silver items bore scratches and showed signs of minor melting. Everything had been thrown away from a spot near the back of the shop area, marking the epicenter of an explosion.

"How did no one hear anything?" Chavali asked.

Colby paced to the back counter with Nasha. "They heard something. They probably saw something too."

Chavali puzzled over this answer, trying to imagine why witnesses remained silent. In her clan, the only reason to keep your mouth shut was to prevent the culprit from being punished. They all had to live with each other. Outsiders, she knew, didn't always care about their neighbors. Criminals often relied upon this to accomplish their goals. In an area like this one, though, she suspected the crafters all looked out for each other.

"They fear someone discovering they assisted the Watch?" She stepped around the back counter where Colby and Nasha both crouched beside the dead man. The sight of his crushed skull disgusted Chavali and she turned aside to see Portia rooting through the merchandise. Sivry examined the window frame.

"Yes," Colby said. "Are you aware of anyone operating in this area who might cause that fear?"

"No. I'm not familiar with this neighborhood." Nasha clucked her tongue. "Please don't touch the body."

"Sorry." Glass crunched while Colby stood.

Chavali noticed broken pottery and dirt surrounding a book. Curious, she lifted the book and found a familiar flower. Eagle Falls had a number of them. Their existence had caused many deaths in that small town, and now more here. She assumed its lack of glow meant it couldn't be salvaged.

"There are signs of a struggle here," Colby said. "The destruction muddies the waters, so to speak, but I'm confident saying this man tried to defend himself and was overpowered, probably with a combination of speed and strength. Some sort of hammer took his life. They landed a single blow and had the discipline to walk away without further violence. One of his own tools probably caused this damage."

"I'd guess this one covered with blood." Nasha pointed to a smith's hammer in the doorway connecting the store with the workshop in back. "Someone strong, then, or using magic to augment it."

"He had a recent customer pay with coins from Grippa." Portia held up a coin with a hole through the center. "I can't imagine those are common here."

"No," Nasha said. "I haven't seen one since I spent the last of mine, many years ago."

"The explosion centered here," Sivry announced. "It emanated, though, bursting out in a circle instead of a sphere." She pointed at the ceiling. "No sign of damage there."

Portia looked up. "Might mean something, might mean nothing.

Either way, they've got the ability to blow things up. From the damage I see, it was a fire or heat-based explosion, and this place reeks of magic. No sign of the dust that seems to enable teleportation. They left on foot."

Chavali picked up a piece of the pot, turning it over in her hands. "This man, the silversmith, he must be the source for the silver dust. That makes him the supplier for the Evidence Storage thieves, either knowingly or not. Was he killed to prevent him from giving information? If so, why so much destruction when a simple murder would suffice?"

"Let's ask him." Nasha placed her hand on the man's cheek and closed her eyes. Her lips moved with whispered words.

Though Chavali understood none of it, the hairs raised on the back of her neck. The spirits' ever-present whispers, usually quiet enough to be easily ignored, rose in volume, intruding on her ability to listen and concentrate.

"Tell us about the last customer you had," Nasha ordered.

Chavali stared in wide-eyed horror as the corpse's jaw opened and words spilled out. "Princess Ambrye." Breathy and hollow, the moaning voice scraped against Chavali's nerves. "Asked about silver dust. Interrupted. Struggle. Death."

"What happened to Ambrye?"

"Don't know. Didn't see."

"What about the silver dust? What did you tell her?"

"Nothing. Interrupted."

Nasha frowned. She saw Colby open his mouth and waved him off. "Describe your attackers."

"Male. Robed. Brown." The corpse paused for several long,

rasping seconds. "Amulet. Ship and moon."

"The Drowned Ones," Nasha spat. She let the corpse go.

Chavali shuddered as the energy released and the whispers in her head faded. She stumbled to catch herself and her hand shook. Once one foot moved, the other did, and she didn't stop until she'd fled the shop and run across the street. There, she leaned against the wall, clutching a piece of the broken pot to her chest.

Spirits shouldn't be forced like that. Nothing should be forced like that. She felt the binding on that corpse, demanding it deliver the information Nasha requested. The spirits of her clan felt it too. They didn't like it either. Their whispers buzzed angrily on the edge of her hearing.

"Abomination," Chavali whispered, unaware the word came out of her mouth. She shuddered again and took a deep breath. They had to work with Nasha whether she wanted to or not, at least for now. Anyone who would use such vile power earned suspicion in Chavali's eyes, though.

She moved a hand to rub her eyes, only then noticing she still held a pottery shard. Colby stood at the empty window, watching her. Waving him off, she turned away from his concern and noticed she stood in front of the ceramic shop. Several broken pots sat in the display, matching the shard she held.

Though the connection made no real sense, Chavali slipped inside the shop and looked around. Broken ceramics littered the floor near the front. Farther back, the shelves held intact pots and plates, both decorative and functional.

A plump woman straightened from clearing debris and leaned on her broom, giving Chavali a weak, tired smile. "Hello. Sorry about the mess. Complete accident. I still have plenty of stock, though. Can I help you find anything?"

Chavali took in the destruction with a frown. When things broke in her clan, someone fixed or replaced it. Among the Fallen, she received a small stipend to pay for things, and anyone who destroyed property fixed or replaced it on Eldrack's orders. She had no idea how it worked in a city. "What happened here?"

The woman's smile faltered. "There was some sort of tussle across the street. Knocked everything down."

"Tussle? I don't know this word."

"An explosion rocked the street last night."

Witnesses who refused to speak to the Watch apparently had no trouble speaking to potential customers. "Really? That must have been terrifying." Chavali crouched and picked up several broken pieces of pottery.

"Thought my heart stopped." The woman nodded and glanced nervously out the window. "They said Mike died. The silversmith across the way."

"That's horrible." Chavali held up a large chunk of a pot with an interesting swirled design. "I like this. How much do you want for it?"

The woman stared at her, then broke into a weepy smile. "It'll cost me three silvers to make a new one, that's plenty."

Chavali straightened and carried her new piece of painted ceramic to the counter. "Will anyone reimburse you for the damage here?"

"Oh. Well. I don't think so. There's…"

"The Watch?" Chavali pointed out the window at the two men standing guard at the silver shop.

The woman sighed. "No. The Watch doesn't do much for us here. Don't get me wrong. I'm all for Princess Ambrye. She's a charm. The Queen is a jewel. But they've got more important things to worry about. And the Watch can't stop the Bloodflies. They might give me a little help to tide me over, I suppose. Can't hurt to ask, can it?"

"No, it can't." Hearing that gang name again made Chavali wonder how many pies the Bloodflies had their disturbing fingers in, and how they managed to keep it so quiet from the Watch. She dug a gold coin out of the small purse at her waist and set it on the counter. "I've heard the Bloodflies are a force to fear. Do you think they caused the explosion?"

"I don't know." The woman glanced out the window again as she touched the gold coin. "The princess was there, though. I saw her through the window. She's a striking woman. My niece wants to be an Inspector when she grows up, all because of Princess Ambrye."

"I hope she wasn't harmed in the explosion."

"I hope not too. I saw a group of rough-and-tumble types go in after her."

Chavali laid her hand atop the woman's as she dragged the coin toward the edge of the counter. Thanks to the woman's thoughts, Chavali saw the incident replayed. Ambrye strode inside the store. Seven men entered a short time after her, each dressed in brown robes and wearing swords. A woman screamed out the word "watchtower."

Seconds later, the glass blew out and fire billowed into the street.

"I don't need change," she said to explain the contact.

The woman blinked at her, then her face blossomed into heartwarming gratitude. "Creator bless you." Her eyes watered.

Chavali pulled her hand away before the woman could blubber over it. "I wish you all the best." Scooping up her pottery shard, she gave the woman a polite wave and left.

Chapter 20

Thankfully, Nasha left the group for another errand as they climbed into the carriage to return and deliver information to Denton. Chavali wished to have nothing to do with the woman and preferred not to explain why. Colby sat across from her for the ride, watching her with concern. Portia and Sivry each seemed deep in thought.

They arrived and Denton saw them immediately. Portia and Chavali related what they'd discovered, passing the story back and forth with ease.

"Who are these Drowned Ones?" Chavali asked.

Denton leaned back in her chair with a scowl. "Bunch of lunatic cultists. Near as I can tell, they're mostly members of a few different gangs operating in the docks district. About a year ago, man name of Shance rose up out of nowhere and organized them around some weird death obsession. They think everyone has to die and be reborn for Reunion to happen. Rant against the Queen a lot, saying the nobles are a plague on the world. I have no idea what the two things have to do with each other."

"Why do you let death cultists own the docks?" Colby asked.

Denton bared her teeth. "We have to be able to prove they're breaking laws before we can arrest them. Or catch them in the act. I'm confident they're the ones supplying Blue Death, for example, but we can't seem to catch them with it. Every time we try to set up a sting operation, they see through it. I can't explain that. We had a tip on a warehouse full of the stuff. I sent a scout to check the tip, and he confirmed. When we got there to raid the place, we found faked vials set up perfectly to fool a scout, and workers who knew nothing about it."

Chavali saw the frustration in Denton's shoulders. Part of her enjoyed that in the woman who'd tortured her for hours this morning. The rest of her needed more information. "We have heard of this Blue Death. What is it, exactly?"

"A drug. No idea how they make it. Allegedly, it lifts the veil between you and the Creator, exposing the world as it really is. In practice, it causes hallucinations and madness. We have to keep a number of cells ready these days, just to hold people high on the drug so they don't hurt themselves or anyone else. We've seen bodies from people who walked off balconies for no apparent reason, and more drowning victims in the last few months than the past five years combined. And when the ones in our cells come off the high, they go into withdrawal and wish they were dead. Even the ones who only took it once. Including the ones who don't know how they got dosed."

Considering the two users they'd already encountered, Chavali wondered whether "hallucinations" covered the truth of it. She also wondered how many people used this phenomenon to mask murders and other crimes, and if the Drowned Ones did that. Shance intrigued her, but she didn't care what Denton knew about him. She wanted to meet him and sample his thoughts.

Setting her curiosity aside, Chavali turned to a subject she suspected lay in Denton's area of expertise. "Do you know why Ambrye would scream the word 'watchtower' while in the middle of being abducted?"

Denton frowned. "It sounds like one of her code words. She's got a lot of them. Wait here. Captain-General Crayton has her code word file." She rose and left her office, not bothering to close the door.

"Anybody think the princess is still alive?" Sivry asked.

Colby said, "I do. They went to a lot of trouble to abduct her. Even crazy people don't do that just to turn around and kill their hostage."

"I expect they took her to dose her and drive her mad." Chavali sighed. "That would be a shame. She has a sharp mind. I believe I might have liked her, given time to convince her I'm not a suspicious, lying criminal."

"You are, though," Portia said, "so that would've been a rough road."

Chavali grinned. "Which would have made it all the sweeter."

Colby sighed while Sivry and Portia both chuckled. "If the Drowned Ones have her," Colby said, "we need to find them. We'll have to go poking around the docks."

Chavali nodded and mused over how to arrange a meeting with Shance. The Blue Death seemed a problem that perhaps could use their attention, but it may or may not require violence. Colby would apply violence as the first solution, under the guise of justice. Portia also tended to follow that path. She wondered if Sivry could be a more effective co-conspirator. She also wondered what madness had compelled Eldrack to send Colby on this mission.

"It was a keyword." Denton returned with a parchment envelope. Red block letters formed a word on one side. Chavali made out the neatly printed "W" and assumed the rest of it spelled "Watchtower." Denton used a small knife to slice the envelope open and removed a folded page.

"If this code word is encountered, I am either missing or dead. I strongly suspect one of my fellow Inspectors is involved." Denton's brow flew up. "Kenna Denton, a Captain of the Watch, should be trusted with this investigation." She offered the paper to Colby, stunned and blinking. "I had no idea she knew my name."

Colby scanned the note for himself. "How much weight should we put on this?"

"Better question," Portia said, a finger raised in inquiry. "How did she decide to come up with a specific code word for that? That's crazy."

"She is organized and suspicious, almost to the point of paranoia," Chavali said as she watched Denton take too long to recover from being starstruck. "Trust it as much as if she stood here."

"If the Drowned Ones have her and an Inspector is involved, then an Inspector is involved with the Drowned ones," Sivry said. "Does that make sense?"

"Who cares?" Portia snatched the paper from Colby and tossed it onto Denton's desk. "We should focus on tracking the statue. That's our best lead."

Though Chavali agreed, Portia voicing such a callous opinion made her raise an eyebrow. She saw Denton's face cloud over with anger and decided to intervene. Because she liked Portia. "I agree. If the princess is not near it, this traitor inspector will be, or there will be clues to their identity. As it's the only true—"

"No." Denton thumped her fist on her desk. "Go check into the Drowned Ones. The princess is the priority, not your statue. The statue won't die if we leave it until she's rescued."

"Of course," Colby said with finality and stood. He glared, managing to target both Portia and Chavali at once. "A life is much more important than any object. We won't let her suffer any longer than necessary." He stalked out of the office.

Denton turned her icy stare on Chavali. "If I find out you've been focusing on the statue—"

"Do not lecture me about priorities or methods." Chavali waved in dismissal as she stood. "We struck a deal with the queen. It did not include you telling us how to pursue our goals."

"The deal isn't void if you find your statue."

Chavali shrugged. "Perhaps. If you continue to treat us as subordinate and inferior, we will reconsider the terms of our deal. We can pay for our stay at the inn. None of us has committed any crime more heinous than being foreign. This thing you think you can hold over our heads to make us dance as you please is an illusion."

She turned her back on Denton and walked out, uninterested in anything else the woman might have to say. Colby stood in the hall, glowering with his arms crossed. Ignoring him, she breezed through the building to the back door and kept walking. Denton would have to scramble if she wanted an inspector to accompany them, which suited

Chavali.

Colby growled her name and she kept walking. A shouting match so close to the Watch building would draw too much attention. If he wanted to yell at her for pragmatism, he would do it where they could have some measure of privacy. Two blocks away, she finally stopped at the mouth of an alley and gestured for the group to enter it.

As she expected, Colby stopped and loomed over her while Portia ducked into the refuge from casual observation. Chavali turned her back on him and took one step into the alley before he clamped a paw on her shoulder.

"Do *not* have this conversation in plain sight," she growled.

He glanced up and down the street, then let go and followed her into the narrow lane between tall buildings. Sivry took up a guard stance, watching the street. Chavali appreciated the woman's willingness to screen what could become a loud, angry torrent of words from passersby.

"I can't believe you," Colby snapped. "Both of you."

"We have a mission," Chavali said. "This mission is not to save the princess. It is to find the statue. Eldrack trusts us to do what is necessary to accomplish this. You, in fact, were of the same opinion only hours ago."

"She's a person!" He made a frustrated noise, then he lowered his voice. "This morning, I was worried about you, a person, and we thought she might be dead. Now we're almost certain she's alive. You can't seriously abandon someone to that kind of fate. I know you're not *that* cold."

"It's not about abandoning Ambrye to lunatics," Portia hissed. "It's about following the best lead we have. We don't know where to find these Drowned Ones. How are we supposed to do that? Walk up and down the docks asking people? Ask the other inspectors when they're now our prime suspects? Did you notice how Nasha suddenly had someplace else to be after we questioned the silversmith? How about Reynolds' other cases he couldn't set aside for a disappeared colleague?"

Chavali crossed her arms and set her chin. "And I met Kalei. She and Ambrye are rivals. Considering Ambrye's skills and showmanship, I would not be surprised to learn the others have some jealousy about her. This sounds like what they call a motive for kidnapping her."

Colby ground his teeth. "Just promise me we're looking for the princess."

"We are looking for the statue," Chavali said. "That is our entire goal. The only side question we must consider is why we found that blue flower here. In a silversmith's shop, of all places."

"I think the person walking this way is an inspector," Sivry said.

"We made a deal," Colby said. "We gave our word."

"We have a mission," Chavali countered.

"I won't go back on my word."

"This I know, but you did not give yours. I gave mine. If I choose to break it, that is my business."

Colby's hands flexed, giving Chavali the impression he wanted to choke her. She had no fear—even without their binding to the Fallen, his manners wouldn't let him. "Just once, it would be nice if you could try honesty for an entire day. Just once."

"Hello!" Kalei called into the alley. "I hope I'm not interrupting anything important?"

Chapter 21

"I see you rarely pay attention at home," Chavali snapped at Colby. She turned and shifted her expression from anger to friendly smile with practiced ease. "Kalei, it is good to see you again. You are here to assist us with locating the Drowned ones, I expect?"

"Something like that." Kalei scanned each member of the group. Her gaze lingered on Colby, who stood with his back to her. "Is everything all right?"

"Just a lover's spat," Portia said. She flashed an obnoxious grin at Chavali. "Pull up a chair and tell us what you know about the Drowned Ones."

Chavali kept her scowl to herself as Kalei and Sivry joined them to discuss the matter. "Where do you think we should look to find them?"

"The docks. We don't really know where they're based, exactly, because they're so good at keeping one step ahead of us. Rumor has it their leader can see into the Creator's realm. Of course, there's all kinds of rumors about him, so who knows what's really going on."

Glancing askance, Chavali saw Colby lean against the wall and work at getting his emotions under control. As annoying and frustrating as she found him and his morals, she could buy him time to calm down. "I wish to hear some of these rumors. Kernels of truth often lie within, yes?"

"So they say." Kalei flicked her gaze over each person again. The corners of her mouth ticked up. "There are several different rumors about him dying and coming back to life, which is the basis for their belief everyone needs to do that. Common threads among them say he was a sailor. His ship went down in a storm with no survivors, but the Creator pulled him from the deep to deliver a message about rebirth. Since he got here, the docks have become a less pleasant place."

Chavali remembered seeing a man mugged when they first arrived. The attacker, as she recalled, matched those she'd seen in the potter's memory well enough to suspect a connection between them. As for the rest, she had no room to scoff at the idea of returning from the dead, no matter the alleged method. "Have you any thoughts on likely places to find at least one of them? If we can catch one gang member, he can lead us to the rest."

"Or I can just track the statue," Portia said. "Either it leads us to her or it doesn't, but it's not about guessing. It's about getting a specific reading on a specific location. Inspector Kalei can help us avoid dead end streets. Stop us from blundering into blind alleys. That sort of thing."

Kalei nodded. "I can do that. I know the city well enough. Are you going to use magic to track the statue?"

"Yes. You can watch if you want. I don't have a problem with that." Portia crouched to perform her ritual.

Kalei knelt beside her, watching every movement Portia made.

Uninterested in the ritual now that she understood it, Chavali waved for Colby to move deeper into the alley with her. Every time they'd locked horns before, a simple conversation had resolved it. Between the two moments, though, they glared and sniped at each other for hours or days. Skipping the middle part appealed to her.

She stopped a dozen yards from the others to look up at him. Tension held his shoulders rigid and mouth thin. "Colby, I understand you generally think me a monster in need of rescue from myself. I cannot apologize for this. I'm a keeper of secrets, a liar, a storyteller, and a con artist. These things will not change because you wish it so. Regardless, I strive to be honest with my clan. You are not part of my clan. There are things I cannot tell you. There are things I cannot allow you to be curious enough about to dig for and discover on your own."

He opened his mouth to say something. She held up a hand to keep him quiet. Much to her surprise, it worked. "But you are Fallen and so am I. It's like clan. A different kind. I trust you to use your skills to my benefit and offer the same to you in return. All I ask in this is for you to trust that my methods are not madness."

His shoulders relaxed enough to show he'd heard her. "You're not always right, Chavali. I know things tend to work out how you expect most of the time, but not always. And I hate it when you put on your cold, callous tramp routine."

Chavali arched an eyebrow. "Tramp? I am *never* a tramp."

He rubbed his eyes and sighed. "I wish you'd disagree with the cold and callous parts too."

"That would be lying. You prize honesty."

"Chastity! Colby! Kiss and make up already. I've got a strong tug, not like this morning. It's toward the docks."

Colby shook his head in disgust, making Chavali feel she'd succeeded. She patted his arm with a smirk and turned to rejoin the others, but he stopped her with a hand on her shoulder.

"The methods matter as much as the goal," he murmured.

"No, Colby, you're wrong. A goal is nothing more than a time and place. It's fleeting and often less glorious than we imagined. Basking in it is fruitless. The journey is the *only* thing that matters." Glancing over her shoulder, she noticed he gaped at her. She'd flummoxed the poor boy by agreeing with him without agreeing with him. Later, after he'd had a chance to think and they had time to argue more, he'd undoubtedly return to the subject.

"This way," Portia said. She led the group out of the alley and toward the docks.

Chapter 22

An hour later, Chavali and Colby stood in the afternoon shade of a boat-builder's warehouse, waiting for Portia and Sivry to return from pinpointing the specific building housing Harris' ring. Kalei had left them to round up a handful of nearby Watchmen for an assault on the place.

"How long do you think it takes to get used to so much fish in the air?"

"Longer than I want to be here."

Chavali laughed. "I thought you would like it here. The Inspectors are treated with much respect and fawning. The Watch is large and powerful. So much law and order."

Colby huffed at her. "I know that if I've noticed the people here aren't ecstatic about the Watch, you've already figured out the reasons why."

"Of course. Too many people are afraid of these brutal gangs. When The Drowned Ones can walk into a shop through the front door to snatch an inspector and blow it up, you know they're doing smaller things all the time. This Bloodflies gang is also much more of a threat than Denton thinks. Clara was genuinely afraid of them, and she runs the black market here. Gangs who terrify people in such positions are not trifles. The Watch fails at controlling one and considers the other a nuisance. Neither is endearing to those who must put up with the gangs on a daily or weekly basis."

He nodded up the street. Kalei swaggered at the head of ten Watchmen, all hulking and armed for war. "A display like that won't help anything." At Chavali's questioning look, he elaborated. "The owners of these buildings pay protection to the Drowned Ones. Unless we burn the gang out so effectively they can't recover, the leaders will assume someone in the area tipped the Watch off. Everyone in the area has been proactively threatened with reprisals, from destruction of property to murder."

Chavali nodded in understanding. So far, her interactions with gangs led her to the opinion they operated in the same ways bullies did. Harris had been in gangs for most of his life. If she could force herself to wander through his stolen memories, she would learn much more about the nuances. But not right now.

Portia popped her head around the corner. "We found it. Warehouse. Only one guard. Sivry handled him."

"By 'handled', you mean...?"

Chavali rolled her eyes. "I'm sure she slit his throat and threw the body in the water," she said to Colby.

"Who slit whose throat?" Kalei asked with a cheerful, too-sweet smile.

Portia snorted. "No one. Just wishful thinking. We've got the target location. Might as well move now, before they notice a wad of guards ready to rumble in their backyard." She beckoned everyone to follow her and pointed out the building.

At the end of the row, the nondescript warehouse building fit between its neighbors. The same amount of paint peeled from its walls, the same number of windows had grime, and the same amount of rust colored its door hinges. Like a good pickpocket, it blended in and didn't call attention to itself.

The Watchmen pushed past Kalei, who didn't argue. They jogged to the front door without waiting for further instructions. Two leveled crossbows at the door. Five circled around to the back. One man stood in front of the door while the last two flanked it. At a nod from a crossbowman, the one man hefted his mace with a ball end as thick as his head and slammed it into the door.

The door crumpled around the mace head and flew inside. The mace-wielder stood aside while the crossbowmen fired without looking. Their bolts disappeared into the darkness within and the other three men rushed inside. Both crossbowmen reloaded.

Chavali stood a good distance away, admiring their efficiency. She noticed Kalei stopping Colby and Portia from joining the guards rushing in. These men seemed to have everything under control, which suited her. She had no interest in breaching unknown locations to face unknown numbers of men interested in killing her.

Bright yellow lights flared inside. Men screamed. Metal clanged.

"I can't just stand out here and watch." Colby shoved Kalei aside and ran into the building.

Portia followed on his heels. Chavali sighed and took a more sedate pace. Kalei caught her arm before she took a second step.

"Let them do their job. Your friends should too."

Chavali raised an eyebrow and yanked her arm away. If Kalei turned out to be the inspector working with the Drowned Ones, her reticence to join the assault would make sense. On the other hand, she could merely dislike violence. "Is this how inspectors earn the adoration of the people? By letting the guards handle the dirty work? Their lives don't matter, after all. No one knows their names."

Kalei clenched her jaw. "No. Fine. Let's go in." She tossed her cape aside and drew an elegant, finely wrought blade with a basket hilt. Sword in hand, she traced an unknown symbol in the air and strode past Chavali. Energy flickered around her body in a cocoon. She ducked inside the building and out of sight.

Still taking her time, Chavali drew her dagger and held it away from her body, as Eliot had taught her. Some of his lessons came naturally now, while others still required her to think. She took a deep breath and hoped enough muscle memory and instinct had been created in the past few months for her to be useful without getting herself hurt.

She stepped into roiling brown smoke masking harsh yellow light. Shouting all around her echoed and bounced together, punctuated by odd screams and grunts. The sounds of fighting added to the cacophony. The smoke burned her nose and throat, prompting her to cover her face with her sleeve. Illusions wouldn't help in this mess.

Something large and heavy crashed to her left. She sprang to the right and hit her head on a metal shelf. The world tilted around her as she tripped over a low shelf and fell. Coming in here had been a mistake. At least she still had her dagger, gripped firmly in her right hand. As she waited for her head to clear, she noticed a pool of dark liquid seeping into the packed earth floor.

Desperate to know who had been hurt, she crawled forward in the acrid smoke, her eyes now watering. Her breath caught as she found a Watchman, blood still dribbling from a gash in his neck though his eyes were wide and glassy. She scrabbled back, not wanting to touch a dead body.

"Colby!" The noise of confusion and battle swallowed her shout.

A dark shape loomed in the murk and she recognized a sword thrust too late to avoid it. The blade sliced a shallow line up her thigh. Fear and anger sent her surging to her feet, rushing her opponent. She threw her body at him. They crashed together into a wooden crate and it collapsed under their combined weight.

His head hit the ground, giving her a precious second to seize. She stabbed her dagger into his chest. It skittered off his sternum and up into his neck. Only as he gurgled did she think to sample his thoughts. By then, she didn't want to. Once, she'd been in the thoughts of person while they died. Never again by choice.

She yanked her dagger out and scrambled to her feet. "Colby!"

Another shadow approached. "Right here." He reached her side. Fresh dark sprays decorated his leathers.

"Where did the smoke come from?" Watchful around them, she put her back to his. Her head bumped the scabbard strapped to his back.

"I don't know, but at least three Watchmen are dead. Portia! Sivry!"

"They will all converge on us."

"That's kind of the idea. The enemy knows the terrain too well."

Someone somersaulted into view and Sivry sprang to her feet in front of Chavali. "I get the feeling we were expected."

"Me too." Portia ran to the group, another shadow on her heels.

When her robed pursuer saw Colby, he stopped short and backpedaled. Before any of them could react, he disappeared into the smoke again.

"Can you disperse the smoke, Portia?" Colby asked. "Because that would help a lot."

"Not my forte, but I saw that Watch mage do it before. Let me see what I can do." Portia crouched in the middle as Chavali, Colby, and Sivry made a protected triangle for her.

"I'd like to know where Kalei is in all this," Sivry said.

"As would I," Chavali growled.

Pure, clean wind rushed from behind her in a great gust, knocking her forward. Chavali screwed her eyes shut and hugged her wounded leg. Remembering the injury made it sting again. When the wind stopped, she opened her eyes. The area around them had been cleared of everything but dark stains on the floor and globes of harsh, sulfurous light. Outside the wide circle, tall shelves lay on their sides, broken crates and boxes covered much of the floor, and several bodies lurked amid the debris.

Five Watchmen tossed wood and other debris aside. Booted feet thumped on metal stairs, retreating upward. Everyone turned to look and Chavali followed Colby as he shoved his way to the one door swinging shut in the rear of the building. She noticed one Watchman limping and another working to free himself. The other three hurried to join the group rushing for the stairs.

"Is this wise?" Chavali asked. "They seem to have been ready for us."

"We may never find them again," Portia said.

"We're in," one Watchman grunted. "Don't waste the blood already spent."

Colby threw the door open and thundered up the stairs. Knowing her skill, Chavali slammed her back against the door and held it open for everyone else to swarm up behind him. "This is beyond me," she told the Watchmen. "I will check for injuries and help your brothers."

The last Watchman saluted her and disappeared into the stairwell.

Chapter 23

Chavali ran to help the nearest Watchman trapped under the debris. Grabbing boards and tossing them, she worked swiftly to free him.

"Ma'am," he panted. "I think my leg is broken." He shoved a metal beam away.

"I am not strong, but I can help you help yourself." She offered him a hand.

He gripped her forearm and used her aid to lever himself standing. Nearby, someone groaned and another heap of debris shifted.

"What happened?" a slurred voice demanded.

"I will come back in a moment," Chavali called out. With her help, the Watchman hobbled to the doorway. He leaned against the wall with the other injured Watchman and shooed her away. As she approached the source of the noise, wood and metal exploded up and out, buffeting her. She cringed away, then straightened to see a man with dark, shaggy hair wearing robes similar to those in her memory of the Drowned Ones.

He shot to his feet and hopped through the debris, ignoring her. When she ran to circle the debris and prevent his escape, he glanced up at her. His gaze snapped to her feather. Before she got a more than a fleeting look at his face in the weird light and settling dust, he leaped in a different direction and fled deeper into the warehouse. To follow him, she had to wade through the twisted metal and wood.

At her feet, someone groaned and she stooped to find a warm hand groping feebly toward her. She hesitated for a moment before abandoning the chase and gripping this man's hand. His half-coherent, pain-filled thoughts marked him as a Watchman.

"I am here. The one with the feather. I will not leave you to die." As she lifted debris from him, she heard him try to answer with a feeble groan. "Hush." Why did she offer to do this? She should have followed everyone upstairs. Now she had to deal with the spiraling depression of this man certain he'd been led here to die by a peacock of an inspector who vanished when the fight became difficult.

"Don't be melodramatic," Chavali said with a huff. "You're going to live. Harbor City has healers like anywhere else, yes? Yes. Your injuries will not kill you." She uncovered his face and wiped blood from his eyes. "It feels bad, but is not. This blood is from a scrape."

You haven't found my legs yet.

"Bah." Movement to the side caught her attention and she caught sight of several people climbing down past the windows. One robed man dropped into sight at the doorway and ran. The Drowned Ones fled, which meant Colby and the others must have reached the top floor.

"Like goats in a fire," Chavali muttered. She kept working to reveal the Watchman's body without releasing his hand. Boots hurried down the stairs as she heaved the final board off. What she found underneath it made her wonder how the guard still lived. A metal shelf strut protruded from his lower gut, and he lay in a puddle of blood.

She schooled her face to avoid letting him see any reaction from her. "I am not strong enough to lift you. We will need help. I must let go, but you will not be abandoned."

His hand relaxed with wordless acceptance. For a moment, she thought he died, but she saw his chest continue to rise and fall. She set his hand down to avoid further injury and ran for the stairs. The door flew open as she approached and two Watchmen ran into her.

"Let them go," she snapped, stumbling to the side. "You have wounded men. One will die without a healer."

Both Watchmen froze and stared at her. She flicked her hand in dismissal, then pointed at the dying man and the doorway.

"Yes, ma'am. Thank you. You should go upstairs."

While they turned to dealing with their own men, Chavali limped up the stairs. At the second floor landing, she found a Drowned One with his skull crushed. With more time, the nauseating stench would fill the shaft. For now, she covered her nose with her arm and stepped over it to find Colby, Portia, and Sivry ransacking the room with three more Watchmen. All had blood on their clothes now, and one Watchman held his arm close.

Couches and small tables filled this room. With the windows all open, Chavali caught a hint of alcohol and sweat under the fishy scent of the docks. One robed woman lay on the floor, blood draining from her leg. Her fingers scraped on the floor as she tried to escape. Chavali swooped down on her and grabbed her neck.

"Are you part of the Drowned Ones?"

Yes. Must escape.

"Where would you go if I let you leave?" She saw a brown door in the woman's thoughts, one so plain and unadorned she would never be able to pick it out among many. "Never mind that. Where will I find Shance?"

The woman gurgled and her thoughts scattered more. Chavali flung the cultist aside and watched her die.

"Useless," Chavali spat. They'd been too thorough and not thorough enough. "Members of the Watch, you have injured and dead downstairs. It would be wise to guard them until help can arrive."

All three Watchmen agreed with her and trooped downstairs.

"I found the ring." Portia held Harris's ring up, recovered from a drawer in a desk. "But no statue. They separated it."

"The princess isn't here either," Sivry said from the other side of the room. "At least, she's not alive. I suppose they could've chopped her up and stashed her in the couch cushions, but that's pretty gross."

"Do you know what else isn't here? This Blue Death drug." Chavali considered what she'd found downstairs, besides injured Watchmen and dead bodies. "Those boxes and crates were all empty."

Portia peered through the ring at her. "This was all a giant trap. Somehow, this Shance guy knew we'd come looking for this and set up an ambush for us."

"And now Kalei is missing." Despite not seeing the inspector race up the stairs with everyone else, Chavali had expected to find her here.

Colby stooped to pat the corpse down. "At least we know the Watch is honest."

"I think four are dead. One more if they can't get him to a healer in time. This one," Chavali nudged the corpse with a boot, "makes only three dead cultists that I saw. There may be another buried downstairs."

"As soon as we charged up here, they all scattered." Colby retrieved a few coppers from the dead woman's pocket and gave up. "This one stayed to delay us. She got in the way and stayed there. Managed to hold out just long enough. There's nothing like a zealot. She knowingly sacrificed herself."

Sivry wove through the furniture to return for the conversation. "I considered following them out the window, but realized I'd be grossly outnumbered." She paused at a desk and rifled through the papers Portia had already checked. Shaking her head, she rolled everything up and tucked it into her back pocket, then covered it with her shirt.

"And now we have no leads," Chavali said. "On anything."

"No kidding." Portia dropped onto a couch and rubbed her face. Her shoulders drooped. "I don't like our odds for finding the Drowned Ones again."

Chavali sat beside her, tired and feeling the ache in her leg again. "This has been a very unpleasant day."

Colby straightened and sighed. "I don't think I've eaten today."

"That would explain why I'm so tired," Portia said.

"I suggest we go back to the inn," Sivry said. "At least for a meal and to talk without inspectors and captains breathing down our necks. I'd also like to look these papers over after I've put something in my belly and can think straight."

They quieted at the sound of boots on the stairs. A watchman poked his head inside the room and looked at Chavali. "Ma'am, I want to thank you. Because you acted and called for a healer right away, Oersen is going to make it. He's on his way back to headquarters for more healing, but he's going to live."

"I'm glad to hear it." Chavali smiled at him, pleased for some small good tiding out of this mess. Of course, Oersen wouldn't have been hurt if not for this fiasco, but at least he didn't have to die. "Did you find any other injured to tend?"

"No, ma'am. The other four are dead. And by the way, Kalei just came back with reinforcements. But not the healer. One of our guys handled that."

"My sympathies for the losses."

He nodded and slipped away.

Colby, Portia, and Sivry all stared at her. Colby's mouth quirked into a grin.

"What?" she snapped. "I'm not a heartless monster. He did not deserve to die."

Portia giggled. "Yep, I need food. A lot."

Chapter 24

Chavali closed her eyes to savor the first bite of a baked potato slathered with butter and sprinkled with herbs. When it touched her tongue, the flavors made her nauseous. She scowled and choked it down, following it quickly with two more bites. As she sipped her hot tea, waiting for her belly to settle, she scanned the room.

The group occupied a cushioned booth in the back corner, affording them some privacy. Chavali took the outside edge with her back to the wall so she could people-watch. Colby sat across from her so his legs could stretch beyond the confines of the table. Portia and Sivry nibbled at crackers in the two inside seats.

"I saw Kalei walk into that warehouse," Chavali said. "I goaded her to do it."

Portia said, "She must've walked right out the other side, though I can't imagine how. I didn't cause most of that destruction with my wind, and there was no straight line from one door to the other. Maybe she waited by the door and once you went in, she ducked out."

"That seems like a lot of effort for no real purpose," Sivry said.

"She could've stuck with us and avoided killing anyone if she was the dirty inspector. Or gone around the back with that first group of Watch, or something else."

Colby, having no trouble devouring his potato, mixed vegetables, and steak, wiped his mouth with a napkin. "It's possible she got a few steps into the mess, realized how messy it was, and decided to go for reinforcements. Since she came back with more Watch."

"Yes, yes," Chavali waved him off. "This is why we left instead of questioning her."

"These inspectors are just a suspicious lot," Portia said. "It's amazing everyone thinks they're so wonderful when they act so dodgy."

Chavali snorted and noticed a man in ordinary clothes with dark hair tied in a tight tail at the nape of his neck. He saw her and his mouth twitched in a half-smile, then he turned away. The man's face seemed vaguely familiar, but she'd seen so many different people since she arrived, he could have been anyone, even an off-duty Watchman.

"I think we should consider our next plan. We have no leads, so we must create our own. Any ideas?"

They quieted as the waitress came by and refilled Chavali's near-empty mug with more steaming tea. The herbs smelled a little different, but Chavali had no reason to complain. She sipped it and nibbled at her vegetables. The small medallion of meat would seem appetizing soon.

"We've got the papers I snatched," Sivry said. "If we take some time to look them over, they might make sense."

Portia set Harris's ring on the table. "This is useless to us now. We do still have access to the princess's quarters and office. I get the feeling she's kind of a tidy person, so going through it all shouldn't take too long.

Also, you made nice with some guards. Maybe you can get some information out of them."

Chavali nodded and thought about what she might ask guards. If the inspectors did anything suspicious, they masked it well enough to go unremarked. Still, the idea had merit. "I have someone I can contact in the Broken Ring, but I must know what to ask him to do. And if the Drowned Ones have the statue, I cannot see how he will be useful. Except he can possibly help us find Harris's killer. This is part of our mission here, after all."

"We still should find the princess," Colby chided.

"Bah." Chavali's stomach seemed better and she set to the task of cutting a sliver of meat. "I don't care about the princess unless finding her will get us the statue."

"She's a *person*. If we can help her, we should."

"Colby," Portia said while Chavali shifted from knife to tea to avoid stabbing Colby. "I get where you're coming from, but if we can find the statue instead, that's our job. And let's face it—if one of the inspectors was involved in Ambrye's disappearance, she's either safe enough or already dead. Besides, we can't help every single person we come across because they're a *person*. We'd never get anything done."

"I'm kind of with Colby on this, but for a different reason," Sivry said. "If we gain favor with the queen, Eldrack can use it in the future. It could open doors for him. I'm not sure how, but I do know that's how things work. Monarchs are just gang leaders operating in the light."

Chavali cradled her tea with both hands. "This is true. And a good point. There is something to be said for the value of a monarch's favor." Her head suddenly seemed too light and too heavy at the same time. She blinked heavily and rubbed her forehead. "Finding the princess is worthwhile for that reason." The room drifted sideways. She sipped her tea again, hoping it would fix this as it had fixed her stomach.

"I suppose that's kind of a win," Colby said with a sigh.

"Fine." Portia huffed. "We're looking for the princess. That doesn't help us decide where to go from here."

"We could..." Chavali shook her head, trying to figure out what she meant to say.

"Are you all right?" Colby asked. He reached for her, offering a steadying hand. A faint glow surrounded him.

Portia draped an arm around her shoulders. "Did you get stabbed without telling us?"

Did she get hurt? Chavali tried to remember. Her thoughts oozed too slowly for her to focus on them. "My leg." To her own ears, the words sounded slurred. Shimmering purple light flickered at the edges of her vision, which meant only one thing. And yet, she felt no prophecy coming. The rest of her vision remained its normal gray-based monochrome. Injuries had never done that to her before.

"Here, drink some more tea. It always helps." Portia raised the mug to her mouth and helped her sip it. Purple streamers shot from Portia's fingertips and hit the ground as snakes.

"We should get her up to the room and check the wound," Colby said. His voice bounced inside her skull. Golden motes danced around him. "It may need to be cleaned and dressed."

As she slumped to the side, too dizzy and confused to do anything but fall, Chavali heard an unexpected voice.

"I'll catch you," Keino reassured her.

Chapter 25

Chavali looked up into Keino's face in full color. Purple rippled around him, covering Colby and Portia. The table turned to brown goo and splashed around her. Bright green plant shoots burst through the wood floor, showering her with splinters. Keino leaned in to protect her from the wood. He ripped a plant stalk out of the ground and tossed it aside.

"This is a dream," Chavali said, too confused to resist as Keino lifted her in his arms.

"No. It's real."

She squirmed against him. "Let me go."

"I'm only trying to protect you. He is coming. Why won't you let me in?" He ran from the plants, racing into purple darkness.

"The same reason I never let you in before." She slammed her elbow into his neck and kicked her legs. He let go and she fell. Plummeting through inky blackness, she wriggled until she could see forward. Something tiny grew until it became the back of a mint-green wagon with a bright red roof.

"This is a dream," she repeated to herself. Her heart raced anyway. If she hit that wagon at this speed, it would kill her. As it grew closer, she took a deep breath, screwed her eyes shut, and braced for a disastrous impact.

Something passed by close enough to buffet her hair and she landed on a shifting, crinkly cushion. She opened her eyes to discover scarlet leaves covering her body up to her neck. The pile rolled beneath her and she clawed in every direction to avoid slipping below the surface. Her efforts sped her slide until her feet hit something solid.

She fell to a sheet of ice with wagon wheels stamped on the surface. On the other side, a fist pounded against the cloudy ice. The ice cracked. Chavali scrambled away. She backed into something and turned to find a creature she'd never expected to see again. Glossy scales formed of black mist outlined a goat-shaped thing with leathery wings and short, stubby horns.

"Pale," Chavali breathed. Pale had murdered countless men and women in Ket and planted all the manipulations in Colby's mind that Chavali had struggled so hard to find and remove over the past months. Had her efforts taken the triggers from Colby and transferred them to Chavali instead of destroying them?

The goat-dragon shrieked in a distant echo and reared up, spreading its wings. Keino burst through the ice, flying through the air with one fist thrust forward, and crashed into Pale. The tangled pair slid across the ice, throwing sparkling showers of snow in every direction. Chavali saw her opening. She scrambled to her feet and fled. The ice heaved in front of her, throwing her to the surface again and shoving her back toward Keino and Pale's struggles. She flailed her arms until she managed to grip the rising edge and held on as it shot into the air. Cold numbed her fingers. Already swinging in the air, she urged her body higher in both directions, trying to overcome gravity and hook her leg on the edge.

When the ice abruptly stopped rising, she flew into the air and landed on the back side of the frozen wall. She slid down to a swirling pool of blood and hit the surface with a splash. The blood buoyed her. When nothing else happened, she caught her breath and swam for the side.

Crawling out onto lush, green grass, she left a trail of blood. Ahead, she saw a ring of wagons. Shadows flickered against the large wooden wheels and bright green and blue walls. A glance behind showed her nothing in pursuit, so she crept close. The desire to see even a hint of her family overwhelmed her fear of their possible condition.

She reached the nearest wagon and touched its solid wood. The subtle mark imprinted in the wood below her hands identified it as her family's. A deep, primal need urged her to get inside. She took a deep breath and peered around the corner.

Flames from a giant bonfire licked the sky. Dark shapes writhed in circles around it. The familiar rhythm of drums pulsed in time with her racing heart. With every step, dread battled anticipation. If she looked hard enough, would she find her sister? Her parents? Seer Marika? Did she want to see their spirits? None of these questions had answers.

Figures sat around the edge, each holding a goatskin drum, arms moving in a flurry to beat out the celebration dance. More figures whirled and jumped in the center, their beaded skirts swishing. They raised their arms in gratitude to...not the Creator. To Estevior, their founder. To

Iparre, Hegoa, Mendeba, and Ekia, their totems. This dance showed the clan's joy for life and wonder.

Every man had the same face, the one Chavali always imagined for Estevior. Every woman bore Istal's face. Their skirts shimmered with a rainbow of iridescent colors. Chavali wanted to count but couldn't. They danced in a blur, one body merging into another, concentric circles moving against each other. When she tried to count the men around the edge, she realized that, even though she could see the wagons on the far side, the people faded into indistinct shadowy haze.

Turning away felt wrong, yet her mind needed to see something solid. She grasped the front corner of her family's wagon and let its firmness ground her. As she raised her foot to step onto the back ledge, shadows wrapped around her and pulled her away. The dancers held her arms and legs.

"Let me go!"

They tightened their grips and carried her over their heads, bouncing in perfect synchronicity with her own heartbeat. She squirmed and kicked, desperate to get away. The hands tossed her into the air and she landed on more hands dancing in the opposite direction with her. Heat washed over her, more and more intense as the dancers passed her from ring to ring, closer to the bonfire.

"I'm your Seer!" She broke one hand loose only to have it wrenched behind her back. "I serve you and you serve me. We are sym—" An arm wrapped around her mouth. Desperate not to burn, she bit down and tasted bitter, angry judgment. They passed her to the next row, who slung her low and smothered her with their bodies. Again and again, they threw her closer and closer until she reached the inner ring.

The dancers held her toward the fire. Heat leached her strength. Fingers of flame lashed out, searing lines across her flesh. She turned away, clinging to her tormentors with dwindling energy.

"I can protect you." Keino's cool breath tickled her neck. "He is coming. Let me in, Chavali. Let me help you."

Chavali didn't know what to do. No choice was good. Keino wanted more than he said. The dancers wanted to punish her for unknown crimes. Pale lived on inside her. And still, Harris's memories remained beyond her reach.

"I want to wake up," she whispered, her face buried in scratchy, beaded cloth. "Please let me wake up." She sobbed with eyes too dry to form tears.

"Hold me close or you'll never wake again," Keino murmured into her ear.

"No."

"I love you."

"I hate you."

Keino's lips brushed her neck. "Coming from you, that means the same thing."

Chavali opened her eyes and discovered she now stood in her family's wagon, Keino holding her from behind. Moonlight streamed in through windows on both sides, bathing them both in a gentle glow. He trailed kisses down her neck and pushed her dress off her shoulder. She heard nothing but the soft touch of his lips against her skin.

For so long, she'd wanted this. Delirious in the silence, she melted into his arms. Without his thoughts intruding, she could forget how much of an ass he was. Every time he'd tried to kiss her in life, she'd been treated to his noxious, arrogant fantasies of claiming and dominating her. The man had always wanted to possess her...in every way...

She blanched and stiffened as she considered what he might be demanding. Such a thing might not be possible, in which case she worried for nothing. The stakes demanded she not take the chance. "No." Pushing away from him, she refused to look at his face. His wounded puppy pout would test her resolve.

He let her go. She stopped several steps away with her back to him, staring at that locked chest again. The chest wobbled. "Did you lock Harris inside?"

"You did that."

Chavali frowned. At the time, she hadn't wanted to deal with all these memories. His life held tragedy and despair. She had enough of her own without taking on someone else's. "I want to let him out."

"What for? He is coming and that bandit can't protect you. No one can protect you like I can."

"I don't need your protection," she snapped.

The moonlight cut off. Cloth ripped and the air thickened. Chavali braced for what she'd see as she turned. She found a hulking, brutish creature with claws as thick as her wrists. Keino's eyes glared at her from its beastly face. The chest clattered and thumped. Chavali backed into it and kept going, her heart in her throat.

"You don't need him," Keino growled. "Only me."

Chavali took a deep breath and raised her chin. She never gave in when he lived and wouldn't start now. "I don't need either of you."

Keino opened his fanged maw and roared with a great gust of hot, rancid wind. The blast knocked Chavali to her knees and churned her stomach. She tasted bile. He blew harder. Clinging to the corner of the chest while being blown sideways, she wished this dream involved less dangling from things. She also wished she knew what to do.

Her dreams had changed so much since she became Fallen. In the old nightmares, she had no choices or options. They'd been nothing more than bizarre, twisted stories with a scripted part for her to play. Lately, she'd been able to think and react however she wanted. In this one, she even felt awake.

Keino's breath changed to gushing salt water. Chavali coughed and gasped, trying to ignore where it came from. The water blasted her fingers until she let go. She tumbled with the current around corners and through rocks. Her limbs cracked against hard surfaces, breaking every bone in multiple places. She screamed. Water rushed into her mouth. She flung her arms feebly, desperate to find a bubble of air.

"Let me protect you, Chavali. All this pain will go away. He's coming, but I can keep you safe."

Her lungs filled with water and she mouthed, "No."

Chapter 26

Please wake up. I can't do this without you. The clan needs you. Come back.

Chavali groaned. Relieved thoughts surged into her head as weights piled on her body. "The Seer is not a pillow," she croaked. The harshness of her own voice surprised her. She opened her eyes in the dim light of a bedroom to find Biholtz, Haizea, and Danel hugging her. Judging by the stone ceiling and the bed, she lay in her own room in the Fallen tower.

"Welcome back," Kelly said.

Biholtz pushed the two younger children off. "Chavali needs water. Danel, you hold the cup. Haizea, you hold her hair out of the way." She slid behind Chavali and took the place of her pillow, propping her head up enough to drink.

Chavali couldn't remember being so tired before. Mint flavored the cool water, soothing her throat as she sipped. She tried lifting her arm and found the effort too much to bother.

"Colby tried to stay by your side. So did Portia. Eldrack threw them out. He tried to get the children to leave but failed."

"He doesn't have anything over me," Biholtz declared. She hugged Chavali from behind.

"Somehow, I suspect she learned to do that from her Seer," Kelly said.

"I also suspect this." Chavali smirked. "I see I have been returned home."

"Apparently, you fell in the common room of an inn, screaming. Portia thinks your tea was dosed with some kind of blue drug, though I don't understand how you didn't notice if it was blue."

"Blue Death."

"Yes, that's it."

Chavali closed her eyes to think. The two users she met had been lucid. Though they'd said lunatic things, both men had walked, talked, and interacted with her as if they heard and understood her. They hadn't collapsed or passed out. Why did it affect her so differently?

"Are you still awake?" Kelly asked.

"Yes."

"Good. You should eat before you fall asleep again. I'll leave that to Biholtz."

"Yes," Biholtz said. "You will."

Chavali opened her eyes in time to see Kelly stand and smooth her white skirts. "This drug is supposed to have withdrawal."

Kelly nodded. "You're well past that. Biholtz and I already nursed you through it. Eat, rest, and try to get out of bed. In that order. Eldrack will come by soon, I expect. He'll want to hear your report, among other things."

Haizea shoved an apple wedge into Chavali's mouth, preventing her from telling Kelly where Eldrack could shove his reports. Kelly grinned and left while Chavali glowered and crunched. Danel took turns with Haizea, cramming food into Chavali's mouth until Biholtz made them stop.

After a gulp of water to wash the food down, the children settled around her and she drifted with Biholtz's soothing thoughts of home and safety dominating her mind. She woke later from a dreamless sleep to the sound of the children stifling giggles.

"I'm awake," she mumbled. "Be loud if you want."

Biholtz popped her smiling face into view at the end of the bed. "How do you feel?"

Chavali propped herself up on her elbows and noted both her ability to do so and the clarity of her mind. "Better. Help me to the bathroom."

"No trouble," Biholtz told the smaller children. "From either of you. Play with your toys while we're gone. And you can eat the crackers."

Sliding her feet off the side of the bed, Chavali chuckled. "You sound like your mother. I remember her telling you and your brother that when you were little." The ache of loss had eased, and remembering those outside her own family hurt less than her parents and sister.

Biholtz ducked under her arm with a smile. "You think so? I had a dream my mamá came and told me to be good and help take care of Haizea and Danel like they were my own."

"Recently?"

"Five nights ago, when Colby brought you back. Penny brought us down here that morning."

175

"No wonder I feel so weak." Chavali wobbled to her feet with Biholtz's help. The girl had grown much stronger working for Marcus and had no trouble shouldering most of Chavali's weight. They lurched up the stone hallway to the group toilets and bathing chamber. Chavali remembered being surprised by the luxury of hot water when she first arrived. Four months later, she had grown to expect it.

While she soaked in the tub with Biholtz brushing her wet hair, Chavali thought over the mission. By now, the princess had to be dead or discovered. The inspectors weren't stupid, and all three couldn't be behind the plot. Two against one should have an obvious outcome. And yet, each had said or done something suspicious.

She wanted to know why the perpetrator separated Harris's ring from the statue and used it to set a trap. This Blue Death couldn't explain it. Users might see the future, but as she well knew, any such visions offered metaphors, not reality. She doubted someone saw an image of the ring being removed from the statue, or anything of the sort.

Few knew about the ring's importance in that context. Kalei had watched Portia perform the tracking spell and asked questions about it. Nasha and Reynolds were, no doubt, sharp-eyed enough to spot the ring on Colby's or Sivry's finger and make the connection. Thinking back over conversations on the subject, anyone walking past Denton's office might have overheard them, including Denton herself.

No, Denton wasn't involved. Chavali believed that. Everything about the woman screamed of duty and integrity. It had to be an inspector, as Ambrye herself surmised. Who knew how the woman guessed as much? Chavali scowled at the cooling water.

The puzzle occupied too much of her mind to let it go. She

wanted to know the answers. Even more, she wanted to find Harris's killer. He deserved that from her. Unless some second team went to finish the mission, she needed to go back to Harbor City.

"I'm finished here," she told Biholtz. "When we get back, I'll need to pack and leave again soon. No matter what Eldrack says, I'm going to finish things."

"I'll get Haizea and Danel home."

"Thank you."

Chapter 27

Chavali sat at her small table, contemplating the task before her. The bag she used for travel sat empty on her dresser, which meant she had to find and pack everything again. Kelly seemed the likely suspect in this crime. The infernal woman always wanted to be helpful. Chavali prodded the pouch of fortune telling prop baubles she often wore at her belt, considering whether to bring them this time.

Eldrack knocked on her door and poked his head inside without waiting to be invited. When he saw her, he smiled and walked in. "You're awake and alone, good."

"Afraid of Biholtz?" Chavali smirked.

"And back to your normal self. Even better."

"I will be ready to leave again shortly, and there is little you could do to stop me."

Eldrack clasped his hands and smiled. "I have no intention of stopping you, only delaying you until tomorrow so you can have another night of rest. No other team was dispatched to finish the mission for you. We get little information from North Cascain, as you know, so you'll need to figure out what's happened in your absence and proceed from there."

Chavali raised an eyebrow. "You let it go for five days? And now wish to wait one more?"

He shifted and looked away. "I'm almost positive the statue is still there. That means you should still be able to retrieve it. The trail to Harris's killer is probably cold, but I have faith in you. Speaking of Harris, I want you to see the healers about that before you leave."

"I see." She regarded this man, a simple clerk who once had been Fallen himself, and wondered what kind of missions he'd carried out. His skill with diplomacy suggested something less deadly than her own. Guarding secrets had to have been a major part of them. "There will come a day when your refusal to answer my questions will become a serious problem. Today is not this day, because I wish to be the one to finish this, but it will come soon."

Pursing his lips, he nodded. "I understand. See the healers before you go."

She'd hoped her willingness to let the secrecy slide would prompt him to speak more. "I have nothing to offer them yet. When I do, I will see them."

"Portia explained the Blue Death. Under its influence, nothing happened?"

Chavali barked a laugh. "Nothing? Not hardly. Among other things, I saw the barriers preventing me from accessing them. Your wishes and needs will not remove them."

Eldrack gripped the back of the other chair, leaning against it and facing her. "What sorts of other things?"

"None of your business."

"Answering questions goes both ways, Chavali."

"You are not in my clan. I have been clear about this."

"And I've also been clear on this subject."

Chavali scowled and restrained herself from throwing her bauble pouch at him. "I saw Pale. I don't know what that means."

"And that scares you?"

Until he asked that question, it had only confused her. A shiver of fear wriggled up her spine. "Of course it scares me. She's dead. There's no reason to see her in a nightmare or vision. Robin would make more sense." The possibility Pale had become tied to her in death made the blood drain from her face. Showing up in that nightmare made more sense under that assumption. She almost preferred the idea of having taken Colby's triggers into her own mind.

Eldrack raised his brow. "Is there something else?"

"Does there need to be?"

He sighed and shook his head. "If you won't tell me about it, talk to Kelly."

Chavali made a noncommittal noise. Kelly didn't know any more about the spirits than Eldrack. The healer had no need for that information. Perhaps she'd speak to Penny about it. The elder clanswoman understood magic, and Chavali had promised to discuss the matter in depth sometime when the children wouldn't overhear. Danel and Haizea, in particular, might get strange ideas about their families from hearing only part of the conversation, and the entire explanation about the spirits would confuse them.

"As I said, I have nothing for her yet. She can wait until I return.

The statue is more important than this nonsense."

"If you could see your own face, you wouldn't buy 'nonsense' any more than I do. And it's fair to say your secrets may have compromised this mission." He sighed again and let go of the chair. "Regardless, I know a brick wall when I run into one. These issues need to be dealt with, whether you want to or not. Get the job done and take care of yourself." Before she could respond, he left.

Chavali rubbed her face because throwing things at the door behind him would accomplish nothing and give her a mess to clean. She thought of Harris for no reason—of his crooked, smirking smile and his shaggy hair. She'd never seen him through anyone else's eyes or dreams, so she had no idea what color his eyes were. From their tone, she guessed green or hazel.

Keino's face intruded and she huffed. The ass butted into everything lately, even errant, disjointed mourning. If the healers refused to bring Harris back, she would never be annoyed by him again. He shouldn't have allowed himself to be killed. Neither of them should. Keino's death had, in truth, been inescapable, but Harris's entire life had been about slipping away, fading into the background, and letting others take the fall. Survival should have been natural and easy for him. Idiot.

Knocking on her door startled her from her thoughts and she wiped unwanted tears from her cheeks. "Come in," she called out.

Colby swung the door wide and let Portia and Sivry in. "I ran into the kids on the way down. Since I know you'll want to go back, I got these two to come make plans."

Chavali smiled. "Thank you for whatever you did when I couldn't. All three of you."

Sivry produced the papers she'd stolen from the Drowned Ones warehouse and unrolled them on the table. "The horse did most of the work carrying you. Portia only threw up once on the boat ride this time."

"I considered staying in Harbor City," Portia said with a smirk. "But then I would've had to spend my time with inspectors, and that sounded like the most awful thing imaginable. Worse than two more boat trips. A lot worse."

Chavali laughed. "Yes, I agree."

"Did you see anything useful on that drug?" Colby asked as he held down two corners of Sivry's pages.

"Nothing relevant to our current problems, no." A common thread between all her interactions with the Blue Death leaped out and demanded she pay attention to it. "Except for 'he is coming.' This also was in the prophecy, and something said by both users I encountered. But I can't say with certainty who 'he' is." It could, she thought, even refer to Keino, though he'd been the one to say it in her nightmare. "I suspect it means Robin, but I can think of other possibilities that make equal sense. It's useless information for now. Something to keep in mind."

She scanned the paper Sivry and Colby held down and saw crisscrossing lines similar to the map in the West Watch building. "What is this?"

"We're not sure," Sivry admitted. "It's like the routing map Harbor City uses to help people get around. If you could see colors, it would be a little less confusing. But it's not that map. Nothing on that map turns like these do. Also, the writing isn't Shappan, and it isn't Cascaini. It's some kind of code using symbols."

One thick line ran from the top right corner with an arrow pointing at the center of the page. It split off into four lines running at squared angles, then each of those split off into another four lines, some diagonal. This continued across the page, covering it in squares and octagons, with another thick line dead-ending at the lower left corner and an arrow pointing at the corner. Every other line had no true start or end of its own.

"I don't know enough to guess what the code might be," Sivry said. "If I had some clue about the purpose of this thing, I could crack it."

"Intriguing." Though some of the symbols seemed vaguely familiar to Chavali, she ignored them, knowing she wouldn't be able to puzzle out anything the others couldn't. Instead, she tapped the arrow in the upper corner and traced the line with her finger. Portia steered her to stay on the same color and she wound through the map until she reached the bottom arrow.

"It's a flow diagram of some kind," Colby said. "This is a system that shows how something is distributed, but I have no idea what. How about the rest of the pages?"

"Lists in code." Sivry swapped pages and showed them scribbled lists of symbols. "Without some syntax to work with or some hints about the subject, I just don't know. This Shance guy is either brilliant or insane. Or possibly both."

Chavali picked up one of the three pages and turned it over, again ignoring the symbols. Instead, she rubbed it between her fingers and sniffed it. "Old paper, unusual ink. Messy hand. I wonder if this is blood?"

"No," Colby said. "It's blue."

Chavali raised her brow and set the paper down, eager to stop touching it. "He used his drug as ink to write lists? I would err on the side of insane. He's unpredictable and prone to strange tactics. Considering his ambush, he set it up to kill, which means he's ruthless in protecting his people, even though he purposely left at least one behind to die or be captured. Perhaps he hoped for capture so he could free her."

"We need to know what's happened since we left," Colby said. "It's late afternoon now, so we should leave first thing in the morning."

Chapter 28

Chavali, Portia, and Sivry once again shared the couch in Denton's office while Colby sat in a separate chair. Denton leaned back in her chair, the scowl she'd sprouted when she saw them fading in the wake of Chavali's explanation for their whereabouts.

"This Blue Death is quite potent for someone with the actual curse of prophecy, it seems," Chavali said.

"Sounds like it," Denton said. "Since you left, we've gone through everything at that warehouse and found nothing of interest. Even though we got nothing but three corpses that revealed nothing new to Nasha, I'm now convinced they had nothing to do with the princess's abduction. Someone dressed those people up at the silver shop to frame them, or something to that effect.

"Since you mentioned the Bloodflies, I've had my people prodding at them to see what they can find. So far, that's resulted in five dead Watch and no leads. Worse, they displayed the bodies publicly and took credit. We've got dockside informants turning up dead too. One of my Watch barely escaped an assault on her meeting with a local. The local was dismembered and left in plain sight. I didn't think much of the Bloodflies before, but they have my attention now.

"To make matters worse, that silver dust from the art evidence theft has now also been stolen. From Evidence Storage. And people on the street know about it. I don't know who's been leaking this information, only that it wasn't any of you, because you haven't been here. All of which means you're it for people I know I can trust. If an inspector isn't involved in this, I'll eat my boot. Consider them all suspects and proceed. You have my leave to do whatever you need to do. There's a traitor using my people. Find them and you'll get your statue back."

Chavali thought over these incidents. Clara, the black market woman, was already terrified of the Bloodflies. They'd been terrorizing people for a while, and only now chose to do so in plain sight. "If they took Ambrye in the first place, they had to have a reason. The Drowned Ones had a motive. A bizarre, deranged motive, but still a motive. Something changed for the Bloodflies, making them *want* your attention, and that of the entire city."

"Which means one of the inspectors wanted attention?" Colby asked.

"Not necessarily," Denton said. "This inspector is working two jobs now. They're bound to have a partner managing the gang in their absence. That person could be behind this."

"We should question the inspectors who know the princess best," Portia said. "I can't see anyone with no personal connection abducting her. But we'll have to be careful so they don't realize we suspect them."

"No," Chavali said. "We should be clear they are the prime

suspects. There should be no doubt they are under investigation themselves. Whether we learn anything useful from questioning them or not, we will force them either to let the gang operate on its own or to take greater risks in carrying out their plans. Either way, mistakes will be made."

"And mistakes are how we'll catch them," Denton finished. "Agreed. The Captain-General has a device he can use to locate the inspectors and members of the royal family at need. Before you ask, yes, we tried to use it to find Ambrye the moment she was reported missing, but it didn't work. There are ways to shield the locator with magic, and we assume she's under one of them."

"Use your device and point us." Chavali raised her chin. "We will find Ambrye and discover your traitor."

Denton nodded and left the office.

"You just gave your word to solve their problems," Colby said. "Did you mean it, or was that another play for Denton's trust to get what you want?"

Though the question chafed, Chavali knew what Colby meant. "Ambrye is an inspector. That makes her clan with the other inspectors. I am disgusted beyond words by this treacherous inspector for putting Ambrye in true danger in the first place, for causing the needless deaths of so many in the Watch, and for actually making me believe these Drowned Ones have anything to do with it."

Portia smirked. "The last one is the biggest deal for you."

"Perhaps." Chavali crossed her arms and chose not to consider those implications. "It is still unclear why Harris died. Should this inspector turn out to be responsible, there will be no safe place in all the world for them to hide."

Denton opened the door and leaned into her office. "Reynolds is here. He's worked with Ambrye and knows her well. I'm having him moved into an interrogation room as we speak. I'll help you find Nasha and Kalei when we're done with him. Those three know Ambrye well."

Chapter 29

Given the delicate nature of questioning a sharp-witted suspect, Colby agreed to watch from the other side of a mirrored window. Sivry, unsure how to help with this, elected to do the same. Portia, Chavali, and Denton entered the interrogation room, this time with Reynolds, the very average, unremarkable inspector, sitting in the chair. He hadn't been strapped down.

Portia leaned against the wall. Denton stayed by the door. Chavali offered her hand to shake with Reynolds.

"I'm Chastity."

He shook her hand without hesitation. "Edsen Reynolds. Everyone calls me Reynolds." His thoughts, crisp and ordered, pre-echoed his words. Chavali learned he disliked his first name.

"You know why you are here?" She kept hold of his hand. If he wanted it back, he'd have to yank it away.

Who are you to be the one asking me questions? Reynolds flicked his gaze to Denton and back to Chavali's hand. He made a tiny effort to retract his hand, but stopped when it became clear she had no intention of letting go. "Someone told me I was under suspicion for Princess Ambrye's disappearance." Again, his thoughts focused on his words, and Chavali saw he chose them with care.

"You are, in fact, *the* suspect."

How can that be? "That's interesting." *And worrisome.* "How did you arrive at that conclusion?"

"Following the evidence. This is what you do for a living, yes?"

"Excuse me a moment." Reynolds held up a finger for Chavali. *Why are you still holding onto my hand?* "Captain, why is a foreigner questioning me? Aren't Nasha and Kalei also familiar with this case?"

"Answer the question," Denton said.

It's a stupid question, and I don't know this woman. Reynolds arched an eyebrow. *I suppose that might be the point. An outsider as interrogator does make a certain amount of sense here. I wonder why this particular one, and why she keeps holding onto my hand.* "Yes, of course. I follow evidence and make deductions. Interrogate. Investigate. My duties aren't opaque."

"Where were you when Ambrye went missing?"

Yes, let's go through the alibis first. Yawn. "I spent my evening at the Wiltoneer, a tavern on the east side, where I had dinner with my aunt, Lina Caerlin. We left in a hired carriage around eight. I dropped her off at home, then returned to my office, where the night desk clerk and duty sergeant can verify I remained all night. In the morning, a Watch carriage took me home and the driver waited while I shaved and changed clothes. He then drove me to the west side Watch office at my request, so I could hand-deliver some paperwork and pick up some reports. I happened to be there when word of her disappearance was released."

Through this explanation, he replayed memories of the evening, night, and morning. He'd slept on a couch in his office for most of the night. His journeys had been all straight, direct routes with no distractions.

Something about this recitation of his time bothered Chavali, but she couldn't decide what. His thoughts being so clean and sharp also frustrated her. Then he thought about his confusion around her holding his hand again. She knew the contact would continue to distract him and let go. In her time as Seer, she'd encountered a few people who managed to keep the spirits corralled away from nuance and lesser thought processes. He appeared to be one of them. That made him dangerous.

Now she had to do things the hard way and pay attention to his body language and inflections. "Are you aware of the raid on a Drowned Ones site several days ago?"

"Yes." Reynolds clasped his hands in his lap and seemed at ease. "I heard about it after the fact. Had I known in advance, I would have offered to help. The Watch has lost far too many able bodies to operations like that."

"Where were you at the time of the raid?"

Reynolds smiled at Chavali as if he considered her a simpleton. "I'm not sure exactly when it took place that afternoon, but when I left my office the one time, I used a Watch carriage to travel to the northeast corner of the city to meet with a witness to a murder I'm currently investigating. After that meeting, I returned to the office in that same carriage."

"And, of course, I must ask where you were both times Evidence Storage was robbed."

"The first time, I was in my office. The duty clerk can verify that. The second time, I was at home. My neighbors can confirm that, as their dog escaped its leash and I helped them catch it."

His answers still bothered Chavali. She still had no idea why. Perhaps Denton, with years of experience at interrogation, could explain later. "How would you characterize your relationship with Princess Ambrye?"

Reynolds smirked. "Close enough to know she prefers the title of inspector. We attended Academy together. Good friends, I suppose."

"Did you know her before the Academy?"

"Not personally. Nasha is much closer, though. I believe they have dinner together from time to time."

Chavali noticed his voice flattened a tiny bit while relating this fact. Something about the relationship between Ambrye and Nasha bothered him. "How well do you know Nasha?"

His eyes narrowed so little Chavali doubted anyone else saw it. "I'm not the only suspect, am I? You're targeting inspectors. Ambrye pointed you at us. How did she do that?"

"You know how she is," Denton grunted.

"One of her contingencies? Really?" He shook his head. Though he tried to look bemused, Chavali saw irritation in the curl of his mouth. "The woman thinks of everything."

"About Nasha?" Chavali asked.

"Oh, as well as anyone else." Reynolds waved off the question. "She's secretive and slinks around all the time. I doubt anyone but Ambrye knows her well. And who knows what they talk about."

"What about Kalei?"

"Upstanding inspector. You'll undoubtedly discover some evidence of minor issues between her and Ambrye, but they're all drama. The two women are cordial and I'd be shocked if Kalei had anything to do with this."

"May I speak with you, please?" Chavali asked Denton.

Denton nodded and they left the room with Portia.

"Why did we stop?" Portia asked. "He hasn't really answered many questions yet or coughed up much information."

Chavali watched Denton, who returned her frustrated scowl. She had a feeling they'd reached similar conclusions about Reynolds.

"You don't trust him," Denton said.

"No. But that doesn't mean he abducted Ambrye. Compared to her, he doesn't seem smart enough."

"I can have him watched and followed, though he can slip my people easily enough if he wants to."

"He will not want to. He will want to be seen."

Portia's brow shot up. "How can you be sure?"

Chavali smirked. "I have known enough arrogant asses in my time to recognize them without effort. He dislikes Ambrye, from jealousy, rejection, or something else. This is enough reason to keep a leash on him. Have him followed. Tell him he's being tracked randomly."

Denton chuckled. "You think like one of them. The princess must have seen it in you. What did you think about him rattling off all those alibis?"

"It seemed off to me." Chavali knew they'd turn out to be true from watching the first one in his mind. No conflicting thoughts had intruded, and the straight-line path offered no room for him to be lying.

Despite that, she didn't believe him. "I'm uncertain why."

"That's how I feel about it," Denton said. "I'll have them verified. Can't do much more than that. Do you want to ask him any other questions? With anyone else, I'd consider grilling him, but he's an inspector. He'll see right through that."

"I agree. His actions after this will be more useful than anything he might say. What of these issues he mentioned between Kalei and Ambrye? I know they are rivals, but he made it sound like nothing in a way that makes me think it's much deeper than I observed."

"I have no idea how you got that from what he said," Portia admitted.

Chavali groped for the right words to explain. "He was...too eager to share? And what I saw of them together was not 'cordial.' It was frosty."

"Kalei has had some charges of excessive brutality filed against her. Besides that, I can get the files to show you, but I also happened to overhear her once accusing Ambrye of intimidating witnesses to Captain-General Crayton in a case Kalei had no involvement in. The point being she had no way to know about it unless she was snooping around to catch Ambrye doing something questionable."

"It sounded to me like Reynolds thinks Nasha did it," Portia said.

"Yes," Chavali said. "So I wish to question Kalei next. Find her, please," she said to Denton. "We will wait in your office."

Chapter 30

"I don't understand," Colby said after Chavali explained her observations in Denton's office. "Why are we going to question Kalei next if Nasha's more suspicious?"

"She isn't. All three of them still strike me as equal suspects." Chavali drummed her fingers on the couch's arm. "Interviewing Reynolds neither discounted him nor fingered him. He's guilty of *something*, but cannot be directly responsible for anything relating to this. His alibis will all be found true. On the other hand, his relationship with Ambrye is negative. Whether it's strong enough to motivate him to abduct her is questionable."

"Which leaves us more or less where we started. Only worse, because we don't have the ring to track anymore," Sivry said with a sigh. "I'm really out of my depth with questioning suspects and interpreting their responses. Is there something useful I can do while you're busy with that?"

"I'm kind of in the same boat," Portia admitted. "I know how to talk to normal people and get them to admit things they don't want to, but these inspectors play on your level." She nodded to Chavali. "And that's beyond me."

"You could snoop around the city generally," Colby said. "Or go back to all the places we know are related to this and check for anything we or the Watch missed. Ambrye made pronouncements and guessed at a lot with just a quick check of that prisoner transport, but she didn't stick around to ask the guards questions. Things like that. Maybe with a more detailed picture of everything that's happened so far, we can make better guesses. And we still need to figure out what that flow map is for."

Sivry and Portia glanced at each other and nodded. "I think we can handle that," Portia said. "We both fit in around here anyway, so that's a good use of our time. We'll meet you back at the inn for dinner no matter what we do or don't find."

"Watch your backs," Chavali said as the two women turned to go. "All three inspectors know who we are already."

Sivry flashed her a thumbs-up and they left. Colby opened his mouth to say something, but Denton returned and passed on where to find both Kalei and Nasha. Chavali and Colby took a Watch carriage to find Kalei first.

"You know I'm at Portia's level for interrogations too," Colby said as they trundled up the street.

"Yes. Why do you think Eldrack assigned you to this mission?"

"Honestly, I have no idea. It's a poor use of my skills. He should've sent me to deliver the statue in the first place."

"This is also my thinking. Something is going on that he won't speak of."

Colby laughed. "You're one to gripe about people keeping

secrets."

"I have had that argument with Eldrack before." Her lip curled. "I would very much like to know how he decides which agents to assign to which mission. So far, he seems strangely prescient about what will happen on any given assignment."

"That's always been my observation. Until Ket, that is. I seemed like a lousy choice for that one too." He stared out the window, watching the scenery go by.

"I liked Harris. I also think if you had been there instead, many fewer would have died and the king would have his statue."

"My goodness, Chavali, that sounded like a compliment about my competence."

She rolled her eyes. "Don't let it go to your head."

He laughed again. "I'll try not to."

Several minutes of companionable silence passed before Chavali elected to say anything else. "Are you from Itreon?"

"What?"

"Itreon. When Nasha mentioned it as her hometown, you recognized the place and lied about how well you know it."

He stared at her. "Do you ever miss anything?"

"No." Chavali smirked. "Answer the question."

"No." He shook his head with an amused chuckle. "I'm not from there. My mother was born there. If Nasha heard my family name, she'd recognize it. Things would get awkward. And I didn't lie."

"By your own standards of honesty, you lied. Flagrantly."

"I should have gone with Sivry and sent Portia with you."

Seeing his smile remained in place, Chavali grinned. "You knew what you were getting into. But I will change the subject anyway. You were a soldier, yes? And this was much like being a Watchman for rural people, yes?"

"More or less. Probably close enough for whatever you're going to ask about."

"What do you think of the inspectors? Generally, not individually. How things work here."

Colby crossed his arms and settled in to think. "I think it's a strange way to arrange the system. The inspectors seem to be able to go where they want, do as they please, and pursue investigations without checks on their behavior. Ambrye preened in front of that crowd, which bothers me. It also seemed like the extent of her regard for dead bodies involved their use as evidence. Nasha likewise seems to view them as nothing more than tools. Reynolds is arrogant, and so is Kalei.

"If one of them wanted to commit a crime, I can't see what stands in their way, other than the ability to track them. Which seems to rest in one man's hands, and anyone can be bought or persuaded with the right pressure or lure. Ambrye has to concern herself with her integrity to a certain point, because she'll eventually become the queen, but she can still get away with plenty. The others have even more freedom."

He paused to think more. Chavali wondered what pressure or lure would force Colby to step over the line of his personal morality and ethics. Nothing came to mind. Even if someone harmed Karias, he would stay true to his ideals. Doing otherwise would break him.

"On the whole, it's practically designed to make the ordinary guardsman feel resentful. The inspectors are popular and flashy. They get all the accolades while the Watchmen do most of the real work. I'll grant the inspectors are all intelligent and I'm sure they do necessary tasks. It just seems like they take more than their share of the payoff."

"Peacocks. They strut. This is the part you don't like. Ambrye performed for the crowd instead of serving them."

"I suppose that's it, yes."

She pictured him on Karias's back, riding with a squad of soldiers under his command. He led from the front, but not as the flag-bearer. Instead, he surged forward to cross swords with their enemy first. He took the blame for mistakes and passed around the glory. His faults did not include hubris. Stupidity at times, yes, and far too much sentimentality, along with his slavish devotion to superficial honesty... She stopped herself from wasting time cataloging every aspect of him she found annoying.

"I am not surprised you feel this way."

"Neither am I, when you put it so plainly."

"Perhaps you should keep your mouth shut while I question Kalei."

Colby rolled his eyes. "Yes, mistress. Whatever you say."

"This is a good response."

He laughed. So did she.

Chapter 31

The carriage stopped outside an establishment called The Gilded Lantern, a blank wall with a heavy oak door flanked by two ornate lanterns and wedged between a women's clothing boutique and a decorative furniture store. Across the street, the stores sold gentlemen's suits and books. Their destination, however, provided no specific guidance for what could be found within. Based upon that, despite never having been inside such a place before, Chavali knew exactly what to expect. She'd seen enough of them in the thoughts of others.

They opened the door and stepped inside a different world filled with warmth and cedar. Gauze draperies hung from the ceiling to create a soft maze strewn with pillow-covered chairs and couches. Ornate lanterns matching those outside and hanging from braided chains provided a soft glow throughout the room.

"Oh," Colby said. "It's a sylajutte."

Chavali smiled at the young hostess who stepped into her path with a welcoming smile. Her light hair had been piled atop her head in an elegant twist with thick curls dangling to frame a pretty face. She wore a flowing gown with full sleeves and a high enough neckline to suggest her assets were not among those available to the customers here.

"Welcome to The Gilded Lantern. How can I help you today?" She'd been trained to speak with the most soothing, pleasant tones possible and had a sweet, melodious voice.

"Please tell Inspector Kalei that Chastity is here to speak with her and the matter is rather urgent."

The girl's smile faltered, presumably for knowing neither of them would be paying for services today. "Of course. Wait here, please." She scurried away.

"It's nicer than I expected," Chavali commented while they waited. "Many of these places are less concerned with ambiance than sex and alcohol."

Colby shrugged and said nothing. He examined a lantern close to his head, using two fingers to turn it so he could see the negative space designs on each side. When the hostess returned, he snatched his hand away.

"She'll see you now."

Chavali followed the girl through the maze. Couples and small groups lounged, playing cards and dice games. Touching seemed to be the theme here. Chavali noticed herself scowling at these people and forced herself to stop. She slipped into a fake smile and didn't care if anyone could see through it.

Kalei sat on a curved couch with her feet up, holding a half-full wine glass. An attractive, shirtless man scooped two empty glasses off the coffee table beside her. One sparkled in the light, as if it had been dabbed with three or four tiny smudges of metallic paint. He bowed himself out of the small space to offer them the illusion of privacy.

"To what do I owe the pleasure of your company while taking some time for myself?" Kalei gestured with her glass to the two chairs opposite the table.

"Are you sober enough to answer questions about Princess Ambrye or should we escort you to an interrogation room to give the wine time to wear off?" Chavali sat in the closer of the two chairs. She sank deeper into the cushion than expected and had to struggle to sit up straight.

"I'm fine." Kalei sipped at her glass, then set it on the table. Her glass also glinted in the light with one small smudge the size of her thumbprint. "What about her?"

Chavali noted a subtle inflection on Kalei's last word, which spoke of disgust. "Where did you go during the Drowned Ones raid?"

Kalei stared at her for a long second. "You were serious about the interrogation room. This is a questioning because I've become a suspect."

"Yes. Quite. Please answer the question. Seven people died there."

"You mean four. The other three were cultists and murderers." She paused and licked her lips. "I realized the raid was undermanned almost immediately and left to round up reinforcements. I thought I could do it fast enough to impact the fight itself, which didn't turn out to be the case."

Unsurprised by this excuse, Chavali nodded. "Can you account for yourself at the time Ambrye was abducted?"

"You want my alibi? Sure. I have no idea when she was actually taken, but I heard it was in the evening. I didn't do anything unusual that day. Worked in my office, had dinner...hm. I go to a few different places routinely and I'm pretty sure it was one of those. Went home. I like to sleep in my own bed as often as possible. Reynolds uses his couch a lot, probably because he can't sucker a woman into his bed."

Though Chavali knew Kalei purposely distracted her from the alibi, she let it happen. If the inspector believed she had the upper hand in the conversation, she might get sloppy. "You dislike Reynolds?"

Kalei barked a laugh. "Who doesn't? He's such a smug ass." She leaned in to share a confidence. "I almost walked in on him with Ambrye once. Overheard him ask her out to dinner in his office. She turned him down and left. He walked out and I pretended not to have heard anything. This was two weeks ago, I think? Maybe three. He asked me if I would kneecap Ambrye for him, for fun."

"Charming. What of Nasha?"

"Creepy." Kalei cupped a hand around her mouth to exclude Colby. "Between you and me, her ability is the most disturbing thing I've ever seen. I've seen her make corpses without a jaw talk, which is really..." She shook herself in an exaggerated shiver. "And you know what? She follows Ambrye around a lot. Always lurking by her office and wanting to talk to her. Like a fawning follower with too much access. Then she pulls her quiet, harmless routine and acts like her weird ability is the most natural thing in the world."

Though Chavali agreed about Nasha's ability, she declined to say so. "I saw that you know Ambrye reasonably well. How would you characterize your relationship with her?"

"Oh, you know. She's the big, bright star. Keeps her distance." Kalei waved dismissively but couldn't keep the bite of jealousy from her voice. "I doubt anyone really knows her."

The inspector seemed far too comfortable. Reynolds, at least, had been wary and chose his words. Kalei tossed her statements carelessly. Chavali decided to change her approach to that of information gathering rather than suspect questioning. "Did you have a chance to examine the odd dust in Evidence Storage before it was stolen?"

Kalei blinked at her. Her entire body tensed. "Dust? No. I have no idea. I don't know anything about dust."

"Really?" Chavali wondered how such a question could have been so wrong for her goal. She'd read Kalei wrong or, more likely, missed something. "You had access to it, did you not?"

Again, Kalei paused. "In theory. All the inspectors can get into Evidence Storage any time we want without signing logs or anything. I didn't have any reason to examine that dust, though. Not my case."

"I thought Ambrye's disappearance was everyone's case."

"That dust has nothing to do with that case."

Rather than pursue this, which Chavali felt certain would lead to Kalei either shutting up or lying, she tabled it. Kalei knew something about the dust and didn't want anyone to connect her with it. "Of course. I am merely curious. Did you find anything interesting in the Drowned Ones warehouse?"

"No." Kalei picked up her wine and watched Chavali over the rim while she sipped. Her regard felt hostile now.

"I see." Chavali stood and smoothed her skirt. "We have taken up too much of your time, Kalei. Thank you for seeing us." When Kalei said nothing, Chavali and Colby left.

Outside the building, Chavali squinted in the sunshine. The sylajutte had no windows and she'd forgotten how early in the day it still was. Their carriage waited. Colby asked the driver to take them to the morgue before they both climbed in and shut the door. Only when The Gilded Lantern left their view through the window did either speak.

"I don't need you to tell me she's hiding something," Colby said.

"Yes, she was obvious about it, which is interesting. I also find it intriguing how little these inspectors like each other. Granted, there are those among the Fallen I do not like, but to have four people with so much power and responsibility who so clearly hate each other seems foolish."

"It probably didn't start that way, and the queen probably can't see it. I'd like to talk to Captain-General Crayton, but it's more out of curiosity than any belief he'll help with the case."

"If you had to pick which inspector is behind all this, who would you finger?"

Colby stroked his chin for several long moments. "I honestly don't know. If Reynolds's alibis all check out, it can't be him. Kalei tensed up when you asked about the dust, which, as she said, has nothing to do with Ambrye's abduction. Nasha seemed nice."

"The dust matter is troubling to me. If she knows what it is, she knows where it came from. I cannot see Harbor City putting a member of the Syndicate in the Watch, let alone hiring one as an inspector. And she would have to be deep enough into the Syndicate to learn about those flowers, which wouldn't go unnoticed. That means she has ties to the Order of the Creator's Path, who sent an assassin after me. I am not disposed to like them."

"They sent an assassin after us all. You happened to be the first one he tried to kill."

Chavali drummed her fingernails on her knee. That assassin had failed, thanks to Marcus's help. She thought back to that first chance meeting with Kalei and recalled her reaction. "When she first saw me, I can't be sure, but I think she recognized me."

"That's something to be wary of. But it has nothing to do with Ambrye or the statue."

"It means she has another agenda. These people. Just once, I would like a simple mission where the guilty party jumps up and down and confesses to everything while I drink tea."

Colby laughed. "Careful what you wish for."

She stuck her tongue out at him.

Chapter 32

Uniformed Watchmen guided Chavali and Colby to the dank basement the city used to house dead bodies. Chavali had never seen corpses laid out on slabs before, not even in others' memories. She had no idea cities did this. The Fallen had to have a room similar to this someplace, where bodies waited for an unknown price to be paid on their behalf.

The thought of her own body in such a cold, clammy dungeon sent shivers down her spine. Months had passed before she woke up from her death. Bodies were supposed to be returned to the world. At least the smell didn't bother her. The stench of death had been washed away from them and mild, flowery incense burned on the counter.

Nasha stood beside a metal table, examining a corpse with a distressingly familiar neck injury. Chavali had killed this man herself in the Drowned Ones raid. All dignity had been stripped from him. The next table held the equally nude body of the female cultist killed in that raid. Nine more tables held corpses, all bare and in wildly different conditions. One seemed fine, aside from the pallor of his skin. Another with neither hands nor feet had been eviscerated and his face destroyed.

"Hello," Nasha said. "I assume you're here to see me and not the bodies?"

"Yes," Chavali said, gesturing toward the door. "May we ask you a few questions?"

"Of course." Nasha leaned closer to the body in front of her and used a magnifying glass to examine the skin inside its elbow. "Have there been any new leads for finding Ambrye?"

"That is why we're here." Giving up on the idea of moving this conversation away from the dead, Chavali sighed and approached. She took care not to touch anything. "Have you learned anything from these?"

"Not really. They all just say Shance tells them what to do and they do it because he was sent by the Creator, and so on. They're lunatics, in life and death. None of these three saw Ambrye recently, so that confirms they were framed."

"What about the rest of these corpses?" Colby asked.

"The intact ones were Blue Death related, overdose and suicide. The rest are presumed Bloodflies victims from the past few days. They seem to be moving aggressively since Ambrye was abducted. The timing is suggestive. I'm leaning toward them as the perpetrators."

Chavali noticed Nasha inflected Ambrye's name differently than Reynolds or Kalei. Her tone held something positive, not negative. Nasha didn't hate the princess. "What makes you think they're involved with Ambrye's abduction?"

Nasha looked up and gave each of them a slow once-over. "Who else would expect Ambrye to go to that silver shop?" She blinked once, then straightened and frowned. "Oh. I see. Yes, that makes sense. Which inspectors are you investigating besides me?"

"Kalei and Reynolds. Both seem to consider you the prime suspect."

Turning away, Nasha moved to a savaged corpse. "Of course they do," she snapped. She took a deep breath and tempered her tone when she continued. "I'm a foreigner and though I've found a place here, my skills are...frowned upon by most. Even my nonmagical skills. Few understand the value of inspecting corpses beyond a cursory examination for obvious causes of death." She held up a severed arm. "I can't compel this body to speak, but by taking my time and checking every injury, I can tell you this man was murdered by a different person than that one. This killer is responsible for several deaths. He's experienced and brutal. That killer is new. It's his first time and he didn't like the taste of it.

"Reynolds and Kalei scoff at this kind of work. It doesn't matter to them and handling the dead is disturbing. Of course they want me blamed for a crime I didn't commit." Setting the arm down again, she gripped the side of the slab and shook her head. "I would never hurt Ambrye."

Real pain came through in Nasha's words. Seeing an opportunity to gain more insight, Chavali covered Nasha's hand with her own. "I can tell you care about her."

I need to go out tonight. Nasha pulled her hand away and rubbed it. "Yes. Which is why I want to find her. Excuse me." She fled the room, ducking out before Chavali or Colby could call her back.

"That was interesting," Colby said.

Chavali clacked her fingernails against the stone slab, then remembered what lay on its surface. She snatched her hand back and headed for the door. "Quite. She's going somewhere tonight. I want to know where it is."

"Do you still think she's a suspect? She seemed like she genuinely wants to know what happened to Ambrye."

"This could be guilt." Shoving the door open, Chavali wished she could chain all three inspectors down and have the spirits rip away everything until she found the truth. In theory, such a thing could be done; she'd done it by accident to two different people. In practice, she refused to stoop to Robin's level by attempting to do it on purpose.

"Though I didn't before, I do agree with her that the Bloodflies are likely mixed up in this. As she said, only someone who knew about the dust would think to abduct Ambrye at the silver shop. Which means we have reason to suspect Bloodflies involvement now." Chavali climbed into the carriage and asked the driver to take them to their inn.

"Ma'am," the driver whispered, "I wouldn't say things like that too loud."

"The name of the inn?"

"No, ma'am. The Bloodflies."

"Thank you." Colby shut the door and settled into the carriage with Chavali. "A driver for the Watch is afraid of the Bloodflies. If we needed more confirmation they're scary, we've got it."

Chavali nodded. "Even if they aren't responsible for Ambrye's abduction, they are a group worth looking into. With how they've accelerated their campaign of fear, it may well destabilize the city enough to affect the country as a whole."

"This mission just became a lot more dangerous. With what we saw in there, we need to take a sideways approach to them."

"Sideways," Chavali repeated as she watched the streets pass by. They had Portia and Sivry out on the streets already, so they might have more options this evening. Right now, though, they had nothing further to pursue. "Except one thing," she murmured. "Instead of sideways, perhaps we need to go backward. I think we can be certain the Broken Ring attacked the caravan in the first place, which means Harris's killer is among them."

"We've ignored that because it's not urgent. It has nothing to do with the princess."

"But now we know that's not true. Given the ring was separated from the statue, and the two matters are connected, the Broken Ring may know more than we give them credit for." She reached up and slid open the window to address the driver. "Change of plans. Take us to a tavern called The Ringer."

Chapter 33

Chavali expected The Ringer to be a low-class dump. The place surprised her with its fresh paint, cleanliness, and mouthwatering aroma. Her stomach rumbled, wanting roasted chicken and whatever else made that savory smell.

"We should have lunch," Colby said. "While we're here anyway."

"Yes," a woman said with a cheerful smile, "you absolutely should." She wore a crisp, clean dress and a small pocket apron, marking her as an employee.

Chavali smirked. "Whatever is making that smell, please, for two. And tell Rylen the woman with the feather is here to see him."

The waitress's smile deepened as she seated them at a table in the back, then left with a promise of swiftness.

Chavali marveled at the idea of a gang operating out of such a pleasant establishment. Either they trafficked in high-priced goods or they had some kind of in with the owner. Or both—the owner could be the leader, and perhaps had elected to engage in smuggling and theft to satisfy the exotic and eccentric desires of her wealthy clientele.

Checking over the other patrons, Chavali wondered how this place operated in plain sight without attracting Watch attention. Anyone who'd heard of the Broken Ring would suspect a tavern called "The Ringer." More importantly, its location placed it near the west Watch building.

Two uniformed officers of the Watch stepped inside and scanned the patrons. They approached the polished bar and spoke to the attractive young bartender. He answered a few short questions Chavali couldn't overhear, then poured both men drinks. When he set paper napkins on the bar for each glass, he used a curious flick of his wrist.

The officers accepted their drinks by picking them up, napkin and all. While one fished in his pocket and tossed copper coins on the bar, the other clumsily palmed and pocketed a piece of paper or envelope from under the napkin. Both men downed their drinks and left. Behind their backs, the bartender smirked and rolled his eyes.

Their waitress returned with plates of food, keeping Chavali from saying anything to Colby. Bribery or information trading kept this establishment safe. The thought of it taking place under the inspectors' noses amused Chavali. They thought highly of their abilities, yet missed this. Or, she wondered, perhaps they allowed it to happen?

Her first bite of chicken and rice cut off all thoughts. At the Fallen tower, they had excellent cooks. This food surpassed their skills. How Rylen and Gina spent time here without gaining a great deal of weight had to be a miracle. Across the table from her, Colby sighed in delight.

"We have an excellent cook here," Rylen said. He slipped into the chair between Colby and Chavali, having come up from behind her. His clothes matched those of the bartender and waitress.

"I agree," Chavali said.

"I didn't expect to see you again so soon," Rylen said. "I also realized right after you walked away that I never got your name."

"Chastity. This is Colby." She chose not to explain his presence, allowing Rylen to form his own opinions. "How is Gina?"

Rylen sighed and looked away. "I was able to see her." His cheeks darkened. "You were right, about everything. Still working on how to get her free. I've got some ideas, it'll just take time to plan."

"Good. Is it safe to speak freely here?"

Rylen twisted in his seat to check the room. He nodded. "So long as you keep your voice down, yes. You're looking for a statue, right?"

Chavali paused, curious how this man could have learned that about her. "Yes."

He grinned. "Word is, there's an exotic woman with a feather in her head looking for a cat."

"I see." She stifled a sigh. With practice, she could force away her accent and become more proficient with Shappan, but she'd never be able to remove the feather or change her skin tone. Then again, she did invoke his name to gain an audience with Clara. The black marketeer may have let him know about the meeting. "What do you know of it?"

"Not much. The Watch got it as part of a seized shipment of art. Beyond that...no idea."

"Would Velsin know more?"

Rylen tapped his fingers on the table and bit his lip. "Probably."

"If Velsin has useful information," Colby said, "we can pay for it. We can afford this meal."

"The meal is on me." Rylen stood. "Enjoy it while I arrange a meeting with Velsin for you."

Chavali watched him hurry away and use the door to the back. She had a feeling Gina had caused that Watch raid, making all these events connected.

"How is it," Colby mused, "that every time you find a random stranger to help, they turn out to be exceptionally useful?"

"Luck." Chavali savored a bite of her meal while Colby chuckled at her.

"I think it's the..." He gestured vaguely in her direction. "You know. With the future-thing. Them pulling you toward people with a stake in a situation and away from those without one. The Creator works through them to put you on the right path."

"Perhaps." She didn't think the Creator had anything to do with it, but could imagine the spirits seeing something on their side of the veil and nudging her at it. "Are you suggesting I would be much less useful without them?"

He paused and spent a long time chewing the bite of food in his mouth. "No. But our lives would be a lot less exciting."

Chavali laughed and looked down at her plate to scoop up another forkful. She froze. Without noticing as it happened, she'd somehow arranged the food to spell out *he is coming*.

"What's the matter?" Colby reached for her hand.

She remembered to breathe and turned the plate for him to see. "They are insistent," she whispered, unable to raise her voice any louder. "What if Robin is here?" In the after-effects of the prophecy, she'd been fuzzy from the medicinal tea and able to see past her fear of him to other possibilities. Now, all other options seemed stupid and foolish. It had to be Robin.

"If he's coming, it means he's not here yet. Right?"

"What?" She stared at him, blank and ready to flee.

"Someone can't be both coming and arrived. They'd change the message if he was already here, wouldn't they? This makes it sound like we need to hurry, not run for home. It's a warning. Before the fact. Like all your prophecies." He finally set his hand on hers and filled his mind with steady calm and reassurance. Karias's rock-solid determination rode as an undertone.

"Oh." His thoughts punched through the panic threatening to strangle her. She considered his argument and nodded. "Yes. That makes sense. Get the statue, find the princess, and get out of the city."

"Right. That's a good plan." Colby squeezed her hand and let go. "I won't let him take you."

"This is a foolish promise to make." She mashed the message with her fork. "You cannot stop him." Her belly fluttered and the food inside it turned to lead. She set the fork down and pushed her plate away.

"He's not invincible or immortal."

"I don't wish to discuss this anymore."

"You can't just ignore anything uncomfortable and hope it'll go away."

She glared, knowing he didn't deserve her anger and throwing it at him anyway. "Do not tell me how to handle these things," she growled. "It was my life. My clan. He took these from me, not from you."

"I know that." Colby sighed and set his cloth napkin aside, then flicked his gaze over her shoulder and nodded behind her. "We'll talk—"

"No, we will not talk about this later," Chavali hissed. She dropped all her emotions, flinging them aside in favor of welcome for Rylen as he returned in a cloak that covered his uniform.

"Velsin will see you. Come with me."

Chapter 34

Rylen led them out the front door and around the block to the alley behind the building. Vegetables rotted someplace nearby, and they interrupted a pair of shambling rag piles in the act of sifting through the garbage. "I'd take you through the back door inside but you're both really..."

"Distinctive?" Chavali offered.

"Yes. Sorry about the scenery, but this is the best option for all of us." He used a key to unlock the back door and led them up a flight of stairs to the second floor. They stepped into a well-appointed apartment. An eclectic mix of framed paintings, sculptures, statues, vases, and carved furniture filled the large room. Sun shone through gauzy curtains over large windows, casting a gentle yellow glow over everything.

On the other side of a wood table with sweeping curves and delicate whorls, a woman sat scribbling on papers. With a name like Velsin, Chavali had expected a man. This woman had long hair in a thick braid and wore a blouse with a deep v-neck. The large gemstone pendant resting on her chest seemed designed to draw attention downward.

She looked up from her work and smiled, flashing her teeth in a brilliant, dazzling display of welcome. "Hello Chastity, Colby. Please sit. We have things to discuss. Thank you, Rylen." She pointed to two chairs with velvet cushions and the same curves as the table.

Chavali and Colby sat, him taking the chair closer to the door and with the easiest access around the table. Chavali returned Velsin's smile with a much dimmer, but still polite, one of her own. "Thank you for seeing us on short notice."

"I'm always happy to chat with people doing the dirty work for the Watch."

Colby showed his surprise. Chavali, on the other hand, expected this and put a hand on his knee to keep him from blurting anything out. They hadn't been trying very hard to keep themselves separate. Anyone regularly informing for or bribing the Watch had to know about their activities here.

"This is an intriguing position. What do you want in exchange for information?"

Velsin gave them a coy grin, showing a hint of the intelligence behind her beauty. Such a combination undoubtedly allowed her to accomplish a great deal. "In your case, nothing in particular. Consider it my way of thanking you for your assistance with Gina and in advance for your discretion."

Chavali stifled a reaction and squeezed Colby's leg to keep his mouth shut. If a woman capable of amassing this much power and wealth decided to give them something for nothing, it meant the payment she wanted would come in the form of acting on the information. Accordingly, such information needed to be treated with healthy suspicion.

"We have no intention of revealing your assistance to anyone."

"Excellent." Velsin clasped her hands on the table, lacing her fingers together. Her braid dangled in front of her cleavage, distracting Colby. "You're looking for a cat statue you believe I possessed until the Watch liberated it from me, correct?" When Chavali nodded, Velsin continued. "How about if you tell me why you're looking for it? There has to be a story behind anything that would send foreigners running to the Watch for help."

"Our employer wants the statue, and his identity is not relevant. Suffice to say his interest is high enough to risk much for its recovery." Chavali shrugged. She suspected someone in this group had murdered Harris and refused to tip her hand until necessary.

"Interesting. Well, let me be perfectly clear. I don't have it. My people didn't hit Evidence Storage. Rumors say the Bloodflies are responsible for that, but they haven't stepped up to brag, so it's hard to be sure. Everything I know with certainty happened before that moment. This whole thing started about two weeks ago.

"I have a longstanding contract with a rather high-placed personage, to provide him with the type of art he prefers. He has peculiar tastes, and the style he goes for isn't common around here. It's hard to get in North Cascain, which means it has to be imported. Taxes on imports of all kinds are ridiculously high, thanks to measures enacted by the queen in an effort to promote local over foreign. Goods from South Cascain are banned completely. Among other things, I provide an import service to avoid these taxes and restrictions.

"This high-placed person hired me to snatch your statue from a specific caravan, for which he had the routing information. To be clear, he doesn't usually bring me this kind of information. He describes what he's looking for and I find it. In this unusual case, he had everything laid out and all I had to do was send someone to do it.

"Which I did. They ransacked the whole caravan and came back with a lot more than I expected. I sent some of my people out to fence the extra goods and Gina..." Velsin made a face. "She fell into what I assume was a trap intended to help the high-placed person get me into a position where he could continue to use my services without paying for anything. Now that the Bloodflies are involved, I've got no stake in the matter, except that I paid people to get all those pieces for me, and now I don't have the pieces to sell and make back the costs."

Chavali listened to all this, trying not to feel anything about the story. Her blood pounded in her ears anyway. This woman had casually sent someone to murder Harris for business. She doubted Velsin knew the names of any of the dead. Velsin might not even be aware of the deaths.

"Was it your people who acquired the pieces from the caravan?" Chavali thought she did a good job of hiding the roiling anger in her belly.

"No. I don't have enough people to run off to Shappa for something like that. I paid a group of mercenaries to do it. Once they returned and handed over the goods, their involvement ended, so I doubt they have any additional information for you."

"We'd like to talk to them anyway," Colby said. His offhanded, casual manner surprised Chavali. He couldn't usually manage to hide his emotions so well. Knowing him well, she saw the tension in his back and heard the tightness in his voice, but a stranger wouldn't notice this. "To be thorough. You never know."

Velsin pursed her lips, then she picked up a pen and a fresh piece of paper. "It's not my habit to give out resources like this, but I want this taken care of at least as much as you do. All I ask is that the information didn't come from me or my people, and you don't hand this over to the Watch."

"Deal," Chavali said. "Are you going to tell us who your high-placed person is?"

Velsin scribbled on the paper. She set her pen down, folded it in half and handed it to Colby. "Prince Warren."

"The queen's son?" Colby asked, surprise again coloring his face. Chavali squeezed his leg harder.

"Yes." Velsin smirked. "Right under Inspector-Princess Ambrye's overly-nosy nose. He's a frequent customer here, and he's fostered rumors about an affair between him and one of my employees to keep suspicion about his real purpose here quiet. That employee happens to be Gina, who you already know. She was content to play the part. He pays well."

"Her arrest must have put him in an awkward position," Chavali said. "Do you think this could have pushed him toward the Bloodflies?"

"Warren?" Velsin shrugged. "No idea. I can't see him getting into bed with those vicious bastards, but if he thought they could make his problems go away..." She shrugged again. "My money says the Bloodflies have your statue. I don't know much about them, other than I don't want to mess with them. I stay away from them and they stay away from me. Those mercenaries might know more about them."

Chapter 35

"I'm glad this carriage and our driver are unmarked," Colby said as they once again settled inside it, headed to their inn.

"Yes," Chavali said. "We should collect Portia and Sivry to deal with those mercenaries."

Colby frowned as he read Velsin's note. "When you say 'deal with'...?"

She glared, daring him to press for further clarification. "Where are they?"

"She gave us an address." He sighed and looked away. "I want justice for Harris as much as you do. That doesn't have to mean killing them. Maybe we should go speak to the prince first. To have time to settle down. Get used to the idea of confronting them."

Chavali's mouth twisted into a scowl of distaste. Colby held the address and had no reason to hand it over, especially if he believed she intended to murder whoever she found there without regard for their individual guilt. Despite her pact with Portia, this situation required Colby's assistance, not his distraction. "Is there any other reason to wait?"

He folded the paper and tucked it into his pocket. "Yes. I don't want to go see the royal family directly after performing an unsanctioned raid in their city. No matter how it turns out—and I'd like to see us take them prisoner—that could be a problem with Denton. Ideally, we should involve her and the Watch."

"Harris was one of ours. The problem is also ours, as is the solution."

"Chavali—"

"No." She held up her hand again. A small, distracted part of her enjoyed the fact this simple gesture kept him quiet. "We are not the Watch. We are not guards, police, or diplomats. Our job includes protecting our own. When that protection fails, we handle it. There is no court to present evidence we do not have for a body that will not be produced. Harris was one of ours and if you will not help deal justice to these mercenaries, at least do not hinder the rest of us in seeking it."

Colby stared out the window. "When we first met, you'd never killed anyone."

"This is not true." Technically, Colby was right. Chavali, though, felt like arguing about it. She could see the line of reasoning he intended to lay at her feet. "I never killed anyone in this condition you call 'cold blood' until Ket. Before I lost my clan, I caused deaths and saw death face-to-face. If you wish to believe my time with the Fallen has somehow corrupted me beyond what I was before, you're lying to yourself. Who I am now, on the inside, is nothing different from who I was then."

"If you don't think you've changed, I don't think you've been paying attention."

The carriage stopped, saving Chavali from having to answer that.

She stepped out to see Portia and Sivry walking up the street toward the inn. Waving got their attention, and she gestured behind herself with a scowl. As if she'd passed some code along, Sivry hurried to open the door to the inn for Chavali and Portia dawdled to distract Colby.

"What's going on?" Sivry whispered as they crossed the common room together.

"Colby has the address for Harris's killers and will not divulge it."

"Where?"

Chavali blinked and realized she knew little about Sivry's talents. "Front pants pocket, right side. Folded paper."

"I'll get it. You go do something else for a bit." Sivry patted her shoulder and left her side.

Blindsided but unwilling to be the problem in the situation, Chavali kept walking. Her feet took her to the stable where Karias lounged in his stall. He whickered at her, inviting her close. She didn't want to talk to him right now, but retreating meant either returning to the common room or walking around on her own. The former would only cause problems and the latter struck her as stupid in a city where she stood out as different and criminals knew she worked with the Watch.

She unlatched the door and rubbed his nose. "Your rider is incredibly annoying."

Karias whinnied at her, his thoughts colored by laughter. *So are you.*

"Thank you." She rolled her eyes and made sure he saw it.

This is the most boring mission I've ever been part of. Please tell me what's going on.

"The mission is too complicated to be summarized."

Then you're missing something. Explain it to me. It'll help you figure things out.

"Perhaps." She picked up a currycomb and brushed him with one hand while touching him with the other. "Art thieves, a gang called the Broken Ring, hired mercenaries to attack the caravan because one of their patrons, who happens to be the prince of the realm, wanted our statue. The mercenaries killed Harris and returned the art pieces. One of the Broken Ring people made a mistake, causing the statue to be collected among other pieces by the Watch in a raid. The prisoners scooped up in the raid were..." Chavali frowned. "Members of the Broken Ring rescued by members of the Bloodflies, the brutal, scary gang no one else will work with. How odd. I did not notice this incongruity before."

Why would one gang take that big a risk to rescue members of another gang? I'm sure there are easier ways to recruit.

"Yes, this is curious."

Keep going. Maybe there's something else you've missed.

"We have three primary suspects for Ambrye's abduction, and all three are irritatingly competent fellow inspectors. Each has been clear they wish to blame the other two. They all seem to hate each other, except Nasha likes Ambrye. Those two, at least, seem to be friendly, though who knows how Ambrye feels about it. Reynolds is a smug ass, Kalei is an arrogant lush who may have connections to the Creator's Path, and Nasha is pleasant except for her Grippan lineage and disturbing ability to speak with the dead."

You'll have to pardon me if I don't find Grippan lineage particularly damning.

"Of course not. Her hometown happens to be the same as

232

Colby's mother, which is an oddly specific coincidence that makes me suspicious of her. Her ability is likewise an oddly specific coincidence that makes me suspicious of her."

How so?

"She forces spirits of the dead to speak through their corpses of events surrounding their deaths."

That is rather strangely resonant with you. But it's not damning either. The world is a small place. Being from that town isn't really a reason to believe her guilty of this particular crime. Neither is your fear of her somehow turning her ability to controlling you or your connection to your spirits. Is she really a suspect?

Chavali took a deep breath and forced herself to analyze the situation. "I can feel it when she uses her ability, so I know she's not simply creating an illusion to make the corpses say what she wishes. And she does not translate them. They speak openly. Anyone can hear it. She did lie to me about her relationship with Ambrye, but I don't know the truth. She cares about Ambrye, this much is certain."

You should talk to her. It sounds like you think she's innocent despite your preferences. Don't forget that someone else could be responsible for her crossing paths with you and Colby. It's not as if you don't have a major enemy. Robin has shown he can manipulate events and people on a sizable scale when he wants to, and we have no idea how long he's been working at it. Neither do we know what resources he has access to.

"Why must you say such thing." Chavali shivered. "The spirits have now warned me several times that he is coming. We need to figure this out quickly and go. He cannot be allowed access to me again."

I suggest asking her point blank about her relationship with Ambrye and prodding until she gives in.

"Perhaps. Before we do that, we know where to find Harris's killers. Colby is resistant to confronting them. He knows I will kill them if given the chance. Portia and Sivry also will. He would rather we did not, but I cannot imagine what kind of justice he thinks they will otherwise be subject to. We cannot take them back to the tower. There is nowhere to try them for this crime. Evidence is not the type we can present to any judge. I doubt he would accept even an edict from the King of Shappa to execute them."

Karias leaned into her brushing without answering for a long few minutes. *He struggles with the concept of execution. He has no real problem with killing in battle, but the cold kill, where no one is fighting for their life... It's difficult for him to reconcile that with justice. Death is so final and mistakes are so easily made. You know he's seen people executed for crimes they didn't commit. He wants to be sure they're truly guilty, and even then, he wants proof they're incapable of reform. It's a high standard, one that's difficult to fulfill.*

"Were I a normal telepath, I could show him."

I wish to be clear that I share his high standard—I'm not comfortable with executions either. That said, I understand how high that standard truly is and I'm aware of how pragmatic you are. You can still show him. You just have to do it differently than connecting him to their thoughts. He's not stupid or foolish, he only acts like it sometimes.

Her anger had receded, and thinking on it, Chavali realized it came from fear. Brushing the horse, thinking, and listening to his cool rationality had calmed her. She set the currycomb aside. "Thank you for this time. It was helpful. I don't understand why Eldrack sent Colby on this mission with us, but I'm glad for your presence."

Thank you for brightening my day. The stablehands are nice, but not much for conversation. Let me know how things work out whenever you can.

Chapter 36

"I want to be perfectly clear I'm coming along because it's my duty as Fallen to keep you three from getting killed." Colby stalked at the rear of the group, his mouth a thin line and his shoulders set in a sullen, angry hunch.

Sivry had the note now, purloined while Portia distracted him in the common room. Chavali walked with both women, the three of them moving with purposeful strides.

"I think the most important thing we learned," said Portia, "is where the Bloodflies congregate. It wasn't hard. Once we hit their controlled area, everyone was clear about not going there, not doing anything to anger them, and not walking around by yourself. We figure it's roughly fifteen blocks of the city that the Watch doesn't have a presence in."

"They're mostly interested in protection schemes," Sivry said. "The group seems to be positioning itself as better than the Watch because they keep crime from happening. Unlike the Watch, which responds after the crime has happened. Anyone who doesn't pay up or who talks to the Watch is either warned or killed. This address is fortunately not in their zone."

"Let's see. Other things we learned," Portia said. "They ramped up a year ago. Some new guy came in and took over the original gang. The most often repeated rumor about him is he's ex-military from Shappa, an assassin who uses magic. Whatever he really is, he's brutal and beat the Bloodflies into shape. His leadership, combined with pressure from the other new-guy-in-the-city gang, the Drowned Ones, has swelled their ranks. They've gobbled up other small gangs and are now a true force to be reckoned with."

"No wonder these people fear foreigners so much." Chavali noticed that, as the sun crept closer to setting, the number of people on the streets dwindled. Soon, they'd be the only ones bold—or stupid— enough to walk around in the open. She hadn't noticed the phenomenon before and wondered if it had become more pronounced in the days following Ambrye's abduction.

"That's it." Sivry pointed up the street at a narrow two-story house nestled among other two-story houses. Each brick facade hugged the street with no yard or garden in front. The houses all shared their side walls, creating an endless line of perfectly spaced windows glinting in the last rays of evening sunlight.

Portia sighed. "Most blocks like this have no easy access to the tiny backyards. Unless one of you has hidden cat burglar skills, we'll probably be best off walking up to the front door."

"These men murdered Harris," Chavali said. "And, let us not forget, everyone else involved in that caravan. They deserve a swift, brutal assault starting with a clever misdirection. Be ready to rush whoever answers the door." She strode to the house Sivry pointed to, the others following in her wake. Sivry perched to the left, Portia to the right. Colby obliged by crossing his arms, glaring at the ground, and leaning against the next house up the street where he wouldn't be seen.

Chavali arranged the neckline of her dress and pushed her chest out, then she knocked on the door. She waited half a minute and knocked again. From inside, a muffled voice said something she interpreted to mean the occupant would open the door soon. She arranged her face into a bright, pleasant smile and clasped her hands in front of her.

The door opened to reveal a bulky, muscled man with a thick beard, shaved head, and scars on his face and burly arms. Sweat soaked his loose clothes and glistened on his skin. He raised his brow and let his gaze fall to her chest.

"Is today my birthday?" He grinned.

She made a guess about the type of man she now faced and smiled brighter, projecting vacuous simplicity. "Hi," she said with an embarrassed giggle. "I'm lost. Can you help me?"

Dark greed lit his eyes. "I sure can, honey. Are you thirsty? Would you like to come inside and get something to drink?"

"Oh, that's so sweet of you!" She offered her hand to him and took his help to step up into the doorway. His thoughts disgusted her. Unwilling to put up with what would soon be violent advances, she tossed his hand aside and drew the dagger at the small of her back.

"What the—" Before he recovered from her abrupt change, Sivry shoved the door open and rammed her sword through his body.

"Attack!" The man managed to shout before Sivry ripped her blade out.

"Ugh," Chavali grunted. "He deserves to die for the things he just thought about me, let alone anything else."

Portia pushed through and hustled her into the living room. Like the outside, this front room matched expectations for the neighborhood with a couch, chairs, and tables of middling quality. Colby stepped in, kicked the dying man out of the way, and slammed the door shut. Thumping on the stairs announced new people joining the fight.

"That was your plan?" Colby spat. "Put yourself in harm's way and rely on us to kill for you?"

Chavali rolled her eyes, giving her a good view of five crossbows pointing at them from the stairs. She grabbed his arm and yanked him behind the couch. Crossbow bolts crashed into the front window, showering them with shards of shattered glass. Portia screamed. Fire exploded in the stairwell. Men cried out. Chavali popped her head up. Colby jerked her down again before she saw anything.

"Stay here," he growled. He rushed out from behind the couch.

Scowling, Chavali followed behind him. She may have chosen to stay behind in several situations, and she may have been a helpless entertainer when they first met, but that didn't make her useless or a coward.

Flames licked at the wall and ceiling around the charred stairs. Colby hesitated at the bottom and Chavali saw his terror of fire surface in the rigid tension of his back and shoulders. Fire had killed him. She plowed into him, forcing him to stumble forward. He recovered and surged up.

Dagger in hand, Chavali stayed on his heels. Though she suspected Portia had been hit by a crossbow bolt, they needed to deal with these men first. She followed Colby as he dashed from one room to the next, searching for their prey. Boots clomping above them made her tug on his shirt and point upward.

"I told you to stay back," Colby growled as he ran for the second flight of stairs and took them up three at a time.

"Shut up," she snapped, keeping pace with him. Part of her training routine included running up and down the stairs inside the Fallen tower. No stupid three-story house would defeat her.

At the top of the stairs, Colby lunged at the last woman of a clump fleeing for the back room. His sword hacked a wide gash across the mercenary's back and leg. The woman screamed and fell. Colby pressed forward and managed to trip another woman. The mercenary rolled and snagged a fistful of Colby's pants, forcing him to engage. Chavali hurried past.

Inside the last room at the end of the hall, four men clustered around a ladder descending from the ceiling. Chavali charged the group, throwing her body at them. One stepped into her path and wrapped an arm around her waist. He tossed her to the side. She thumped into the wall and turned to see him brandishing his sword at her while the first man swarmed up the ladder and threw a trapdoor open to daylight.

Chavali's world narrowed to the man holding the sword against her. She watched every movement of his eyes, his feet, his wrist, and his mouth. He lunged. She hopped to the left, slashing with her dagger to knock his sword aside.

He chuckled, low and throaty. His foot shifted. Chavali leaned away from his next strike and let her muscles do what Eliot had trained them to do. She shoved his sword arm aside, stepped into his personal space, slammed her knee into his privates, and slashed her dagger across his shoulders. The mercenary howled and found the floor with his face.

She whirled and saw the last of the remaining three men scurry up the ladder. Ignoring Colby, who could take care of himself, Chavali grabbed the ladder and ran up, alert for a trap at the top. When she reached the roof, she popped her head up cautiously and saw all three men fighting against Sivry. They battled near the edge, pressing Sivry toward it.

Without thinking, Chavali hauled herself up and darted in to help. Sivry saw her and pivoted. The three men noticed her too late to prevent Chavali from plowing into one. Her momentum carried her and the mercenary over the edge. Together, they hit the fire escape catwalk. The mercenary took the brunt of it, Chavali landing on top of him.

He bucked to knock her through the open railing. She snared a fistful of his pants and wound up dangling by that grip. If she dropped her dagger, she had no weapon. If she kept it, he only needed to regain enough wits to cut her hand or his pants off. Chavali dropped the dagger and grasped the catwalk.

His face twisted in a mask of hate, the mercenary stabbed at her hand. She let go. Swinging to the side, she glared up at her opponent. He smirked and stomped on her fingers. Though she wanted to let go and make that pain stop, Chavali gritted her teeth and reached up. She grasped his ankle and pulled with all her might. Her effort surprised him and he fell over, cracking his skull on the wall behind. The blow dazed him long enough for her to hook a foot over the side and scramble back onto the catwalk.

Chavali pounced, snaring his sword arm and slamming it against the metal beneath them. He howled and dropped his sword. She kicked it over the side while he wrapped a hand in her hair and pulled. She squealed. He rolled and smashed her face into the metal. Reaching up, she caught her hand on his chin and pushed.

His thoughts told her how much he wished he could take his time killing her. She caught him thinking about the knife sheathed in his boot a moment before he wrenched her head to the side to reach for it. She kicked his hand, knocking it away from his foot. The catwalk trembled with another impact, then the mercenary's thoughts went blank with shock and he released her hair.

Chapter 37

Chavali gasped and rubbed her scalp. She turned to see Colby kicking the mercenary off his sword. The body flopped off the edge to land with a thump in the house's backyard.

"Are you all right?" Colby dropped to one knee beside her and wiped his thumb across her cheek. *You could've been killed.*

She flinched away from his touch, more because it hurt than to avoid his thoughts. Blood smeared his fingers. "I am not seriously injured. Portia?"

Colby's eyes widened and he jumped to his feet, then threw the window open. He climbed through and vaulted over the dead bodies he'd left in the hall to reach the stairs, shouting Portia's name.

"Chastity, come up to the roof," Sivry called.

Chavali took a deep breath and climbed through the window. She shambled to the ladder and found the man she'd fought, still groaning and trying to inch his way to freedom. Feeling less than charitable toward these men, she stepped on his back, driving his face to the floor again. She snatched up his sword and held it to his neck while she covered his cheek and ear with her other hand.

"Are you the leader of these men?"

"No," he groaned. His body shook.

She plucked an image of the leader from his thoughts. "You attacked a caravan in Shappa, yes? You were hired to do this." His thoughts confirmed this hadn't been a mistaken attack. "I am interested in the fate of a particular man traveling with that caravan. He has dark hair, longer than yours, a pretty face, and not enough sense."

His thoughts flickered over his memories of the caravan attack. They'd used an ambush against the second wagon. The first wagon had continued, isolating itself, and the rest of the caravan stopped without knowing what happened. He flashed over the rest of the battle. Most of his time had been spent using his bow to take down the men who fought back. Though he shot two men who met Harris's basic description, neither were him.

Toward the end of the assault, this man noticed the leader breaking away from the battle to investigate a stand of trees on his own. When they regrouped later, after the remaining women had been defiled and killed, he carried a bag the right size to contain the cat statue's box.

Chavali let go. This man had murdered many people, and probably more than she ever wanted to know about, but not Harris. She stood and prodded the wound she'd caused, surprised by its depth. He'd die soon without help. Listening to him whimper made bile rise in her throat.

All these mercenaries deserved pain and suffering. They deserved horrifying deaths. She had no time to give them what they deserved. With a growl, she slammed the tip of his own sword into his back. He groaned, shuddered, and died. She yanked the sword out of his body and climbed the ladder. At the top, she again found Sivry facing mercenaries. This time, Sivry held her sword on two men sitting on their knees, hands clasped behind their heads and backs to Chavali.

She took a deep breath and strode across the roof, hope and dread warring inside her. When she reached the trio, she took the last step so she could see both men and recognized the leader as the one with blood oozing from his nose. The other man had a minor cut on the side of his face. Sivry held her side, but Chavali saw no sign of bleeding.

"This is a curious situation." Chavali felt her energy leaving her. Her limbs wanted her to sit and relax. She summoned her anger, letting it loose to bolster her through this.

"Who are you," the leader grunted, "and what do you want?"

"What do I want?" She saw Colby clamber onto the roof, his hands, face, and clothes smeared with dark stains. "I want to trade you for my friend," she told the leader, loud enough to be sure Colby heard it as he jogged to them. "You murdered him to take what he carried. Killing you will not bring him back, I know this. I would hear you tell us why you attacked that caravan in Shappa, though. To hear you say the words out loud."

"The house is burning down," Colby said. "Portia's trying to stop the fire. We need to get out of here."

Chavali cursed the timing. She wanted to linger over the subject, to explore it and terrorize these men. "I want this one. He killed Harris."

"We don't have time for this." Colby clamped his hand around the subordinate's neck from behind. "We're going to give the Watch a description of you and tell them all kinds of things. If you keep your head down and find honest work, you'll be fine." He tossed the man to the side, sending him to the neighboring roof.

"What are you doing?" Chavali growled. She slid her arm around the leader's neck, making sure to touch his cheek with her hand. "These men have murdered many. They cannot be trusted. Tell me about the man you stalked into the woods for the statue."

This is about that guy? The incident replayed in his mind with gruesome detail. He did terrible things to Harris for the crime of not having the statue on him and lying about where he'd stashed it. Chavali's eyes burned as she watched Harris endure horrific torture before he died. Never once did Harris betray Eldrack and his trust, which ought to mean a great deal to any healer that required convincing of his worth.

The memory segued into thoughts of escape. Seeing how he planned to do it, Chavali threw him to the ground, planted her foot on his back, and rested the tip of the sword on the nape of his neck. "If you think I will not kill you, you are mistaken," she spat.

"Let him go," Colby said. "He's lost his team, he's losing his house, he's losing everything. That's punishment enough." He wrapped his arm around her waist and lifted her off the ground.

Powerless to resist Colby's strength and conviction, Chavali didn't bother struggling. "I saw his memory." She glared at Colby while the leader scrambled to his feet. "He interrogated Harris to determine where to find the statue. It included tearing his gut open while he still lived and showing him his own intestines. And that was not the worst of it. Through it all, that disgusting creature *enjoyed himself.*"

Colby went still. He set Chavali down and gripped her shoulder, his gaze boring into her. "Are you lying to me?"

She let him see the pain she felt from watching such a terrible act through the eyes of a man who'd taken pleasure in such a sadistic task. "No. I would not about such a thing."

He turned. The leader had managed to get several feet away already and ran with every ounce of strength he could muster. Colby gripped his sword until his knuckles went white and chased after the man. His sword reached far enough to cut the leader's leg open, causing him to tumble forward.

Chavali chased after them, needing to see this man's justice served. When Colby planted a foot on the leader's back and held his sword ready to plunge into the man, she froze and held her breath.

"There are some things," Colby said, "that cannot be forgiven. Not by anyone, for any reason. I hold close my duty to be merciful, but you deserve no such thing."

"Wait." Chavali touched his arm. "If you would rather, I will do this. I will not see you laid low by such a monster."

Colby looked at her and smiled. "I appreciate that. But this is my job. Not the one I do for Eldrack. The other one."

Chavali nodded and crouched beside the leader. She touched his face. Pain, frustration, and fear chased each other in his mind. She had a thought to ask him a question with no relation to any of this, just to be thorough. "Are you affiliated with the Bloodflies in any way?"

What? "No." *Those bastards edged us out of our territory.* He pictured their original home base and fervently wished he could go back to that time and place.

She pulled her hand away and nodded. Colby plunged his sword into the man's back. The leader gasped and gurgled. His hands shook, like Harris's had. His eyes widened with the realization he would die, like Harris's had. Colby stabbed him again, this time in the lower back, and stood aside to watch him die.

"That man was my friend," Chavali murmured to the dying man. "He was my family." She whispered a potent curse in the clan tongue, for his soul to be chained in one place for all time and tormented by the free spirits of the dead. As the final words left her lips, his final breath rattled out.

Chapter 38

Colby dragged the body to the burning house and tossed it onto the roof. He helped Chavali climb down the next house over and they met Portia and Sivry at the corner. Portia and Sivry both had minor injuries that needed either bed rest or a healer, leading Chavali to hail a carriage for a ride to the inn.

She swallowed her grief and told Portia and Sivry what she'd discovered, keeping the details of Harris's grisly death to herself. Whenever she next found time to speak with Karias, she'd tell him to help excise the poison from that wound. Eldrack also needed to hear everything, though he likely knew the extent of the damage already. If the healers had to put him back together, they also knew.

"I wish to speak with the prince before retiring tonight."

"How can you think about that now?" Portia held her arm, which had been grazed by a crossbow bolt. Flying glass had cut her face and neck in several places.

"The one thing I want more than anything else right now is to leave this vile city. I will not leave again without the statue. Until it is late enough to assume Nasha has gone out, I wish to be busy."

"I'll go with her. You two get some rest."

The carriage stopped at the inn and Portia and Sivry climbed out. Chavali watched out the window while the carriage trundled up the street, headed for the royal palace. She rubbed her eyes, trying to force the images away. Harris's last words rattled her at least as much as his eyes.

"We should talk to the queen first," Colby said into the silence. "She seemed to trust us and I think she'll help. If Warren is actually doing what Velsin says, he'll try to wriggle out of an interview. With the queen pressuring him, he'll have to either talk to us or flee. Running would reveal a lot." He paused. "Are you sure you're up for this? We could take some time, get you some tea. There's no reason we have to go now instead of an hour from now."

"I'm fine."

"I didn't ask if you were fine. I know you're fine. You're always fine. I asked if you can do your job. I can't do the things you can do, Chavali. I can't pick up this slack for you. Being there isn't good enough. You have to be able to handle it."

Chavali stared out the window, wishing he didn't have a point. Crawling into a bed and hiding sounded preferable to confronting a prince about his illegal art habit. Him sneaking around and buying illicit goods mattered so little in the grand scheme of things that she wanted to laugh in his face. His culpability in Harris's death had no bearing on anything because the killer no longer lived.

She took a deep breath and tried to summon a reason to care. Harris's pain taunted her and she wanted to know why he'd suffered through that. "Wait." She frowned, one question rising above everything else. "Velsin said the prince had the information already. He specifically wanted the statue and already knew where to intercept it. That statue was locked in a box for a very long time. I watched Eldrack open that box with the Seal of Shappa, an object only that monarch—and, apparently, Eldrack—have access to. No one outside the Fallen knew about it. It was never outside Eldrack's office except in its box. Yet Warren knew he wanted a cat statue. *How did he know?* We must find the answer to this question."

"Yes." Colby lifted his hand, the gesture purporting to offer her some measure of comfort.

She waved him off. His version of "comfort" would be a sunshine-laden speech about justice and virtue, or warm, fuzzy feelings of righteous glory. Sometimes, she found that helpful. Not now. "I do not require coddling."

He sighed and turned away from her. "You're so difficult."

"Yes." She climbed out first when the carriage stopped, smoothing away a grim smile. Guards in royal livery conducted them inside the grand, carved double doors and through the wide, airy marble and metal entry to a well-appointed sitting room. Everything bore the heron device of the family. The place reminded Chavali of a grander, more ornate version of the Lady of Ket's manor house.

She sat on a velvet couch, finding it soft and comfortable. Colby stood behind her at attention. They waited in tense silence. She didn't want to talk to him and he didn't trust her to do her job. The queen would pick up on that and use it against them if she could. The prince would too. Chavali tempered her breathing, pushing everything aside to focus on the critical matter at hand. The royals would still pick up on the tension, but they wouldn't be able to read her and figure it out.

When the queen entered the room, attended by two servants and four guards, she wore richer clothing than their first meeting. Jewels glittered from her neck and head, rings winked on her fingers, and metals woven into the fabric of her formal gown shimmered. Despite the finery, Chavali saw the circles under her eyes and grief keeping her face and shoulders taut.

"Your majesty," Chavali said without standing, "I apologize for interrupting. We have questions for Prince Warren, but felt it prudent to approach you first."

The queen turned to her attendants and waved them away. "I'm in no danger here." She stepped into the room and seated herself in the chair opposite Chavali. One guard remained in the room, standing at attention beside the closed door. The queen sighed heavily and leaned her head on her hand, projecting weariness and vague irritation. "What's he done?"

Chavali heard an unspoken "this time" at the end of the queen's question and knew this conversation would go better than anticipated. "A person who specializes in importing goods outside of official channels has claimed him as a client."

"That's a very diplomatic way to tell me he's been getting his latest art pieces from smugglers."

"I have no wish to offend."

"He swore he'd stopped." The queen sighed again and covered her eyes in shame. "I caught him in a lie about a beautiful piece a few months ago. Tried to convince me the artist was local. I can't understand this obsession he has. I'd be much less annoyed if he gambled his money away. And the part where he's faking an affair is straining diplomatic relations with Grippa. He's been promised to a nobleman's daughter there. I just don't see why he can't wait to indulge himself in six months."

The absurdity of Prince Warren made Chavali forget everything else for a moment. She worked hard to stifle a snort. "The statue we came in search of is the matter at hand. We do not believe he had any direct involvement with your daughter's abduction, but he may have periphery information that can lead us to her."

"Bring him," the queen said with an imperial wave of her hand.

The guard at the door opened it and leaned out, passing along the order.

"Tell me how much damage he caused by demanding that statue."

Chavali pursed her lips. "Many have died. Beyond this, I cannot yet tell you."

"Do you have names? Are there families that need to be compensated?"

Again, Chavali paused. "I know only one, and you are already compensating us. We will have the rest sent to you to handle in whatever fashion you feel is appropriate."

The queen's gaze flicked from Chavali to Colby as back. "That's the reason you came. Because the person carrying your statue was killed, and you were close. Was he your husband? Brother?"

Once, Chavali had pretended to be Harris's wife. She had no need for such a fiction here. "No. A close friend. Someone we all four cared about. Those directly responsible for his death, a band of bloodthirsty mercenaries, have been dealt with. We...would appreciate some kind of pardon for the accidental damage caused in pursuit of that justice. A house burned down."

"It's not my habit to excuse people for wanton murder."

"Majesty," Colby said, "I understand you're an adherent of the Order of Spilled Blood." At least his tendency to over-research local nobility and royalty had some use. "I'd like to be clear that these men were primarily killed in self-defense. The fire was started accidentally, and it's the reason the rest died. We may not have tried very hard to save them, but knowing what atrocities they were responsible for, we can hardly be blamed for that."

After spending a long few moments in deep thought, the queen waved to her guard. "Inform Captain-General Crayton his foreign consultants are not to be prosecuted for any crimes surrounding a house fire this afternoon. It need not be investigated."

The guard leaned out to relay the message and opened the door to let Prince Warren in. Like his mother, the prince wore finery. He carried a fine cloth napkin he used to wipe his fingers, leading Chavali to believe they'd pulled the queen out of a formal dinner. Warren noticed Chavali and Colby and his face lit up with expectation.

"What is it? Have you found Ambrye?"

"No." The queen pointed to the chair beside her. "Sit. Answer their questions. You will stay after they leave."

Warren blanched and gulped. "Am I a suspect?"

Chavali smiled at him. "No. Please, sit." When he'd lowered himself into the chair, wringing his hands, she focused on the singular piece of information they needed. "We need to know who told you about the cat statue you hired Velsin to retrieve for you."

He blinked at Chavali, then furrowed his brow. "Cat statue? The one you demanded as payment for finding Ambrye?"

"Yes. How did you know about it, and how did you know where to find it?"

"Where to find it?" He looked to his mother, who gestured with exasperation for him to answer the question. "I don't understand. I didn't find it. The statue is still missing, isn't it? And I know about it because you asked for it in payment." He held up his hands. "Wait. I haven't hired Velsin in over a month, I swear, and that was for a painting, not a statue."

He seemed so honest in his denial. Chavali scooted forward and reached across the table to grip his hand. The guard tensed, but the queen waved him off.

"Tell me everything you know about the statue," Chavali said.

Warren gulped again and his mind failed to form a picture. He thought about seeing Chavali the first time, through a one-way mirror, and hearing her basic description of the box and statue. He racked his brain for any further information and pictured Velsin. In the context, Chavali knew he didn't remember hiring her for a statue within the past year. The last time he did, it was to find someone to make a partner for a small dragon.

"I...uh..." He stammered and tugged his hand, confused by the contact.

"He knows nothing." Chavali let go and stood. Velsin hadn't lied. Warren wasn't lying either. "Thank you for your time." She hurried out of the room. Colby made apologies for them behind her.

Chavali didn't stop until she reached the outside air. The setting sun cast long shadows, much like the questions she couldn't answer. She leaned against a scalloped column in front of the doors to wait for Colby.

They'd missed something important. Velsin said Warren hired her to find that statue, yet Warren hadn't done any such thing. Velsin could have lied to her, she had to admit, but it made no sense for her to do so. If she needed more time to destroy documents or get someone into hiding, that made Velsin an idiot. She struck Chavali as an intelligent person with a good head for her business. Revealing her client to them cost her nothing.

Before she could chase the thought further, Colby gripped her shoulder. "You need a break. I could use one too. We should go back to the inn and get something to eat. Lunch was a battle ago and neither of us finished it."

"I want to talk to Nasha again."

Soft footsteps on the path to the left made Chavali quiet and turn to see who approached. Princess Bricene, dressed as elegant as her brother in a dark gown, jumped when she saw them. "Oh, goodness. I was just stealing some fresh air and didn't see you there." She patted her chest with gloved hands.

"Our apologies for startling you, Highness," Colby said as he stepped into view with a bow.

"Oh, no, it's my fault." She beamed at him. "Head in the clouds. Mother ran off and dinner dissolved into slurping. Half the room emptied." Her eyes twinkled with mischief. "I hope I didn't interrupt a romantic liaison?"

"No." Chavali wished she had her pouch of baubles to fidget with. People found it interesting and distracting, and she found it soothing. She considered walking away, then realized they'd barely spoken with Bricene. The girl probably knew things the rest of her family didn't. "Would you mind answering a few questions for us?"

"Oh." Bricene smiled, her face a perfect picture of helpful cooperation. "Certainly. Anything to help find my big sister."

Several questions came to mind. Chavali chose to start with affirming something simple and move on from there. "How long has your mother's, ah, *gentleman* been away?"

"Oh, goodness." Bricene tittered nervously. "Heard about him, did you? She tries so hard to keep him a secret. I think he's been gone for at least a month now. He's supposed to be back for the birthday celebration."

"Do you know the other three inspectors familiar with Ambrye? Reynolds, Nasha, and Kalei."

Bricene shook her head and seemed relieved to move away from the topic of the queen's lover. "Not really. They don't come here much, and I don't have business with them or the Watch. Warren knows Reynolds, I think. Not terribly well, but I see them chatting at parties sometimes. I've seen Nasha and Ambrye with their heads together. Sometimes, I get the feeling Nasha manufactures reasons to stop by, but I don't really know. She's so foreign and strange. I overheard her tell Ambrye she had a special place all picked out, but I don't know what for."

"Ah." Chavali let the last comment settle in her mind. If she'd picked out the location she intended to hold Ambrye, why tell the princess such a thing? "When she said this, did she seem..." She wished for an excuse to touch Bricene's skin. With guards nearby, reaching for the girl's neck or face would be taken poorly.

"Weird and creepy about it? Yes, a little." Bricene covered her mouth in distress. "Oh, goodness, you don't think she was—" Bricene moved her hand to her chest and shifted to a whisper. "That was the day before she disappeared."

Colby bowed to her. "Thank you, Highness. We shouldn't keep you any longer."

Though Chavali didn't feel the interview should be over, she had no interest in Bricene. The girl clearly wanted to be involved somehow and had no compunctions about using melodrama to insert herself. She let Colby chivvy her to their waiting carriage, wondering if the girl's initial resistance to their deal with the queen had more to do with a desire to figure things out as a junior sleuth outside her sister's shadow than concern about charlatans.

Chapter 39

Chavali sat with Colby, Portia, and Sivry at the inn, not tasting the food she chewed mechanically. After the fiasco with the Blue Death, she insisted upon watching the bartender fill a ceramic pot for her with hot water and a tea infuser, then carried it to the table herself.

"This case has too many points that make no sense. It is distracting."

"Chastity," Portia said, her arm now in a sling, "you're forgetting to use contractions."

"Of course I am," Chavali snarled. "I have seen—" She snapped her jaws shut and ground her teeth. They'd taken care of the Harris part of this mission. She needed to set that aside and focus on the statue part. Holding up her hand, she counted off the things bothering her about the case. "Grippan coins in the silver shop. Velsin and Warren both are not lying, but cannot both be true. Bloodflies attacked a prison transport to free Broken Ring. The Drowned Ones have a flow map and are too good at predicting the future."

Flipping her thumb out for a fifth, she came up blank.

"Everything else is my—" She groped for the right word and found nothing in Shappan. "*Tuizil*. A feeling of wrong. Reynolds' alibis are covering all the time. Kalei and Nasha do not have this. No one could possibly have this, yet I saw his thoughts. What he said was what he thought. Helping a neighbor fetch a loose dog? It sounds like...*simatu*."

Colby covered her hand with his and squeezed. *Settle down. We're all upset about what happened to Harris. When we get home, you can scream and take some time for yourself. I'll even let you hit me as hard as you want. Right now, we need you to keep yourself together. We're a team, remember? Working for all the same goals.*

"If Nasha told Ambrye she had a place, I wonder..." Portia tapped her fork on her plate and squinted at the wall. "I don't know." She shrugged. "But I do know there's such a thing as illusions."

Chavali blinked, wondering how she could be so stupid as to not think of that. She could create illusions herself. That ability had served her well in so many situations and she'd spent plenty of time as Fallen learning to use them more effectively.

"Someone under a guise of illusion could have fooled Velsin into thinking she spoke to Warren. They would need...to be familiar with Warren and either be a mage or have one in their employ."

"Kalei has some magical skill," Sivry said. "There are plenty of people with money, though. So that doesn't really help us. Besides, we don't know all of what she can do. Illusion might be outside her skills."

"Nasha also has magical skill we do not know the extent of." Chavali drummed her fingers on the table, glad Colby had withdrawn his hand rather than continuing to inflict random encouragement on her. "For all we know, Reynolds can do this."

"It's probably late enough to find Nasha." Portia set her fork down on her cleared plate. "We'll have to talk to Denton to find her. Do we have anything to give her to show we've been doing more than attacking mercenaries?"

No one spoke up. Chavali churned through everything they knew. "This place the mercenary leader showed me, I wonder if it matters? Pushing out a gang is not strange, but this gang seemed the type the Bloodflies would want to absorb. What if they wanted the location more than the people?"

"Where is it?" Portia asked.

"I don't know." Chavali closed her eyes and conjured the fleeting memory she'd pulled. "It was a shop, I think for meat? Fish? Something like this. Two floors upstairs for a living place. I did not see the outside."

"I can think of two butcher shops in Bloodflies territory," Sivry said. "We can go look them over."

"I think I will recognize it from the outside, but not in the dark."

"I don't want to go down there in the dark if we can help it," Portia said. "Not even with Colby along. If we're going to tangle with those guys, I want to have a small army along for the ride."

Sivry nodded her agreement, pain keeping her face taut. "We might be able to sneak around in the area, but if they really wanted the shop for some reason, I don't think we'll get in without a fight. Portia and I aren't in the best shape, and there's only four of us."

"We go to see Denton, and then find Nasha. I will think of something to report on the way." Chavali took a last drink of her tea and stood with the others. Though they'd cracked one question she raised, the answer only created more questions, and the other issues still loomed.

In particular, the Grippan coins stuck out as odd. They knew the Bloodflies framed the Drowned Ones for the events at the silver shop, but why take the extra time to plant Grippan coins? They threw suspicion on Nasha for purchasing the dust in the first place, except no one had used the dust since then. The last use happened prior to that incident, and the dust must have been purchased more than a day earlier. Why would the shop owner not empty the coins and take them to be exchanged as soon as possible?

Prince Warren's impending marriage popped into her head. His soon-to-be family might have sent him coins for any number of reasons, including his known interest in art. His intended may even have visited and left them behind by accident, prompting him to use them for illicit transactions.

Were they wrong about the illusion? What if, instead, someone had modified Warren's memories? Robin could do that. Chavali had seen no sign of his influence, but she spent little time in Warren's mind and had no idea if she'd notice in such a fleeting contact. Pale's stamp had been subtle. As her teacher, Robin's would be moreso. Any such manipulation would have happened before they arrived, which meant Robin could have been here and gone with the intention to return.

"He is coming," she murmured as they walked into the Watch building. She shivered.

Chapter 40

Chavali told Denton they had a theory to check on and declined to offer details. Denton grumbled and told them where to find Nasha. Half an hour later, the group walked into a clinic in the worst part of the east side. The shabby building sheltered a collection of squalid shanties. In the fading twilight, people dressed in grimy rags scurried past without giving the well-armed team a second look.

Antiseptic and soap permeated the inside of the squat stone building. An older woman in frayed white robes greeted them with a soft smile reminiscent of the Fallen healers. Several voices moaned in pain nearby, muffled by distance and the thick white curtain separating the rest of the room from this small entry.

"Do you need healing?"

"Actually," Portia said, "yes. Both she and I do. How much do you charge for that?"

"We charge nothing, but accept donations." The woman gestured for them to follow her past the curtain to a room full of beds. Half of the forty cots had occupants tucked under worn sheets, most asleep or unconscious. One whimpered, her hand raised and grasping the air. Others moaned as they rocked or shuddered. Nasha sat on the edge of a bed with a woman sobbing into her pants leg.

Sivry passed the woman several coins. "Our injuries are minor, but we'd be better off without them."

"Thank you for your generosity. We only have one healer in the clinic right now, so you'll have to wait a little bit, but I'll let her know you're here." The woman shuffled past the beds toward Nasha.

While Portia and Sivry sat together on the nearest bed, Chavali watched the old woman with curiosity. She approached Nasha and gestured to Chavali and the rest of the group. Nasha turned and saw them. Nodding, she got the older woman to take charge of her patient and hurried to the group.

"What are you doing here?" Nasha whispered.

"I could ask the same," Chavali said, crossing her arms.

"I have a small gift with healing. They let me examine the dead in exchange for spending time here." Nasha peeled away the bandage on Portia's arm. "How did you get shot with a crossbow bolt?"

"Where did you hide Ambrye?"

Nasha scowled at Chavali and covered the wound with her hand. "I didn't. How many times do I have to tell you I wouldn't hurt her?"

Chavali snatched Nasha's other hand under the guise of preventing her from working until she answered the questions. "When was the last time you saw Ambrye?"

Too long ago. Nasha's mind filled with a highly intimate moment between the two women.

Stunned by such an obvious reason for Nasha's cagey responses that she never saw coming, Chavali let go. "You're having an affair with her?"

Nasha's already pale face whitened. "Please don't say it so loud. Ambrye has to remain available for a state marriage."

"Why didn't you tell us in the morgue?" Colby asked. "No one would have overheard. We could've already shifted focus to Reynolds and Kalei."

Nasha pressed her lips together and Portia sighed with relief. "I don't know. I'm used to keeping it a secret, I guess. You can't tell anyone. Please."

"I sure won't." Portia examined her healed flesh and flexed the muscle. "This is good work."

Chavali wanted to believe the deep, soulful love Nasha felt in that moment made her innocent. "How do we know you didn't kidnap her to be together? If she no longer had the responsibility of her position...no, even I don't believe this. She would've fought you. She relishes her duties. You know this too well to dupe yourself into thinking she could be convinced otherwise by any means."

Nasha moved to Sivry and sighed. "I found a place for us to escape to, a quiet little house in a sleepy town away from here. We could spend time together there, away from prying eyes and ears. When I told her about it, asking her to buy it, she laughed. When would we ever go? Even if either of us had the time, going together would raise eyebrows.

"When she's the queen, she won't be able to run off for a week to relax in the countryside. I'll move into the palace and become one of her spies, or something along those lines. That's the best option I have."

In spite of herself, Chavali let her mouth curve into a smile for the fleeting moments of happiness they'd find. Later, she could be jealous. "It's a good option. We need to find her first, though. Do you have any thoughts, now that you know we don't suspect you?"

Sivry groaned and flopped on her back. "You have no idea how good it feels to not have that ache anymore."

"No," Nasha said, "but if you need my help, you have it. Whatever I can do to find her. Anything at all. If you want to arrest me to make someone else think they're in the clear, I'll sit in a jail cell for you."

Chavali considered the idea, which had merit. Glancing at Colby, she caught him mulling it over and suspected he'd agree. Before she could voice her support, she heard the muffled jangle of chainmail through the curtain. "Inspector Nasha? Chastity?" a woman called out, breathless.

Both rushed to the curtain to find two uniformed Watch officers panting, catching their breath after a run. Chavali crossed her arms and waited. Nasha's hands flexed like she wanted to grab the guards and shake them until information came out.

"Ma'am, Inspector. Captain Denton sent us. Inspector Ambrye signaled from a warehouse three blocks away. We're to escort you all there."

"Signaled how?" Nasha asked. "Are you sure it was her?"

"Yes, ma'am. We're the officers that saw the signal. Someone threw a shadow of three fingers against a candle flame on the window of a warehouse. We saw the shadows wave like she does when she's requesting a breach team to open a door for her. Can't imagine who else would do that."

Chapter 41

Denton had to coordinate a massive influx of Watch in Bloodflies territory without anyone noticing before the assault. Colby, Portia, Sivry, and Nasha crouched with Chavali and ten Watch officers in a dark alley, waiting for the signal. It stank of rotting fish and bodily waste. No one allowed anything but the soles of their boots to touch the ground.

"We're the front breach team," Colby said, keeping his voice down. He pointed to two men and two women among the Watch. "You four are kicking the door in. We'll go through next, followed by the rest. Chastity and Portia are the rear for our team. If there's heavy resistance, our job is to secure the entry point. If not, we move in and cover the teams coming in after us. Denton says the place is a clothing workshop. Lights are on, which means regular employees may be working inside. We don't know. Anyone who doesn't fight back gets escorted out.

"There will be a team that stays outside to take prisoners. There will also be two backup teams for us, another team going in through the roof, and three more teams going in through the side door. Inspector Reynolds is with the side door breach team. Captain Denton is on our backup team. Our goal is to take as many prisoners as possible and liberate Inspector Ambrye. Ambrye is expected to be upstairs. Any questions?"

"Any other Inspectors involved?" A Watch officer asked.

"Inspector Kalei is collecting more backup squads. She'll join us late." Colby glanced from face to face in the dim moonlight, then nodded his satisfaction.

"Signal," Sivry said. "Let's go."

The four Watch officers filed out with Colby, Sivry, and Nasha behind them. Chavali waited with Portia while the rest of their Watch slipped out of the alley. She ran in the darkness, keeping pace with Portia and the man in front of them. The front door assault began as Chavali crossed the street.

The men and women of the Watch synchronized a massive hit on the door, with heavy maces and boots. Three pieces of the wooden door flew inside. Colby, Sivry, and Nasha slipped through the door frame, followed by the door smashers, then the rest of their team. Denton caught up to Chavali and Portia and led them inside.

Long worktables formed channels from the front to the back of the room with an empty row breaking them into two groups. To the side, tall shelves held bolts of cloth and boxes. Magical lights lined the ceiling in strips ten feet overhead. Cloth covered the tables, enchanted needles falling as the twenty workers dropped their work and hopped to their feet, eyes wide with terror. Near the front corner, a platform attached to four cables and a lever to operate a winch offered access to the floor above.

Watchmen streamed in from the side, crossbows and swords

ready. Colby and Nasha led the way to the metal stairs in the back. Denton nudged a worker toward the door.

"Let's get these people out," she barked.

Ten Watch stepped up to help the workers funnel out while the rest moved to the back. Colby gripped the railing for the stairs and took the first two steps up in one stride. Nasha hopped onto the first step. From the middle of the room, Chavali turned to watch the workers reach the front door.

The assault went as planned. Then several Watch screamed and grunted near the front door. Chavali saw men and women fall with crossbow bolts sticking out of their bodies. The workers charged with swords they must have hidden beneath their clothes and more crossbow bolts flew in. Portia dove into the shelves and flung bolts of sizzling energy into the attackers.

Shouts from the stairs announced more attackers coming from above. Chavali ducked under a table and had no time to spare for keeping track of everyone. She threaded her fingers through the spirits, cajoling them to produce illusions for her. Conjuring memories of bonfires, she crafted the crackling first, and threaded it around the edges of the room. Flames chased the sound, spreading along the line as low flickers and growing to the ceiling in the span between one heartbeat and the next.

Denton's voice, barking orders, faded into the background as Chavali focused on maintaining the two-part illusion. Explosions rocked the floor beneath her feet and splinters flew through the air, foiling her ability to keep such a delicate working in hand. The flames disappeared. The crackling remained. With her opaque sheet gone, she saw a cloud of dust and debris tumbling from the front door.

"The exits are blocked!" a woman shouted.

Metal clashed. Men and women screamed and grunted, drowning out other shouts. Chavali stayed low and crept closer to Denton. The floor erupted, fire blowing up through it inches from Chavali. Tossed by the flying wood, she landed in a heap, a spear of broken floor between her arm and her body.

She pushed herself up and shook her head to get her hair out of her face. The floor had collapsed, bringing Watch and Bloodflies alike into the basement. Bolts of cloth, scattered by the explosion, burned in clumps. Bodies littered the debris lining the concrete walls.

They'd been duped. Chavali tasted blood and smelled smoke. Denton groaned nearby. Others moaned in pain. True fire crackled and snapped. Crossbow bolts thunked into flesh and wood. Screams and shouts rang out. A hand pushed out of the debris at Chavali's feet. She scrambled to help them, hefting a piece of wood and tossing it aside.

The man she revealed, his face streaked with blood and lined with pain, shoved a sword at her. She dodged the clumsy attempt. Finally drawing her dagger, she tucked her feet up away from him, then kicked out, connecting the heel of her boot with his forehead. She swept her foot to the side, knocking his sword away, and lunged in with her dagger. The blade found flesh. He gurgled and went limp.

Chavali rolled to the side, seeking Denton. Over the roar of the fire, more shouts rang out. She recognized Colby's voice among them, calling her name.

At once, she appreciated his concern and wished he would shut up and go fight. "I'm all right!"

"Sivry, good enough!" Sivry shouted.

"Portia here. Not dead."

Members of the Watch called their names out. Only half-listening to the roll call taking place, Chavali checked a boot she found. A gory mess of a severed leg stuck out. Holding down bile, she shoved it aside and kept crawling. Rounding a burning pile of cloth, she saw Denton propping herself on her elbows and shaking her head.

In the distance, she noticed Colby leaping through flames and out of sight, calling for Nasha to wait. Chavali ignored him. He could take care of himself better than she could. She scrambled over debris to Denton's side, heaving chunks of wood off the captain's legs.

"What happened?" Denton asked, her voice slurred with confusion.

"They set a trap. We fell into it. The warehouse holds many dead bodies now. Everything is on fire. The exits are blocked. It sounded like twenty-some are still able to shout. How many are able to fight is unknown." Chavali checked Denton's legs, then prodded her side where dark smears suggested blood. Denton hissed, the reaction too muted to cause true concern. "You seem generally fine. I am scratched and bruised. And lucky."

Denton coughed and spat a dark gob to the side. "Watch! Whoever is able, defensive perimeter. Those with light injuries, search for survivors."

"I feel I should remind you there are no windows on the first floor, except in the door we smashed to enter. That doorway is now blocked by debris."

"Great." With Chavali's help, Denton wobbled to her feet.

Portia rounded the nearest fire. Blood matted her hair and she plucked a shard of glass from her arm as she spoke. "We've already seen how well I put out fires. I can make a hole, though. Where do you want to go?"

"Up," Denton said. "The Bloodflies are up."

Portia set her jaw with grim determination and ripped a sleeve off her shirt. Chavali helped her wrap it around the fresh injury and tie it off. That done, Portia pointed in the direction she intended to make a hole. "I can't hold it for long, so you'll have to run. I may not make it all the way through with you. I'll try to send others that way as I can."

Denton nodded and took a deep breath. Chavali thought this was stupid. The moment Portia forced the flames aside so they could jump over them, Chavali followed Denton anyway. They darted over uneven ground, hopping from one section to another. Four Watchmen managed to scrape themselves up fast enough to join the mad dash before the fires surged into place and cut them off again.

At the stairs, Chavali made a basket with her hands to help Denton jump to the floor above. She traded the task with the Watchman behind her, one she recognized from the Drowned Ones raid, and both he and the next boosted her up to reach the base of the stairs. All four men helped each other and the small group of six ran up the stairs, blades drawn. Chavali coaxed the spirits to provide another four Watchmen in the line.

Denton kicked a door open and they piled through. Bloodflies leaped in, too late to block passage. They all filled a hallway, Chavali falling back to let a more competent swordsman fight side-by-side with Denton. Chavali checked inside the first room they passed, seeing no sign of the princess in the disheveled office. Her illusory Watchmen would be no help here, so she let them go. Eventually, practice would guide her to make more effective illusions.

Ahead of them, the Bloodflies turned down a hallway and ran. Denton pursued, but stopped only a short distance down the new hall.

"They're splitting up. We're here to search for the princess, not hunt down Bloodflies. Stay together. Chastity, you're our eyes. Stay in the center and call out whenever you see an enemy."

The Watchmen surrounded Chavali and she walked sideways and backward, keeping up with them and trusting them to keep her from walking into walls. The group turned one corner, then another. She saw movement.

"In there." She pointed at a side room, then turned away, expecting it to be a diversion. "Behind us!"

While Denton and the men engaged four Bloodflies from two different directions, Chavali felt a prickle on the back of her neck. Snapping her head around, she noticed a woman lurking in a dark corner too late. The woman leaped at her with bare hands and knocked her to the floor.

Chavali rolled with the blow as Eliot has drilled her to do. In the confines of the hallway thick with battle, they hit the wall hard enough for the woman to lose her grip. In her moment of disorientation, Chavali grabbed the woman's hair and cracked her skull against the floor once, twice, and a third time.

Getting to her feet, Chavali rammed an elbow into the woman's gut for good measure. As she stood, the Watchmen relaxed with blood on their blades.

"I said to take prisoners," Denton spat.

"That one'll live," a Watchman said, pointing with his sword.

Following the line of his blade, Chavali saw a gang member on the ground, whimpering and holding his belly. "I doubt it. This one, on the other hand, should be fine if her brain does not bleed."

Another Watchman rolled the woman over and wrapped a tie around her wrists, binding them behind her back.

"We need to keep moving," Denton said. "If the princess is here, we'll be lucky to find her alive after all this."

"She's not here," Chavali said, knowing it was true. "This was too well-constructed a trap. Our goal should be to capture prisoners for interrogation and to survive. Someone has to know where she is."

"This wasn't for nothing," Denton said. Chavali had a feeling she said it more to convince herself than her men.

Chapter 42

More Bloodflies popped out of offices as they crept through the labyrinthine halls. Denton kept the small group moving. Chavali noticed some directions had no Bloodflies in them, which seemed odd until the ceiling collapsed behind them, forcing them to stumble forward and separating one Watchman out. Before anyone knew what had happened, Bloodflies swarmed on the Watchman, cutting him down.

"We're being herded," Denton said. She kicked a door in and led the group inside a long, narrow room. Windows formed the top half of the back wall, overlooking a wide room full of crates and shelves. More windows dotted the far walls, though they didn't seem to be the type that opened.

Flames licked around the edges of a square hole in the floor. Judging by the cables and winch mechanism, it connected to the platform below. As Chavali watched, fire swarmed over a stack of crates beside the hole.

"Defend the door," Denton barked. "Use it as a chokepoint. Chastity, can you do anything about or with this wall of glass?"

"Besides look through it?" Chavali scanned the room for anything useful. The purpose of the room appeared to be for someone to pace back and forth while supervising workers without the ability to yell at them. She suspected furniture and other useful items had been removed.

"Who *are* you?" From her tone, Denton wondered why Sivry, Portia, and Colby treated her with enough deference to make her seem like their leader.

"I am a fortune teller. Battle is not the best deployment of my skills."

"I can see that."

Chavali noticed the cables swaying in the hole and ignored whatever else Denton said to approach the glass and press her hands to it. Someone scrambled over the edge and rolled to his feet. He wore close-fitting, dark clothes over a fit, but not heavily muscled physique.

"That man is...wearing a mask? Why would anyone wear a mask for this?" Chavali pointed, her finger touching the glass.

Denton stepped next to her, cradling her arm. "He expects to escape and not be identified."

"No one could be so stupidly arrogant as to believe we would take no prisoners. Any of them could identify him."

"Incoming," a Watchman said.

Chavali snapped her head around to see Bloodflies rushing the doorway. Denton jumped to join the three Watchmen bracing for the attack. Chavali took a deep breath and focused. She had to help. Her life hung on this line as much as theirs. Sparing a glance through the window again, she saw another figure crawl through the hole and dodge a thrust by the masked man as he lurched to his feet.

She threaded her fingers through the spirits and goaded them to fill the hallway outside the room with inky darkness. Shouts and curses filtered through the clanging and grunting. She left the spirits controlling the darkness and watched the two men in the larger room. In the flickering light, she recognized Reynolds as the second man.

They traded thrusts and parries, the two men seemingly well matched. Reynolds needed a diversion to best the masked man. Chavali looked down at her dagger, then at the glass. She slammed the blade into the thick glass. Her strength proved only enough to scratch the glass, but she had no intention of giving up.

Jamming her dagger against the glass over and over, she chipped away at a small hole. While she worked, the two men in the room danced around the tables, crates, and spreading fire. Their narrow blades slashed through the air, clanging together. The masked man leaped onto a table and cartwheeled down it to avoid Reynolds's strikes.

Chavali had never seen such theatrical dueling before. No Fallen she'd watched fight ever twirled in the middle of a fight. No one in her clan ever wasted effort or energy on somersaulting. Something about the fight seemed almost staged, as if both men wished to put on a performance.

Her dagger crunched through the glass, creating a hole without cracking the rest of the pane. She growled, wishing she could curse whatever craftsman made glass too strong to break properly. Checking behind her, she saw the Watchmen holding their own. The one she recognized from the Drowned Ones raid backed out of the doorway and Denton took his place without giving up even half a step to the Bloodflies.

"Help me bind this," he gasped to Chavali, holding his bloody arm.

"You thought you could get away with taking the princess," Reynolds said, his voice distant, "but you won't."

Chavali looked up from ripping away the hem of her dress to see the masked man near the window, fencing with Reynolds.

"I can get away with anything I want!" The masked man shouted.

"I can help you break the window," the Watchman whispered.

Chavali wrapped the cloth around his arm, nodding her agreement and watching his thoughts to understand his plan.

"I already got away with taking her," the masked man spat. "You'll never find her. Especially not now. I've achieved everything I wanted and you don't even have a clue what's going on." He kicked Reynolds, forcing the inspector to stumble back and over a burning crate. "Fire is only the beginning and it'll be your end, Reynolds! No one will escape."

The Watchman gripped his sword as Chavali tied a knot. She nodded and knew how to help him. As she wrapped her hands around the chainmail covering his bicep, she noticed his eyes widen in fear. Turning, she saw the masked man holding up a small object.

"I'm going to burn the world! Drown it in flame! Starting with this building!" The masked man cackled, the sound full of madness, and edged toward a window. If he turned and ran, he could throw himself through the glass and escape. Assuming he survived the fall.

Chavali had no idea what the masked man's object was. She laid her hand across the Watchman's cheek and he didn't notice; he feared his own death too much to care about a strange woman touching him. That object contained a magical explosion, one that could level the entire block if triggered. A similar device probably had been used for the prisoner transport and the silver shop attack.

"I won't let you do that," Reynolds bellowed. He charged the masked man, plowing into him and reaching for the explosive.

Despite his fear, the Watchman pushed Chavali to the floor and curled his body around hers. The building shuddered before the roaring boom reached her ears and shoved them both into the wall.

Chapter 43

Chavali shook her head and coughed from the dust and smoke in the air. Her ears rang and her vision swam. Warmth slid down her cheek and a line on her forehead blazed with agony. The Watchman's weight pinned her down. She suspected she had cuts and bruises all over her body. Her ankle, stuck in place, twinged with enough pain to be twisted or broken.

She brushed hair out of her face and probed her head wound, finding a piece of something sharp embedded in it. Her feather remained intact, at least. Above, she saw stars. For several heartbeats, she stared without comprehension. Then she realized the roof had been blown away.

The Watchman groaned and shifted over her. Nearby, more voices woke.

"Again." Denton's voice cracked. "I hate being blown up. Don't you dare," she growled.

"I do not know your name," Chavali told the Watchman on top of her. "I cannot get up until you do."

"We're not dead," he muttered. "I'm Mils. Give me a minute."

"Chastity! Where are you?" Colby's panicked shouting sounded far away.

"My keeper," Chavali said with a grimace. She gripped the edges of the thing in her forehead.

Mils batted her hand away and shifted his body, grinding her leg against something sharp. "Let me do that. It's shallow, but it's going to bleed a lot. Can we tear off any more of your dress?" He helped her sit up and she saw the wound through his eyes. His concerns centered around her bleeding too much over time.

"A sleeve."

He helped her rip the sleeve off her dress and bunch the fabric up. "You helped us at that warehouse raid. Oersen is a friend of mine. He's fine because of you."

Several feet away, Denton lurched onto the back of a member of the Bloodflies while the other two Watchmen struggled to their feet. Chavali peered over Mils's shoulder and saw the glass and wall had been smashed. Beyond it, the room had been blasted apart, leaving a gaping hole at least thirty feet wide. This building no longer had a roof at all.

"Reynolds sacrificed himself to prevent the blast from taking out the rest of us." As she said the words, Chavali couldn't understand them. The man she met held too much lofty arrogance to perform such a selfless act.

"Chastity! Answer me!"

Mils yanked the object out of her head wound. The unexpected pain blacked her vision long enough to miss him tossing the thing aside and pressing the cloth to her head.

She gasped for breath. "Call out to him, please."

"Chastity is up here! She's hurt. Denton is..." Mils checked on the captain and smirked. "Denton is up and arresting people!"

"Why did you tell him that?" Chavali leaned against the debris of the wall and worked to catch her breath.

Mils grinned. "So he'd work harder to make a way up here. We all need to get down."

Too weak to laugh, she echoed his grin. "You're a man after my own heart."

"Thank you, ma'am. Hold this." He lifted her hand and pressed it against the cloth on her forehead, then helped her free her legs. "I don't think your ankle is broken, but you should avoid putting weight on it until you can see a healer."

"This is good to know. And you? Are you hurt?"

"I think my armor protected me from the worst of it. You should consider wearing some if you plan on assaulting too many more buildings in the future."

"Thank you for the advice."

They heard a crash. Debris tumbled down the hall, followed by Colby bursting into sight. His gaze flicked around, taking in the scene. "That blast barely affected the downstairs," he told Denton as he knelt beside Chavali. "The stairs are clear and stable, and there's a path to them now. We have three prisoners, and the team outside has called for more help and healers already. Looks like four prisoners, actually."

Chavali smacked his hand away when he reached for her head wound. "My ankle is twisted. I know how much you enjoy carrying damsels."

Colby looked to Mils. "Is it bad?"

Mils tried to stifle his grin and failed. "Yes, it's pretty bad. She'll need constant attending."

"Don't be an ass." Chavali tried to roll her eyes. It hurt too much. She changed the subject instead. "Reynolds and the mysterious leader were blown up. What of the others?"

Colby thanked Mils politely and scooped Chavali into his arms. He explained while he carried her to the stairs. "Portia and Sivry are safe but injured. They're waiting for the healers. I caught up with Nasha and Reynolds as they ran into a hail of crossbow bolts. Reynolds somehow dodged them and I dragged Nasha behind a burning crate. She took three bolts, but was able to keep herself going with her healing gift.

"We didn't see where Reynolds and the leader got to, but we did cut down the men with the crossbows. They'll be digging bodies out of this rubble for days, I expect. So far, it looks like at least ten Watch died. Twice as many were injured. No one knows how many Bloodflies were here, but they've already verified twenty-six dead."

Chavali cringed as he took the stairs and had to jump down from the bottom step. They crossed the broken floor covering the basement. At the other side, Colby lifted her and two Watch helped her hobble to Portia and Sivry. Sivry held her leg, which had been splinted. Portia lay on the street, her sleeve gone and the flesh of her arm blackened and puffy.

"I'm glad you're not dead," Sivry ground out through clenched teeth. Agony pinched her face in a wretched grimace. "Broken leg. Portia's only half here. Meditating against the pain, or something like that."

Shouting rang out as Chavali let the Watch officer help her sit. The voices came from behind them. Nasha rounded the corner of the building. Sweat glistened on her unnaturally pale face and she half-dragged her left leg.

"Go," Chavali said, waving to her helper, "get her before she falls over. She needs to lie down." She watched two officers and Colby cajole Nasha into letting herself rest with them.

As Colby helped her sit beside Chavali, two more Watch hustled to them, carrying a body. "Is there a healer around here?"

"No," Chavali said, "but leave him here and we will do what we can."

They set the body down, Reynolds's empty, glassy eyes staring at Chavali.

She frowned. "He is dead. But I don't understand. He should have been blown apart. There is no sign of the explosion on him."

Colby turned the body over, revealing a crossbow bolt in his gut and a stab wound in his chest. Wet blood drenched the front of Reynolds's clothes. Something on his sleeve glittered in the light.

Chavali touched the sleeve and ran her thumb over the shiny spot, then showed it to Colby. "Is it the silver and blue dust?"

He nodded. "Yes. What does this mean? The leader teleported away with him before the blast? Why take him?"

"Accident?" Sivry suggested. "Maybe he didn't mean to, but didn't have that much control over it."

"One way to find out," Nasha said, her voice taut with denied pain. She covered his face with her hand and closed her eyes.

The spirits roiled in Chavali's ears. Her skin crawled. She wanted to flee, but needed to stay and hear what happened from Reynolds's own mouth. Clenching her jaw, she refused to let anything move her.

"Tell me who killed you," Nasha said.

"Prince Warren," the eerie, reedy voice wheezed.

"What?" Nasha opened her eyes and flicked her gaze from face to face. She seemed to be searching for an explanation for this bizarre accusation. "Tell me everything that happened after the explosion."

"I sat up. He stood and shot me with a crossbow. He took off his mask. I expected Jeric. Prince Warren demanded the locations of Inspector Ambrye and the statue. I lied to him. He spoke. He stabbed me. I died."

"What did Prince Warren say after you lied to him?"

"Congratulations, Reynolds. You've killed not just Ambrye, but the queen and Bricene too. Good work, you arrogant moron."

"Where is Inspector Ambrye?"

The voice buzzed, droning loud enough to make Chavali cringe more. "I don't know."

Nasha let go with a grunt. "Of course not. But Reynolds knew. He had to know to lie about it."

With the pressure of the spirits easing, Chavali sucked in a breath and felt light-headed. She leaned back to lie on the ground. "Someone check if Jeric is one of the prisoners. I wish to speak to him, very much. Shield him from the knowledge of Reynolds's death if possible. If he is dead, his corpse may have enough to go on."

Chapter 44

By the time Denton dumped Jeric at Chavali's feet, healers had swept through. Though the Watch healers couldn't match those working for the Fallen in skill, they swiftly eased pain and stopped bleeding. Sivry still sat with a man pouring his soul into mending her leg so she could walk. Portia's arm had been bandaged.

"Chastity, meet Jeric. You asked for him, here he is."

The scruffy man knelt before her, his hands bound behind his back and ankles chained together. He wore a pair of torn, ragged pants and nothing else. Dark smears and minor injuries—no longer bleeding but still untreated—decorated his chest and arms.

"It's nice to meet you, Jeric." Chavali had no reason to be coy or question him normally. She slapped a hand on his shoulder, hitting an already purpling bruise and making him wince. The spirits flowed down her hand as they always did. Except it felt strange. They rushed, greedy and far too eager. When she tried to move her hand, they wouldn't let her.

"Chastity?" Colby reached for her bare arm.

"Don't touch me!" She fell to her knees, pressure building inside her head. She thought the spirits would blow her skull apart.

"Let me protect you," Colby said, but his voice sounded wrong.

"I don't need to be protected."

"Chavali, please. You've already been hurt. You almost died tonight. Let me in. Let me protect you. I promised I would. Let me keep my promise."

"Keino," Chavali breathed. "Leave me be."

Colby's face contorted with rage. He planted his hands on her shoulders and pushed. "I've only ever wanted to keep you safe!"

Chavali fell back and plunged into water. She hit the bottom and opened her eyes to an impossibly blue sky. Keino stepped into view over her. She kicked away from him, pushing herself across a roof.

"Chavali, I don't understand. Why are you afraid of me?" He wore his lost puppy face, the one that always made her want to slap him.

She scrambled to her feet and checked for the edge of the building. Backing away from him, she held up her hands. "I'm not afraid of you."

He clenched his hands at his sides. "Don't lie to me. You always lie to me! Why do you always lie to me?"

The time to think and reason with Keino's spirit had passed. Chavali turned and ran. She leaped over the edge of the building to land inside a smoky bar reminiscent of Clara's but a different place. Her momentum carried her into a table. She knew she had to keep moving. Rolling to the floor, she slipped away from his grasping hand.

"Look at you." Keino groped the bar to get his balance and loom over her again. "Your clothes are ripped and bloody. With me protecting you, things like that won't happen."

Recalling the one thing she'd done that kept him from bothering her for the longest, she kicked between his legs and scrambled for the back door. Without looking back, she flung herself at the swinging door and stumbled into a butcher shop. Everything about it matched what she'd seen in that mercenary leader's mind. She knew the back room had stairs and ran for them.

Keino grabbed a handful of her dress. She squawked and twisted in his grip. Her hand flew, slapping him across the face. He let go. Patting the counter for a weapon, she backed away from him.

"You have to let me go, Keino. I know you love me. I know you care. You don't need to prove anything. It's always been about me, not you. I can't handle you. You know that."

He matched her pace, following her. "But that was before. It's different now. He's coming and I can't be there for you unless you let me in. I *promised* you. I have to keep my promise. Please, let me keep my promise."

Her fingers found a wooden cutting board. She lifted it and threw it at him with all her might, then turned and darted through the open doorway. He shouted his anguish as she ran up the stairs.

Jeric passed her on the stairs, headed down. She flattened herself against the wall for him and stared as he passed. His presence had only two possible meanings. One, he died and she took his spirit somehow into the fold of her clan. Pale had somehow been drawn in, so it could happen, but the second option seemed much more likely—she was inside Jeric's mind.

She watched Jeric and Keino meet on the stairs, neither offering the other an inch. Those two idiots would be stuck tangling with each others' egos long enough for her to explore more. At the second floor, she opened the first door she found and fell through a trapdoor into a dark, dank room.

Cabinets and drawers lined the walls. Shelves held casks and bottles. Chavali wished she had time to go through everything. Wary of Keino following her through at any moment, she grabbed bottles and scanned the labels, hoping for some scrap of information to let her identify this place later.

Keino's boots hit the floor two shelves away. "Stop running away from me," he growled.

"Stop chasing me." The bottle in her hand felt like a good weapon. She backed away without running, letting him close the distance.

When he reached her, she swung the bottle. The glass broke when it hit his head. He grunted and stumbled to the side, sputtering red wine and knocking over a shelf. It hit the next shelf and the next in a chain reaction of crashing bottles and casks. Liquor drenched him.

Chavali, now on the third step of the stairs, raised her broken bottle and glared at him over it. "Do you want to test Eliot's training? You know he's a good teacher."

"I love you."

With a disdainful curl of her lip, she fled up the stairs. This door dumped her into a dark alley. Two figures stood nearby. Jeric passed a pouch to the other person. Chavali moved closer and recognized Kalei.

"If you tell anyone where you got this dust—"

"Relax, honey. I'm the only one who knows. Just me. And we're going to keep it that way."

Kalei sighed and handed him a different pouch. When he gripped it, a small puff of silver dust laced with blue flickered in the light. She covered the top. "Be careful with that. Don't let anyone see you with it that you don't need to, and don't leave a damned trail with it."

Jeric smirked. "Sure thing, honey." The scene separated into two memories taking place side-by-side. In one, Kalei rolled her eyes and stalked off. In the other, Jeric grabbed her rear, snugged her body close to his and nipped her nose like a lover coaxing a reluctant partner.

Chavali had no interest in the rest of his fantasy, but she'd lingered too long. Keino stepped into view while one Jeric dropped the pouch of dust and pushed Kalei against the wall. The other Jeric kicked the wall in frustration and stalked away. Chavali raised her broken bottle and made an effort to ignore Jeric's fantasy about ravishing Inspector Kalei in favor of avoiding Keino's fantasy about ravishing her.

"Please. He's coming. I'm begging you to let me help you face him." A large purple bruise marred the side of Keino's face.

"I have no intention of facing him."

"You always have to do things the hard way." He swept a foot to trip her.

She managed to stumble around it, lurching to the side. The bruise told her she could hurt him. If he could be hurt by her actions, then the time for running was over. Rising to the balls of her feet, she watched him. When he threw a punch, he telegraphed it with his eyes. Her mind naturally twisted this false body far enough to the side to avoid it. Three more times, she let him attempt to attack her and leaned to avoid it.

The follow-through for his third punch gave her an opening. She slammed the broken bottle into his back and scraped it along his flesh. Blood, redder than she'd ever seen before, sprayed across her face.

"Why would you do that?" he cried.

"You cannot have me. I am not yours, I have never been yours, and I will never be yours. I belong to me. Only to me."

He staggered as if she'd slugged him. Unwilling to give up the advantage, she followed and slashed with her bottle. The jagged glass sliced through his arms, filling the air with more blood.

"Chavali," he whimpered. "I love you."

"You're a fool. That's not love. What you want was never about love." Without using the broken bottle, she cut him again, this time on the thigh. She flung the jagged glass at his sad, pleading face. "Protecting me was your *job*, not your calling. Be gone, Keino! Leave me be. Join the rest of our ancestors and be nothing more than one of many."

Chapter 45

Chavali blinked and saw Colby, distress written so plainly across his face she wanted to laugh. Darkness framed him and she realized she lay on the street. "I am fine."

He rolled his eyes. "Of course you are."

Jeric lunged between them. "She said she's fine. Back off."

Colby scowled and shoved Jeric. The chains on the thug's wrists and ankles caused him to fall on his side with a groan.

"Don't touch her," Jeric growled.

Chavali propped herself up on her elbows, not sure what to make of Jeric's behavior. "Shut up," she snapped. "We are going to try this again. I want to know what bar you have access to the basement of."

"What?" Denton squinted at Chavali as she hauled Jeric to his knees again.

"It stocks wine that you like a great deal. Where is this place?"

"She's cracked up," Denton said.

"I'm not sure I disagree," Colby said.

"All of you, quiet," Chavali snapped. "You," she waved to Jeric, "answer the question."

"It's called...Finley's." Jeric gazed at her, begging with his eyes.

Kalei, followed by at least thirty Watch, jogged into sight. The inspector's gaze fell on Jeric and she slowed. Several Watchmen broke away from her group to assist with the cleanup effort. Those remaining with Kalei approached, probably expecting Denton to give them orders.

Chavali wondered how long she'd been fencing with Keino in Jeric's mind. She saw Sivry sitting with a wrap around her leg, the healer long gone. Reynolds's body had been removed. Activity around the site had slowed, and now the Watch had guards posted around it. The other prisoners were gone.

"Inspector Kalei, I wish to speak with you," Chavali said, gesturing for her to come forward.

"Ask me anything," Jeric said. "I'll find the answers for you." To Chavali's surprise, he ignored Kalei as the inspector stepped into view again. With such a vivid fantasy about her, Jeric ought to have thrown his attention in her direction. Instead, he stared at Chavali, eyes hungry for the sight of her.

"Find the answers?" Colby said, his arms crossed over his chest. "What are you playing at?"

Jeric glanced at Colby, expression flickering with annoyance. He switched to the clan tongue, a language he had no reason to have ever heard, let alone understand and be able to speak. "Why is he here, and who does he think he is?"

Chavali paled. She reached a hand toward Jeric, but stopped short, terrified of his thoughts. "Keino?"

"Yes. Isn't this incredible? I can use this man's body! We can be together now and I can protect you."

She had to remember to breathe. Though she strove never to speak their clan's language in front of outsiders, she had no other way to communicate without giving away everything. "The man you inhabit, he's a murderer and he'll be put in prison for the rest of his life no matter what I say or do."

Jeric's face fell. "I've always done everything for you."

"I know." Getting back into flesh changed something in Keino. Maybe the limitations reminded him who he really was. Through this stranger's guise, Chavali saw the man she cared about, the one she fondly remembered slapping and showering with verbal barbs. Once, she'd thrown hot tea in his face. He came back and still wanted her. She treated him worse than a dog and he always came back for more. And now she had to watch him die. Again.

"I never doubted you." As she had in life, she wanted to push him away to save him. Nothing could ever work between them. His words and adoration won her. His thoughts repulsed her. Fear kept her from trying to overcome the problems between them. "But you have to let me go, Keino. There is still clan, and you're tormenting us all. Please, Keino. Let me go. It's the one way you have left to protect me."

He hung his head. "I love you, Chavali."

Her eyes burned. "I love you, Keino."

"I tried to stop him."

"It wasn't your fault. I don't blame you and never will." Tears slid down her cheeks and she brushed her fingertips across his face. "Goodbye."

Jeric crumpled forward, his body limp.

Denton stooped beside him and checked his pulse. "He's dead. What did you do?"

"What was all that nonsense language?" Kalei asked. She seemed relieved by the sight of Jeric's body, which didn't surprise Chavali at all.

Nasha stared at Chavali, wide-eyed. She opened her mouth and Chavali shook her head. Nasha stayed quiet.

Wiping her cheeks, Chavali clamped down on her grief. Finally, she got to say goodbye to someone in her clan. After months of suffering through his attempts to reach her and protect her, she'd convinced him to stop. Weight lifted from her shoulders, but she wanted a chance to sit and mourn. She'd take that time later. For now, she had a princess to save and a statue to liberate.

She glared at Kalei, someone she would have preferred not to have seen any of that exchange. "How much did he pay you for the silver dust Reynolds used to teleport?"

Kalei stepped back and blanched. "What are you talking about?"

"The silver dust." Chavali stood and squared her shoulders, gripping her anger and letting it burn away everything else. "Which is mixed with the dried and crumbled blue flowers from Eagle Falls. With the right magical trigger, it allows teleportation. And you sold a pouch of it to that man, who now lies dead on the street after my interrogation of him."

Kalei took another step back. "I've never heard of Eagle Falls."

"Really. I wonder what would happen if I went to chat with the local Order of the Creator's Path caretakers and asked them about these things? Shall we go do that now?" Chavali knew exactly what would happen: they'd deny any knowledge and blame Kalei. "I am sure they will be happy to explain everything at this hour."

Kalei flinched, showing she also knew what would happen. She closed her eyes and took a deep breath. "She's right. I sold them the dust and they reported how the trials went with teleportation."

"Those three men dead in Evidence Storage? Those murders hang around your neck."

"Take her to holding and put her in magic dampeners," Denton said. She waited until two of the Watch grabbed Kalei by the arms and hustled her out of sight. "We'll deal with her later. I want to know what happened to this man." She pointed to Jeric.

Nasha touched Jeric's body and nothing happened. "I don't understand. What did you do? What was that language?"

"I did very little and that language is none of your business. The mechanism that caused the prophecy came into play here, and I do not control that." Chavali hugged herself, rubbing her sleeveless arm.

Colby, Portia, and Sivry all stared at her. Seeing fear in their eyes hurt. Chavali turned away and found herself face-to-face with Denton.

"Fine. Never mind this guy. Do you know where the princess is?"

"I believe I know where the statue is. This place he mentioned, Finley's." Chavali suspected Ambrye could be found in the butcher shop, but in her mind, the statue ranked higher in priority. With Reynolds and Jeric dead, and Warren sent to the wrong location, they had time. "It should be in the basement, though I do not know exactly where."

Denton scowled. Soot and blood still streaked her face and the uniform over her armor. "When all of this is over, I expect you to tell me everything."

Chavali nodded, though she had no explanations to give. She

couldn't say why Reynolds abducted Ambrye, or why he chose to have his gang liberate Broken Ring members. Warren remained a mystery to her. In no way would she hint about anything relating to the Fallen or offer more detail about the spirits or her clan. The "everything" Denton wanted didn't exist.

"Let's go to Finley's," Denton said. "It's not far. I need a squad!" She stalked off, barking orders to whoever would listen.

Covering her face, Chavali struggled to keep the tenuous control she'd created over herself. The hand on her shoulder didn't surprise her until she saw who it belonged to. She found Nasha searching her face.

"Was that the language of the dead?" Nasha whispered.

"No. It will not help you in your duties."

"Did you destroy his soul?"

"I don't know. Whatever happened, it was accidental. It has never happened before."

Nasha nodded and glanced back at the other three. "I felt it. Whatever you did, it resonated with my power. If you want to talk about it, I might understand better than your friends."

"Thank you. I appreciate the offer."

"I want to be there when Ambrye is freed, but I'm barely keeping my eyes open at this point. I'd be a liability in a fight. I'm going home. If you find her tonight, would you tell her...tell her...I don't know. Tell her I can only half-die once a day."

Mustering a smile for Nasha, Chavali nodded. "Go. Rest. I will send her to you."

"Thank you."

Chapter 46

Chavali matched Colby's brisk pace as they followed Denton and her squad of uninjured Watch officers. They reached Finley's, a pub full of cheery, drunk customers who stood aside for Denton and her people. Most picked up their mugs of beer while being hustled out of the way. The bartender offered a feeble protest that Denton ignored.

They trooped into the basement, everything matching Jeric's memory. While Denton, Colby, and Portia opened cabinets and drawers, Chavali ran her fingers over the bottles until she found the one she'd picked up to attack Keino. Sivry limped alongside her, knocking on casks and feeling the undersides of the shelves.

"Do you like that vintage?" Sivry asked as she pried a small painting from the underside of a low shelf.

"I have no idea." Chavali tried to think of a way to explain what this bottle meant to her and failed. "This reminds me of someone I knew. Before."

"You can probably get away with taking it."

Running her fingertips over the label, Chavali shook her head.

"I'll buy it. I have no need to take from this place."

"Found it," Colby announced. He held up the cat statue, no longer inside its box.

Denton snatched it away. "That's evidence."

"That's our payment," Colby said.

"You didn't find the princess yet, and the queen will have to go through proper channels to liberate it and hand it over." Denton tucked the statue under her arm and headed up the stairs. "I'll have my people police up the rest of this art."

Chavali cleared her throat. "I have a guess for where to find the princess."

Denton stopped and glared at Chavali over her shoulder. "You might have said that before."

"What happened was disorienting." Chavali shrugged and refused to be intimidated by something as meaningless as an empty, vague threat from a guard captain. "I had to let my thoughts settle first. And it is only a guess. This location was much more firm."

"Let's go," Denton snapped. She handed the statue to one of her officers and gave orders to gather all the art and take it to Evidence Storage.

On the way out, Chavali overpaid for the bottle and asked the bartender to have it delivered to their inn. Portia and Colby kept their distance. Sivry limped alongside her. As they neared the butcher shop, commotion in the upstairs apartment drew Chavali's attention. Shadows danced across the window in a confusing display. Something broke the front window, showering the street below with glass.

Denton and Colby sprinted for the front door, crashing through it together. Portia raced in behind them. Chavali kept pace with Sivry and noted a heavy man's boot lying in the biggest puddle of thin glass shards.

They ducked inside and found a dying man bleeding on the floor of the butcher shop. Colby and Denton faced off against three more men in the back room. Chavali picked up the man's sword, thinking it better to hold than leave for a fleeing man to take.

"Your timing is less than impressive," Ambrye said from the top of the stairs. She fended off two Bloodflies with the top half of a broken coat rack and a small frying pan.

Chavali smirked and held up the sword. "Ambrye, catch!" She tossed the blade, hilt first, up the stairs.

Ambrye threw her frying pan at her opponent and ducked. With a swipe, she snatched the blade before it hit the floor. Chavali followed the blade up the stairs, drawing her dagger as she ran. When she set her foot on the top step, the two Bloodflies noticed her and panicked. One turned and ran, the other lunged at Ambrye.

Chavali hustled past the princess to catch the fleeing man. She already knew the layout, making it easy to cut him off as he tried to lose her in the maze of rooms. On his way through a door, she tripped him and dropped a knee onto his back. Part of her wanted to slit his throat. That part thought spilling more blood would fix things and make her feel better. Even though this man had nothing to do with any of the deaths she needed to mourn, ending his life would still help because he'd done awful, wretched things and deserved it. When everyone who deserved death found it...nothing would change.

She sighed and hit him in the back of the head with the hilt of her dagger. North Cascain had laws and methods to handle these things.

There would be a trial with Ambrye as the star witness. His punishment would fit his crime, not the crimes Chavali desperately wanted someone to pay for.

"I see you figured it out," Ambrye said. She smiled as she tossed the sword onto the body of the woman she'd just stabbed with it. "I expected you to. But I thought it would take less time."

"We were interrupted and detained." Chavali stood and smoothed her ragged, ruined dress. "Reynolds was more vicious than expected. And Kalei helped him without knowing how the pieces fit together."

Ambrye nodded. "Reynolds is an ass. Is he in custody, or did he flee?"

"He is dead. Shall we?" Chavali gestured down the stairs, where Denton tied up two prisoners. Colby wiped his sword clean. Sivry rifled pockets. Portia poked around the back room, peeking inside cabinets. "There is another man to take prisoner upstairs," she told Denton.

"Congratulations on cracking this case, Captain Denton." Ambrye saluted Denton.

Denton blushed and returned the salute. "I'm sorry it took so long, Inspector."

"We'll discuss it later. Over a drink or five." Ambrye grinned and led Chavali outside. "Now, tell me everything you know, Chastity."

Chavali arched an eyebrow. "Or you can tell me what you know and I can supply the missing pieces."

"I knew you were sharper than you pretended to be. Walk with me until we can find a carriage." Ambrye set off up the street.

"Go slower. It has been a very long day." Chavali set her own pace, slow enough for the others to catch up if they wished to.

"If your dress is anything to go by, I'm not surprised to hear that." Ambrye slowed and took a deep breath. "Ah, fresh air. Let's see. Where to start."

"Before you begin, I should tell you Nasha wishes to see you. She went home after being injured earlier. Start with the silver shop."

Ambrye's self-assured facade cracked with concern. "Is she all right?" When Chavali nodded, she cleared her throat and began. "I went to the silver shop to speak to the owner, and several gentlemen managed to take me by surprise. I was overpowered, hooded, and brought to this place.

"The first person they let me see was Reynolds, who made it very clear he hadn't come to rescue me. That man gloated about how he'd managed to beat Inspector Ambrye who was too good to let him try to woo her. He wanted to rule the city because obviously everyone would bask in his brilliance." She rolled her eyes. "Some time ago, he inserted himself into the Bloodflies and took over as their leader. It was a minor gang then, a nuisance. They quietly took a large section of the city over, absorbing or pushing out other gangs. I can't tell you how badly I wanted to punch him in the face personally. Shame he's dead already.

"Later, I saw my brother there. At least, it looked and sounded like Warren, except he seemed off somehow. I can't explain that. Regardless, Reynolds and Warren had a conversation in what I assume was code, about drowning and burning and all sorts of things. I've had plenty of time to puzzle over it, leading me to conclude they had some plan to murder my mother and little sister."

"Prince Warren?" Chavali frowned. She glanced back and saw

Colby, Portia, and Sivry following at an almost-discreet distance. "The short version of what happened while you were trapped boils down to Reynolds leading us on a merry chase. We finally caught up to him by walking into his trap at a clothing factory. He staged everything, except Warren switched things out on him and the end game did not go as he planned.

"They were able to have a few moments in private and when Nasha interrogated Reynolds' corpse, he revealed that Warren killed him, in addition to demanding where you were being held. He said he meant to come kill you, as well as the queen and Bricene. But if he already knew your location, why did he ask and why did he believe the false location Reynolds gave him? Why did he not check the place he knew first?"

Ambrye waved for the others to join the conversation. "I'm not sure what's going on with my brother, but something is definitely strange about his behavior. At any rate, most of my guards left before nightfall, giving me a chance to work against the ropes they'd used to tie me up. It took a while. When I got free, I discovered what I think a lot of people already knew—those people can fight. Reynolds trained them well."

"Yes," Chavali said with a sigh and a tug on the ragged shoulder of her dress. "We also discovered this the hard way."

"I'm starving," Ambrye said. "And there's a carriage. Let's continue this at the Watch headquarters."

"Excuse me for asking, Highness," Colby said, "but wouldn't you rather go to the palace?"

"No. I want to be in the thick of this, and I want to hear other reports. I'll send word so my mother knows I'm safe."

Chapter 47

Finally able to relax, Chavali struggled to stay awake in Ambrye's office. She sat next to Sivry on a couch with Portia on the other end. Colby lounged in a cushioned chair and Ambrye sat in an executive chair behind her desk. They ate sandwiches and fruit cobbled together by a clerk, and listened to reports from a stream of uniformed Watch officers coming and going through the open door.

"Highness." A servant in palace livery barged in, elbowing Mils out of the way as he delivered his report on what he'd seen with Chavali during the clothing factory raid.

Mils hadn't changed out of his uniform yet and gratefully accepted an apple wedge from Chavali. "That's about the end of it anyway, Inspector."

"Yes, dismissed. Go get some rest, officer." Ambrye rapped the end of her pen on the pages strewn across her desk.

The servant tapped her foot impatiently, then scanned the room. "This is a private matter, Highness."

"Then it should have waited. Do you have any idea how many

people died tonight?"

Denton ran in, letting herself thump against the doorjamb. "Prince Warren just blew up Finley's. I have three more Watch dead and five injured. Some of the recovered art was also lost."

"But not our statue," Portia said. "I'm sorry you lost more men, I really am. I think we all appreciate the food, and goodness knows I could use some sleep. But you owe us that statue. We made a deal. We found you, we get the statue."

Chavali watched Ambrye sit back in her chair, the wheels in her head turning. "Warren's not a mage. How did he blow it up?"

"No idea." Denton said. "No one saw anyone with him."

Ambrye drummed her fingers on the arms of her chair long enough to make Chavali think she hit a dead end in her thoughts. "Any idea what he went there to get?"

Denton nodded and said nothing, pretending to need time to catch her breath.

Even in her current condition, Chavali could see what was going on. "You're not giving us the statue because you intend to use it as bait for him."

Ambrye's mouth twitched in annoyance. "Too sharp by far," she muttered. "He clearly wants it, and badly. Interestingly, so do you. What is it?"

"A statue. Of a cat." Chavali met her gaze, not flinching.

"It doesn't matter what it is," Colby said. "Someone's decided it's valuable enough to kill for. Give it to us. We'll take it and all this chaos will leave with us."

"An attractive proposal, but it doesn't solve my problems and I'm not sure I like your approach to solving your problems."

"Highness, this is about the queen's birthday celebration tomorrow," the servant snapped. "It's *important*."

"I might remind you," Chavali said, "that I took a prisoner while you killed your captor."

Ambrye's lip curled. "I think we've had the discussion about lethal weapons before, Chastity."

"Highness!"

Everyone quieted and stared at the servant. She clenched her hands at her sides and huffed.

Ambrye sighed and rubbed the bridge of her nose. "What is it that can't wait until morning?"

The servant raised her chin. "Your day has to be scheduled."

"Get out of my office. I'll be bathed and dressed in time for the party. The rest of my day tomorrow isn't your concern." Ambrye waved the woman off.

When the servant hesitated, Denton grabbed a fistful of her tunic and dragged her out.

"We cannot wait forever," Chavali said. She stood, content they could offer nothing else tonight. Sleep tugged on her and she knew everyone else present felt the same. "More to the point, we will not wait long. If Warren does not take your bait within a reasonable time, we will take the statue whether you wish it or not."

"He'll take it. Whatever else is motivating him, he can't resist intriguing art. Besides, I know he's familiar with the artist. I've seen a piece like it before." She waved them out.

Chavali froze. "A piece like it? Where?"

Ambrye raised her brow and looked Chavali over. "I don't remember. I see a lot of unusual pieces in my work and can't keep track of everything. It wasn't recent, and I think it probably wasn't a crime scene."

"I see. Interesting." Chavali turned to go. The others were on their feet and shuffling out. She stopped and chose to remind Ambrye that she knew something damaging. "Don't forget your appointment." Without watching for Ambrye's reaction, she followed the others out.

They climbed into a Watch carriage and Chavali leaned against the wall. She faced Colby, who held a hand out to her. Though he undoubtedly meant the gesture to show his trust and faith in her, she lacked the energy to deal with him. Shaking her head, she took a deep breath and focused on not falling asleep.

"What really happened with Jeric?" Portia asked, her voice soft and weary.

Chavali's eyes snapped open. She'd known this would come up, but had hoped it would wait until they had a chance to rest. Scrambling for an answer to make the question go away, she rejected a dozen explanations. "I lost control of my telepathy."

After a long pause, Portia closed her eyes. "You need to stop relying on it."

Rather than explain anything about it, Chavali nodded. "Agreed."

The carriage stopped at Eidel's Landing and Chavali wished she felt confident about staying awake long enough to enjoy a cup of tea. "We should take separate rooms. I do not wish to wake anyone tonight. It has been too long a day for this."

Sivry yawned and shrugged. "The queen is paying for it. We

might as well."

They had to ring a bell to get service, and the man who shambled out in a robe handed over Chavali's bottle with her key. She set it on the table in her spacious room. The letters on the label formed words. If she asked, Colby would read it for her and tell her. This one time, she wanted to puzzle the letters out herself.

She stripped off her ruined dress and washed her face and hands with cool water from the pitcher by the window. Her weary mind wandered to Mils, wondering if he kept the strip of cloth she'd used to save his life or tossed it. The healer who took care of her forehead and ankle had trashed the bloody sleeve.

Tomorrow morning, she'd take a bath. For now, she feared she'd fall asleep in the tub. The bed called to her. She eyed it with suspicion. Her last night at this inn had been unpleasant. Things had happened since then, and her dreams would, no doubt, be tortured because of them. Not sleeping, though, would make things worse, so she climbed in and cursed it for being comfortable. She closed her eyes and fell asleep within seconds.

Chapter 48

Sucking in a breath, Chavali sat up in the darkness. Her dream fell away, leaving her with a vague sense of unease about Pale, Keino, Harris, and Robin. She remembered water, the chest, and the smell of rotting flesh. Drowning.

A gloved hand clamped over her mouth from behind. "Ssh," a man said.

She froze, fear surging through her. If he wanted her dead, she'd be dead already. Robin wanted her alive. He wanted to use her. He...left her in her room at the inn? Chavali blinked and raised her hands. She hadn't been bound, gagged, drugged, or removed. Her terror receded. This couldn't be Robin.

"Don't scream," he whispered. "I'll let go if you promise not to scream."

Chavali kept her hands up and nodded. When he pulled his arm away, he knelt on the floor in a shaft of moonlight and gazed up at her. Loose dark hair, long enough to reach past his chin, framed a young face she'd seen before but couldn't place.

"You're beautiful," he murmured. Reverence lit up his eyes and smile.

"Thank you." So long as he wanted to compliment her, she had no reason to call for help. Unfortunately, she couldn't tell how he'd react to anything she might say. If he knew she didn't recognize him, he might fly into a rage. "Why have you come?"

"You're the Guide of Lost Paths."

Of all the titles she'd taken or been given, this was the first connected to nothing she knew. Still uncertain of his intentions, she elected to play the role and frowned at him. "How do you know this?"

He beamed and set his hands on the edge of her bed, in easy reach. "They told me you'd come. I've waited so long."

Though she feared a repeat of what happened with Jeric, Chavali reached out and touched his hands. The spirits surged around him, drinking his thoughts and passing them to her. Nothing went wrong. "Your wait can't have been too long."

Long enough. I've dosed so many searching for you. "Nearly a year. Everything I've done has been to find you. What did you see with the Blue Death?" *It didn't harm you or make you need more. You're the only one. It has to be you. They said you wouldn't understand, not at first. I have to show you the truth.*

She realized where she'd seen him. In the common room of this inn, she saw him right before she had that demented vision. He'd spiked her tea with Blue Death. Before that, he'd been the cultist she almost caught in the warehouse raid. Shance, leader of The Drowned Ones, knelt in her room, treating her like a prophet. If Denton knew, she'd explode. Chavali smiled at him. Anything that would irritate either of the two people holding their statue back suited her.

"I saw many things." Since he expected her to be unaware of her status, she had no need to pretend to know more than she did. "Why do you think I am your guide? You have seen many things, haven't you? Why is it me and not you?"

He slipped up to sit on her bed and cupped her chin. "It can't be me. You're the only one who fits." *The ancient legends of the deep said you would come.*

"What do I fit?" His touch bothered her, draining away her amusement.

"The one who sees the future without scars." Caressing her cheek with his thumb, he watched her lips and thought about kissing her. "When her eyes are opened and the veil lifted, she walks unscathed. She drowns in her dreams, yet stands in the light." *I watched you toss and turn in your sleep. You gasped for breath and clawed for the surface. I know you dreamed of drowning.*

His depiction could apply to many, but the uncanny way it seemed to fit her—as well as the fact he'd watched her sleep—made her blood run cold. Chavali touched his hand, trying not to let him notice how hers shook. "What makes you think I bear no scars?"

He leaned in and brushed his nose against hers. *I shouldn't touch you, but I want to.* "The Blue Death didn't kill you," he whispered. His breath smelled of damp earth, fresh after a cleansing storm. "It made you stronger." *This is wrong. You're the Guide, and I must protect you, not defile you.* His lips touched hers, then he turned away.

She leaned into his hand, afraid he'd become violent if she pushed him away before he convinced himself to go. "What am I to do?"

"You've seen what will come. Blood, fire, flood—there's no way to stop any of it. Tomorrow night—I guess it's really tonight, isn't it? I'll show this city what's coming. They'll all see. They'll be prepared." He took a deep breath and met her gaze again, too close for her to focus on him. *I am nothing more than an instrument, a tool to help us all. He's here.*

The only thing that stopped her from jerking away was the force of his hunger for her as he pressed his lips to hers and slid his hand down to hold her neck.

Stop. Stop! I can't. I have to! She's not mine. She's the Guide. He broke off the kiss before she had to pretend to enjoy it. "I'm sorry." Snatching his hand away, he hung his head.

"You—" Her voice cracked. She cleared her throat and tried again, restraining herself from wiping her mouth. "You're forgiven. But you should go now."

"Yes. Yes, I should." He slid off the bed and crept to the window. Gripping the sill, he paused and looked over his shoulder. "The Sleeper will wake and devour from below. There will be no escape for those closest. When the time comes, take your children and flee. Run as fast and as far as you can on the white horse. Don't leave them behind, Sorgeia. Hold them close or their doom will be worse than your nightmares."

Chavali watched him slip out through the window. The pane clanked shut after him. She gathered the blankets and fled for the darkest corner of the room. Huddling there, she waited for her body to stop shaking. Shance could have slit her throat. Anyone could have crept in and killed her. Robin could have stolen her in the night and no one would know. Shance wanted to—

She couldn't stop shivering. Gathering the blankets around herself, she lurched to her feet and flung the door open. Colby had the room across from hers, so she only had to take three more steps before pounding on his door. Unstoppable tears coursed down her cheeks. Too many things had happened in too short a time, and the chest she locked them inside refused to shut one more time today.

When Colby didn't answer right away, she conjured images of him lying on his bed with his throat slit. Karias would know. Besides, he'd been resting all day. He could protect her for the rest of the night. She ran to the stable and fumbled with the latches until she yanked his stall door shut and threw herself at the horse lying in the straw.

What happened? Sleep frayed the edges of his thoughts, reassuring her Colby still lived.

She leaned against him and held the blanket tight, sobbing hysterically. He curled around her, offering a protective cocoon, and thinking of vague, soothing comfort. Much later, she fell asleep again.

Chapter 49

Creaking hinges woke Chavali to a warm world of horse and straw. She blinked and looked up in the early morning light at an older man in tall boots, carrying a bucket. He started when he saw her and stared.

"Um. Excuse me, ma'am. Was there a problem with your room?"

Don't panic. He's here to feed me. This is the inn's stablemaster.

Chavali hesitated, then shook her head. Until she knew if the window had a lock she'd failed to check, she had no reason to complain about a break-in. "I had a nightmare. This horse's owner is here with me."

It must've been one awful nightmare.

"Please, take care of your chores. Don't let me throw your schedule apart."

The stablemaster bobbed his head and dumped his bucket into Karias's feed bin. "I hope your day goes better than your night, ma'am."

"Thank you. Good day to you as well." He backed out and closed the stall door.

Are you going to tell me what happened or rush off to face the day?

"Someone broke into my room."

Why didn't you go to Colby?

"I did. He slept through me pounding on his door. We were all so tired, I'm not surprised. We went straight from one raid to another. Three different places. We found the treasonous inspectors, located the statue, and freed the princess. So many people died last night." She rubbed her face.

Which thing was the one that sent you to me in that state?

"All of them." Chavali leaned against his side and petted his nose. "I miss Harris. He was annoying and stupid, but also surprisingly loyal and a friend. Something happened with the spirits that scares me, and I think Robin will be here soon, if he isn't already. And this man in my room last night."

Too much at once. Tell me whatever you can about the spirits and the intruder. Are they connected?

"I doubt it." She had no idea how to explain what happened with Jeric and Keino. "One of my clan managed to...he crossed into a man I wished to question. Possessed him. When I convinced him to leave the body, the man died. He was..."

Someone you cared about in life.

"Yes."

Which is plenty to upset a person on its own. But you're not just anyone, so you set it aside and soldiered on. I imagine you endured several other, smaller things all day and night until your intruder?

"We dealt with the mercenaries who attacked Harris's caravan."

She shuddered with the memory. "I saw how he died. It was wretched. The monster who tried to get him to talk is dead now. But I saw it through his eyes. He considered it fun. Now I have this memory in full color and I cannot unsee it."

Time will blunt it. You know that better than most, I suspect. Tell me about the intruder.

She rested her forehead against Karias's flank, letting his scent steady her. The scent of horse reminded her of clan. "This man, he was in my room when I woke from a nightmare. He sat on my bed and watched me sleep. He thinks I am some kind of prophet and he struggled not to touch me. I wish to scrub him off my skin."

How will we find him to keep him from doing that again?

Karias's no-nonsense, pragmatic leap to hunting Shance down and dealing with him soothed her more than any assurances of safety could have. "He's the leader of The Drowned Ones. He dosed me with Blue Death before, and now believes my reaction to it makes me the Guide to Lost Paths, whatever this means. He spoke of fire and flood, and plans to somehow show everyone in the city how brilliant or how right he is. Something like this. He's the sanest madman I've ever met. A zealot."

What do you think he'd show everyone? How would he do that? Think about who he is and what he stands for. You saw his thoughts, I gather, and listened to him blather. He told you more than you think, because you were upset at the time. Let the cool, rational Chavali take over now and see what she has to say.

Chavali stuck her tongue out at him, but she replayed the incident in her mind, focusing on his choice of words. "He's been dosing people to try to find me, because it was foretold to him somehow that a woman would have the reactions I had. He said I survived when the veil was lifted. By which he meant when I had the Blue Death."

Is it possible he means to try to dose the entire city with Blue Death somehow? If that's what he thinks it does, it sounds like that would "show" people something.

She opened her mouth to scoff at such a ridiculous idea. Then she closed it. The Blue Death was the primary tool in his arsenal. His gang thrived more because he always knew what was coming than from skill or brute force. "But how would he dose so many people? He dropped it personally into my tea. He cannot do that for everyone in a short period of time. It would take months. He said he'd do it tonight."

I don't know. You should bring this up with the others. They'll have more ideas.

"They have decided to fear me for what happened with the prisoner last night."

You've decided to fear you for what happened. They're following your lead. Wash up and walk into breakfast with your head high and confident. Tell them you were tired and hurt last night, and after a good night's rest you know it won't happen again. Unless that would be a complete lie, in which case you should avoid the subject. I hear you're good at that.

The mischief in his tone made the corners of her mouth quirk up. "That would not be a complete lie. Until I can speak with Railan, it may also not be the complete truth."

Then it's probably best to keep your hands to yourself for a while.

Chavali snorted. She scratched behind his ears, which made him blissfully happy. "Thank you. For being here."

I'm glad I can help. This is still the most boring mission ever. Also, you should go. Colby's waking up.

"I will try to convince him that he needs to ride you across town at some point today." She stood and wrapped the blanket around her shoulders. "I look forward to the opportunity to tell you the long version of what happened yesterday."

Karias whickered and stuck his head in his food bucket.

Chapter 50

"I think we should go directly to the queen to get the statue back," Portia said.

Chavali sat with her back straight and head high, sipping tea. She'd bathed and dressed, taking her time and carefully setting aside everything she felt about what had happened yesterday and last night. Once she took a small bite of her eggs and sausages, her stomach demanded more and she devoured the meal at speed. She now poked at a bowl of fruit, brought when the initial plate failed to satisfy her.

"Between us," Chavali said, "we could probably convince her. I still don't understand Warren's motivations, though. If we knew that, we would know how to find him and end this properly." She had yet to determine how to present her information about Shance without discussing the fact he'd been in her room. Beyond that, him dosing the city with Blue Death technically had no bearing on their mission.

"His behavior is so erratic," Sivry said. "I don't think we're going to understand it."

"There is a real possibility we face two different people here.

Warren on the one hand and someone impersonating Warren on the other. And we cannot rule out mind control of some kind."

"It struck me," Portia said, "that Ambrye said he's not a mage and Denton said he didn't have an accomplice with him at Finley's."

Colby had yet to speak to or look at Chavali this morning. He kept his attention on his plate and ate methodically. She wondered if he tasted anything and if her rejection of him last night had something to do with this. She already knew Karias couldn't communicate much with him, so he had no idea about the things she told the horse. He also shouldn't be aware she slept in the stable.

"Could he be a mage without his highly-observant, inspector sister noticing?" Sivry asked. "She didn't notice Reynolds or Kalei."

"Going back to the prophecy," Chavali said, waving a chunk of melon speared on her fork, "there *is* supposed to be a traitor in the royal house and one of them is supposed to die. It also predicts water and fire. It does not seem Ambrye was genuinely in danger during her time with the Bloodflies, so this has not happened yet. We've certainly seen plenty of fire, but no water, unless you count Portia's unfortunate relationship with travel over it."

"Water!" Colby snapped his fingers. "That flow map we found in The Drowned Ones raid—it could be a water distribution system map, and if it is, it's got to be for Harbor City. Why would they have that?"

Chavali froze with the bite of melon halfway to her mouth. Everything Shance said clicked together. "They intend to dose the city with Blue Death by dropping it into the water system. This is a perfect way to get it into many people at once."

Colby blinked at her. Sivry stared thoughtfully at the wall. Portia nodded. "That makes perfect sense, especially with all their rebirth and revolution stuff. Of course they'd do that. But why haven't they done it already?"

Groping for some reason beyond the one involving her intruder, Chavali stuck the melon in her mouth and chewed.

"The queen's birthday celebration is today," Sivry said. "There's probably a city-wide party we haven't paid attention to because we've been chasing gang members and mercenaries all over the place since we got back yesterday morning. I bet they'll do it while everyone is partying, expecting security to be lighter than usual on the water system."

"Especially with how many Watch were killed recently," Chavali said with a sigh. She didn't want to appear grateful for this alternate explanation.

Portia flicked her gaze to Chavali. "I hate to be the one to ask this, but is that our problem? I know it sounds bad, and a lot of people will probably die. We could just tell Denton our suspicion and leave it. The statue is our mission, which means focusing on Warren. This water supply issue is a big deal, but it has nothing to do with the statue."

Colby sighed and shook his head. "You already know what I think. But let me add a reason you'll appreciate instead of trying to appeal to your sense of decency." He spat the last word, making it clear he suspected none could be found around this table. "Denton is going to have her hands full already. Whether Warren makes a play for the statue or not, the queen won't be able to deny giving it to us after we save the entire city."

"Agreed." Chavali waved for their waitress. When the woman arrived, she asked, "Tell us, when does the celebration begin? We have heard some about it, but few details."

The waitress smiled. "Two hours after midday, there's a parade through the city. It winds its way through several neighborhoods with music and entertainers, ending at the palace. Even where the parade doesn't go, people pour into the streets. They dance and sing and tell stories. At dusk, everyone raises a toast to the queen, no matter where they are. Then there's feasting. You have to get invited to go to the palace feast, but we'll be open."

"Interesting. What do people toast the queen with here?"

"There's a special mix you add to water. It has four ingredients, one for each season we've lived through since the last celebration. The queen chooses different ingredients every year, and the palace sells the mix for a few days before the celebration. Something about they way they create the mix makes it taste best for only a short time after you add the water, so we mix it on demand."

"Thank you," Chavali said. "That's a fascinating custom."

The waitress bobbed her head and walked away.

"Shance could contaminate the water anytime," Portia said. "People drink water every day. Why choose a celebration?"

"He wants everyone to be dosed around the same time," Sivry said. "I think we've established he's a lunatic."

"This means we have some time to discover where that arrow is on the map and deal with The Drowned Ones, but not much. Odds are good we will have to travel a fair distance."

Chapter 51

"Are you sure?" Denton huffed and passed a folder off to a clerk. "That sounds like a crazy plan."

"It fits all the facts," Colby said. "We don't know if Warren is involved with it, but I remember that he said something about people drowning in flames. Since it seems he and Reynolds framed The Drowned Ones for Ambrye's abduction, it's plausible Warren is at least aware something will happen tonight. He may be planning to use what he expects to be chaos to cover his attempt to murder the queen."

"There's only one tiny flaw in your plan," Denton said. "The palace is served by its own, private spring. The rest of the city gets its water from the river. It was set up that way to prevent the royal family and government from being victimized by exactly this type of scenario. There's an intake for the city on the northeast side with its own Watch post. Assuming they get in, none of that will have any effect on the palace."

"Warren may know nothing more than the timing," Chavali said. "Even if he knows some details, he could be counting on general chaos to make an assassination simpler."

Denton rubbed her face. "Alright. I'll get you a key for the intake site. You bring me proof you stopped something there and I'll get that statue for you whether Inspector Ambrye wants to hand it over or not."

"May we also borrow horses?" Chavali asked.

"Yes, that's fine." Denton walked away, muttering about palace security.

"Horses?"

Chavali flashed Colby a grin. "It would be a shame if we arrived too late for lack of transport. The city is quite large, after all."

"You're an awful rider, but it sounds like haste is a good idea. Maybe we'll get lucky and arrive before them."

"Two horses, then," Sivry said. "Portia and I will get the key and meet you at the inn." She looped her arm through Portia's and they both followed in Denton's wake.

Colby watched them go, suspicion tugging the corners of his mouth down. Chavali shrugged and hurried out to commandeer a carriage. They needed to move faster than her legs could manage. Colby shut the door after telling the driver to hurry and sat across from Chavali, his arms crossed over his chest.

"That felt planned."

"It was not."

Colby stared at her in disbelief.

Chavali shrugged.

"Tell me what happened with Jeric."

Leaning back in the seat, Chavali sighed. "I cannot."

"You *will* not. There's a difference. Clan this, clan that." He rubbed his face, rasping the dark stubble he hadn't bothered to shave off this morning. "Chavali, I'm afraid of you. I don't want to be afraid of you. Please, explain what happened and why it won't happen again."

Hearing him confirm her suspicions hurt. "It's too complicated to explain. You have to trust me that there is nothing to fear."

"Then why are you afraid of yourself?"

"I'm not!" She snapped her jaws shut and looked away. "The things I fear...you're not clan. I cannot speak of these things to you. I have explained, more than once, why this is, and you agreed to honor it. Don't press. Leave it alone. What happened to Jeric will not happen to you."

He watched her in silence for so long she wanted to squirm. "What would it take to become a member of your clan?"

"What?" She stared at him, blindsided by the question.

"Is there any chance you'd add me to your clan?"

Searching his face, his shoulders, and his hands, she saw no sign he meant the question as a joke or distraction. "Why would you ask that?"

"Biholtz already treats me like an uncle, and so do Danel and Haizea. Marcus acts like I'm his son. But more importantly, you've helped me in ways I never thought I'd need, doing something I can't do for myself. I want to return that favor. Every time I try, you invoke clan and stop talking. If selling my soul to your clan is the only way I can do anything that will come close to evening this debt, then I'd appreciate you telling me if it's possible or not."

Chavali knew her father would have appreciated Colby's reasons. Papá always liked those who wished to pay what they owed. She smirked. "It's not selling your soul. But it is learning a new language, obeying your

Seer, and keeping our secrets. There is always a price to be paid for whatever you gain."

"Obeying the Seer." He relaxed and echoed her smirk. "I doubt I'd be very good at that."

"Yes, this probably disqualifies you."

He chuckled. "Can we discuss this at home? Or do I need to drop it completely?"

She saw the inn, mid-morning sunshine glinting off its front windows. "I will consider your request and we will speak more when there is time and privacy. If you still wish to pursue it, the entire clan must approve. Including me." Part of that process would mean consulting with Karias. The binding into her clan might affect him in unexpected ways and the horse-spirit had the right to know and object.

The carriage stopped and she fled the carriage, eager for warm light to chase her fears and confusion away. Her mind whirled around the idea of adding Colby to the clan. From spending so much time in his memories, she knew him well enough to say he'd be an asset. But with him as clan, someone morally opposed to lying would have access to their knowledge. She'd have to explain the spirits.

While she stood back, Colby released and saddled his massive horse. Karias watched Chavali and she knew he wanted her to touch him. She hesitated, expecting to be chastised, then rubbed his nose while Colby tightened buckles.

Did you tell him about your intruder?

Instead of speaking, she shook her head.

Good. It'd be too much for him to unpack right now. Where are we going? Will it be exciting? Interesting? Full of pastries?

Chavali grinned. "May this trip across town be less interesting than we expect."

"That would be a pleasant surprise." Colby led Karias outside and to the street. Portia and Sivry clopped toward them on dark horses. He climbed into the saddle and pulled on heavy gloves before offering Chavali a hand up.

She settled in front of him and patted Karias's neck. "We're only hoping to thwart a plan to contaminate the city's water supply with a strange, hallucinogenic drug prior to the city-wide party this evening. How could anything go wrong?"

I see. Have I told you recently how much I appreciate your efforts to keep my secrets for me?

Colby snorted and picked up the reins on either side of Chavali. "Karias, we're headed northeast. To the river."

Chapter 52

Harbor City dwindled to a few small houses perched on the water's edge. The group followed a narrow road in the warm midday sunshine, headed north. They crossed over an enormous land bridge to the other bank. The road curled around the base of the bridge and brought them into a square tunnel. Iron bars ran from ground to ceiling and wall to wall, barring passage except for the gate standing open with two dead bodies on the ground.

Everyone dismounted. Colby and Portia rushed inside to check the immediate area while Sivry and Chavali tied up the two horses. Karias waited with them until Chavali stepped to the gate and crouched beside the uniformed guards, both killed by several crossbow bolts. She pushed one man's eyes shut, then touched his forehead.

"They didn't guard this place very well," Sivry said.

Portia stepped out of the nearby guard shack. "There are two more inside. Looks like they put up a fight. Probably overwhelmed."

Colby returned from delving deeper into the tunnel. "It turns and there's a door standing open."

"It seems safe to say they're here." Chavali stood and wiped her hand on her skirt. She had a feeling this dress would fare no better than yesterday's had. "This body is cold, but not very. They haven't been here for long. We should hurry."

Colby led the way as they jogged through the tunnel. Karias had to lower his head to trot through, and he stayed in the rear. They passed through an open door into a wide passage with a catwalk suspended over rushing water. Water sloshed into the cave and split, half diverted by a stone culvert to the city, half allowed to continue to the lake.

The spirits buzzed in Chavali's ears. Their angry whispers should have been drowned out by the roaring and splashing of the water below. She resisted the urge to swat at the air around her head and made fists instead. Karias nudged her, reminding her about his presence. She took a deep breath. They'd charged into worse and come out fine.

The catwalk ended in stairs taking them down to a stone landing overlooking the river. Chavali didn't see the two robed men until Colby charged at them. She barely heard the sound of their swords clashing over the water. She crouched and waited, trusting the other three to handle two Drowned Ones.

Peering over the side, she noticed a man in coveralls dangling from the edge of the landing, barely visible in the dim light. As soon as Portia knocked one cultist off his feet with magic and Colby chopped the other in half, Chavali rushed to help the man. She snatched his arm and he gripped hers. Sivry dropped to her knees and took his other arm. They pulled him over the edge, back onto solid ground.

"Thank the Creator for you," the man gasped. "I thought I'd fall in for sure. I work here. These people, they came in and threw people in the water to be killed by the purifiers. I don't know who they are."

"How long were you there?"

He rubbed his arms. "A quarter of an hour, maybe?"

"Did they have crates or boxes?"

"No, ma'am. Two of them had small backpacks. All of them had weapons. That's it. I didn't see anything else."

Chavali frowned. She couldn't quite see the cultists' plan, but thought of another question to ask. "How does this place work? What is the last thing that happens before the water is split into pipes for the city?"

"It goes through an enchanted filter membrane."

"Is there access to the water after this membrane but before the splitting?"

He scratched his head. "I don't know. Maybe? I don't work on that side."

"Go, the way back is clear. They left no other guards." Chavali accepted his thanks, then watched him flee across the catwalk. "They didn't bring the drug with them."

"They know how to make it on the fly," Portia said. "They're not going to drop the stuff into the water, they're going to change the water into Blue Death. And no one will notice because of the special mix they're dumping in for the party."

"There must be some kind of access on the other side of the membrane. They would not want to risk the filter undoing their efforts. Or they may be planning to disable or destroy the filter."

"One way to find out." Colby hauled the next door open and led them through it.

337

The noise lowered, reduced to mechanical humming and errant splashing. Another metal catwalk, this one wide enough to cover the entire cavernous chamber, suspended them above a series of pools glowing with reflected magical lights. At one end, water rushed in and swirled into the first pool, thick with foam. Metal arms churned, slowing the water through pool after pool, gradually changing its color from light to dark, until it reached the last and funneled out through a pipe as wide as Karias.

Colby charged across the expanse, Sivry and Karias on his heels. Chavali followed Portia, not seeing the enemy until Colby and Karias crashed into five robed people. Portia traced an arc in the air with two fingers and pointed. Magic coalesced into a dart at her fingertips and slammed into a cultist, knocking him off his feet. Sivry dashed in behind the horse, cutting another down.

By the time Chavali reached them, every cultist lay dead on the metal floor. The fight had been too swift for prisoners. Someone to question would have been useful, but they'd make do without.

As Colby took the lead out of the room, Chavali slowed and scanned the cavern. Something seemed off about an irregular curve on the other side. Though she risked losing the group, she knew they'd follow a straight line until they found the cultists and make plenty of noise fighting them.

Halfway across the room, she realized that odd shape was a person. Dagger ready, she ran to engage them. The man stood, his eyes wide and hands raised. His uniform marked him as a worker. Chavali slowed and sheathed her dagger, showing she meant them no harm.

"I am helping the Watch," she said as she neared them. "Are you injured?"

The worker relaxed with relief. "You're here to stop them." Another worker stepped into sight, also relieved.

"Yes. Can you tell me where is the filter membrane, and how can we reach the other side fastest? And do you know if there is access past the filter?"

He nodded. "Yes, ma'am. There's a hatch just beyond the filter, for repair purposes. There's a maintenance tunnel back here that'll take you straight there. Don't touch anything moving." The two workers showed her a door around the corner. "We fled the filtration room when they got there and locked it so they couldn't follow this way."

Chavali turned to get everyone to come this way, but they'd gone on without her. Despite the relative quiet, they must have gotten too far away before she said anything. She drew her dagger again and took a deep breath. "The way back to the front gate is clear. Unlock this door for me, please. Then go. If any of these people escape, I would not see your corpses because of it."

Both workers nodded and one unlocked it by waving his hand over what had to be a magical sensor. "Good luck, miss. Creator watch over you." They fled.

Holding the door cracked open, Chavali tried not to think about what she would face alone. The others took the long way, but they moved faster and could fight better. With luck, they would all arrive at the same time.

Pulling the door open slowly, she found a dark tunnel, the ceiling too low for her to stand. She eased the door shut and crept past turning gears and pumping pistons. Splashing water, clunking metal, and a low hum reassured her no one would hear whatever small noises she made. The spirits swarmed around her, buzzing loud enough to make her believe they had crossed into this world as a cloud of bugs. Bright light ahead showed her a man standing at the other end, from about his waist down.

Unfamiliar with this type of encounter, Chavali stopped several feet before reaching the man. Beyond him, she saw large pipes and movement without understanding the situation. The spirits prevented her from hearing voices. For all she knew, the cultists had already started whatever ritual would doom the city.

Though she cared little about thousands of random strangers, she cared a great deal about stopping Shance and getting the statue. Besides, it would make Colby happy, a fact she found oddly motivating. He wanted to be clan, of course, and she valued him as a trusted friend, as well as wanting to keep Karias in her life. This explained everything.

She took another deep breath in a long chain of many and sprang for the man at the tunnel mouth. This leap proved disastrous as, though she sank her dagger into the small of his back, she tumbled forward with him and they fell down a flight of stairs she didn't expect. He cushioned her bumpy ride, at least.

Shaking her head to clear it as she yanked out her dagger, she saw she'd landed at the feet of several cultists. She tried to scramble away and wave her bloody dagger to fend them off. When she hit the legs of another cultist, she froze. A woman punched her in the face, knocking her to her side. Someone kicked her in the gut. Someone else knocked her dagger away.

Two men grabbed her arms and hauled her to her feet. Someone covered her mouth to keep her quiet. She saw a tall woman perched on the edge of a giant pipe, just past a square frame vibrating with energy. Beside her, a round hatch stood open.

This woman didn't fit here. Her hair was too dark and her skin tone wrong for North Cascain. The lines of her profile and the slope of her shoulders...

The woman looked straight at Chavali and her strangely familiar face fell with wretched, awful disappointment. That face belonged to a Blaukenev. In her dream, when Chavali had seen the women she knew all looked like Istal, this was the face they wore. The moment slowed as she tried to understand.

Her head exploded with pain. Chavali screamed into the cultist's arm. Rippling columns of smoke appeared all around the cultists. Dead clansmen and women stepped out of them, glaring at her and provoking no reaction from the cultists.

At once, every clan spirit—or whatever word truly fit—shouted at her. Their words tangled into incomprehensible cacophony and they stalked toward her. Cultists snapped their heads around and charged away. The woman on the pipe stuck her hands inside it. Her lips moved with words too soft for Chavali to hear over the shouting and fighting.

Chavali struggled against her captors, frantic to get away from the spirits. Why did they stand against her? She'd never abused them or done anything against them. Robin had, but they could hardly blame her for that. The agony in her head intensified and she screamed again, fighting against it to free herself. Panic took over. She squirmed and twisted. Her captors let go and she fell to the floor. The nearest spirit shoved a spear into Chavali's side, sending a spike of agony through her. She screamed again, her voice already rough and cracking.

They still shouted. Chavali writhed on the floor, unable to get up, unable to flee, unable to fight. Another spear pinned her foot to the floor. She caught sight of a magical dart hitting the clan woman in the chest, knocking her off the pipe. Sivry leaped onto the pipe and kicked the access door shut.

A clansman grabbed Chavali by the hair and yanked her to her feet. He and another clansman threw her across the catwalk, sending her crashing into a knot of cultists fighting against Colby and Karias. She collapsed at their feet and her body bowed as a clan sword swept through her leg. Her mouth opened but only a hoarse whisper of a scream came out.

The fight raged around her. She lay on the metal floor, gasping for breath and too weak to stop herself from twitching. Another Blaukenev kicked her in the face.

Chapter 53

Wake up, Chavali. I don't understand what happened here. You need to wake up and explain it. Please wake up. You look terrible and I'm afraid this is worse than whatever happened with Jeric.

Chavali groaned, aching everywhere, including her throat. She wanted to sleep forever. Someone held her sitting up. Afraid of what she'd see, she kept her eyes shut and listened to Colby's mind.

Thank the Creator you're awake. Drink this. It's clean water, I promise. We stopped them before they got very far. They may have tainted some water, but not much. Definitely not the whole city. We stopped them.

Cool water soothed her throat in small sips.

You bled from your eyes, ears, nose, and mouth. Please be better than fine.

"I will live," Chavali croaked.

Colby wiped her face and neck with a damp cloth. *I'm glad to hear that.*

Someone nearby coughed, the sound wet and ugly. "You may

have stopped us here, but it doesn't matter," he spat. "We've still won."

Chavali reached a hand toward the voice of a dying man.

Are you sure you want to touch him?

"Yes."

Colby's thoughts disappeared and her fingers found bare skin. The spirits, once again her allies, fed her the cultist's mind. *Shance will prevail at the palace. He has to. In the name of the Guide of Lost Paths, he will succeed.*

She recoiled from him. Opening her eyes, she saw they hadn't left the filtration room. Her body had been propped against Colby's knee. Sivry and Portia stood over several cultist prisoners, tying them up. The nearest had wounds too severe for him to survive much longer. The other eight cultists knelt with their heads hung. Bodies littered the floor.

"Did anyone get away?"

"Yes," Colby nodded, "at least two of them. What happened to you?"

"They aren't done. Shance is at the palace. They know about the spring feeding it."

Colby sighed. "We'll have to go. If we hurry, we can stop them from drinking anything. You're in no shape to help, though."

"Nasha will be there."

He gritted his teeth and surveyed the situation. Chavali watched him think, unable to do so herself. "Portia," Colby said, "can you tie them up well enough to keep them here until the Watch can pick them up?"

"We have enough rope for that, yes. It'll take me a little time, but I can send a tendril of magic through it to make it bind securely enough so no one will escape for the next several hours."

"Get moving," Sivry said. "I'll help her. We'll catch up."

Colby scooped Chavali into his arms. "Ride swift. If we don't get there in time, it may be a madhouse." With that, he turned and jogged away, Karias following behind him. "I swear, Chavali, if you tell me you can't explain this because of clan, I'll leave you here."

"I cannot explain it because I do not understand it. I need to think, but my head hurts too much for this."

"That answer, I can accept." He reached the front gate and clambered onto Karias's back. "To the palace, Karias. As fast as you can." One arm around her, holding her close, he tugged on the reins, signaling he had as good a grip as he could get.

The horse launched into a gallop, carrying them over the land bridge and into the city. Shouting and singing assaulted Chavali's ears and Karias had to slow. He snorted in annoyance and Chavali looked around in horror. The festival had begun. They'd taken too long, and now revelers clogged the streets.

Colby growled in frustration. "We have to get there before the toast."

"Karias will get us there in time." Chavali patted Colby's thigh. "Patience sometimes is the best course. Other times, it can be stupid. Wisdom is knowing the difference."

"That's the strangest thing I've ever heard you say."

She let a giggle burble out. "I am in pain."

Colby left a long pause while Karias picked his way through the mass of people. "Tell me what happened in there."

"My clan tried to kill me." The words tumbled out. She wanted to snatch them out of the air before his ears swallowed them.

He tightened his grip around her waist. "I don't understand."

Casting about for some way to explain without explaining, Chavali covered her eyes and let her fingers brush the base of the feather in her forehead. "Neither do I." That woman had been clan, she knew it. That made no sense. She knew every member of her clan. No one living should be unfamiliar. She'd recognized some of the dead attacking her, but not that woman.

The people of her clan did not leave to strike out on their own for more than a few days. Once, when Chavali was young, Edrigu fought with his father and ran away that night. Two days later, he returned to the clan, still angry but unable to bear the time away from his Seer. Somehow, this one woman left before Chavali was born and never returned. And she happened to be some kind of mage who looked like Istal.

"Did you see the woman on the pipe? The one performing the ritual?"

"I couldn't tell it was a woman, but yes."

"You couldn't tell? How could you possibly not tell?"

"I can't see how you *could* through that dark cloak. I thought it was Shance."

Chavali let her mouth fall open, then snapped it shut. If she saw a Blaukenev on that pipe but no one else did, what did that mean? Did she hallucinate everything in that room? Was she somehow affected by proximity to the Blue Death despite not being dosed with it? How could she explain all the pain? Colby said she'd bled from her eyes and ears. Her mouth and nose made sense, but her eyes? Did the Blue Death cause that?

She opened her eyes to see a woman offering them flowers. Colby took the sprig of small blooms with a friendly smile. She shouted something at them, lost in all the music and singing. Karias pushed past her and wove through a knot of already drunk men.

Colby twirled the flowers in his gloved fingers and sighed. "This celebration feels very wrong right now."

"I would rather dance to my doom than find it any other way."

"After suffering through one of the other options, I suppose I can't fault that opinion." He handed her the flowers. "But let's not start that dance yet."

Chavali smirked. Keino had tried giving her flowers once. The memory felt fuzzy, as if what happened yesterday finally allowed her to put distance between them. "No. Not today. We have other things to do yet." She tucked the flowers behind her ear.

Chapter 54

No matter which side streets Karias chose to take, they found throngs of people. The entire city danced and drank outside as the sun sank to the west. They passed carriages stuck in the madness. One held a couple in the throes of passion, unaware or uncaring the windows had been left uncovered. Another had been turned into a rolling market stall, carrying men selling wood and cloth wands, masks, and other party favors.

As the afternoon slipped by, Harbor City shed its inhibitions. Paper confetti rained from the rooftops and tall windows. In one street, someone juggled live, still-squirming fish. Couples took a step to the side to indulge in each other. Children shrieked and ran freely. Bonfires crackled in the streets. Alcohol flowed. Hands wandered. Chavali had never seen such a spectacle, and she suspected the same for Colby.

They finally reached the front gate for the palace with the sun half-hidden by the horizon. Chavali grinned when she saw who'd pulled guard duty tonight. Mils waved them through the gate.

"Is Denton here?" Colby shouted over the din.

"Inside! On duty!" Mils ran behind Karias as the horse surged up the drive to the front doors.

Though the doors stood open, they saw no one but a handful of guards. "Where is everyone?" Chavali called to Mils.

"Upstairs! Almost time for the toast!"

To Chavali's surprise, Karias galloped straight into the building and up the wide hallway, his hooves clacking against the marble. They'd seen only the front sitting room before and now plunged past it. Two wide, sweeping stairs curved around a landing ahead, and the horse charged up them. They reached the landing in time to see a glittering crowd in velvet, fur, and jewels raising goblets to the queen, who stood on a dais.

Everyone cheered as the sun sank below the horizon, drowning Chavali's scream of warning. They drank while Colby leaped to the floor. He managed to stop two people in the back who'd paused to nod to each other. For everyone else, it was too late.

Chavali scanned the dais and saw the queen, Ambrye, and Bricene. Warren wasn't there. She turned back and saw Mils still running in their wake. "We need to find Prince Warren," she told Karias. As little as she wanted to think now, she needed to. Denton was inside, on duty, but not in the room with all the people. "Down the stairs."

The horse whickered and left Colby behind. Chavali gripped Karias's mane and resolved to spend time learning to ride properly as they vaulted down the stairs. They slid to a stop in front of Mils.

"Where did Ambrye put the statue?" She asked Mils. "I know she brought it here to bait Warren."

Mils stuck his foot into the stirrup. "The vault."

Karias turned his head to glare at the man.

"Let him ride," Chavali snapped.

Using Chavali's thigh to lever himself, Mils hopped up and swung his leg into the saddle like a trained horseman. He snatched up the reins with his arms around Chavali and pulled to the side. "This way. Denton is guarding it personally."

Chavali didn't need to check Karias's thoughts to know how irritated he was. His ears lay flat and his eyes promised murder.

"We're in a hurry," she grumbled.

Karias huffed and launched into a gallop down the hallway. He negotiated a flight of stone stairs down better than she expected with his height and girth.

"Do you often ride horses through buildings?"

"This is my first time."

"Mine too." Mils snapped the reins and Karias plunged down a hallway in the basement. "I thought I told you to wear armor the next time you assault a building."

"I have taken your suggestion under advisement."

They turned down another hallway, then a third. Denton stood at attention by herself at a large metal door. Karias slowed to a walk and stopped in front of her. Leaning and twisting, Chavali checked both angles of approach and frowned.

"This is a little flashier of an entrance than I expected from you, Chastity. Are you stealing my men now?"

Mils hopped down from Karias's back and saluted. "It looked urgent, Captain."

"I don't understand. Warren isn't at the toast. Why is he not here?" Chavali took a deep breath and climbed down. Her limbs protested and her head swam. She leaned against the wall. "How is this vault protected?"

"The palace has a number of wardings to prevent magic from working well," Denton said. "The vault itself has similar protections to Evidence Storage, only more robust. I'm not privy to the specifics. How did things go at the water facility?"

"We arrived in time to stop them from polluting the entire system, but they did it by performing a ritual on the water itself, changing it. Some people here will have a very strange night, but not many. I regret I have no proof to give you, other than bodies and prisoners at the facility itself. As soon as you have a chance, a squad should be dispatched there. I do not know the count of men you lost there. A worker told us the cultists threw people into the water."

Chavali stared past Karias, trying to understand. Where could Warren be if not here? Waiting for the chaos to begin, perhaps, but why? With him in hiding for having blown up Finley's, he shouldn't need a distraction beyond everyone assembling for the toast. He didn't have to sneak away from the festivities after appearing with his family in plain sight.

Denton's mouth went thin. "I'll be glad when you leave my city."

"As will I."

"What are we waiting for, exactly?" Mils asked.

"Prince Warren. He wants the statue."

"Won't he see us all standing here and decide to try another time?"

Chavali blinked at him. "Yes." She beckoned for Karias to step to the side. "We should make the vault appear unguarded." With time to prepare, she felt confident about her ability to create a solid, realistic illusion. She twined her fingers through the spirits and pictured what she wanted. An illusory wall covered the four of them, making the hall appear empty.

"We must be silent now, and wait." She put a hand on Karias's neck, hoping he'd hear Warren coming with enough time to prepare for him.

You and me are going to have a chat about who gets to ride on my back. Oh yes, we are. It'll be a long chat. One full of a number of thoughts that words don't fully encompass. We'll have this chat when Colby isn't around so I can throw you off my back and into a giant mud puddle.

Chavali rolled her eyes and touched her ear, then nodded up the hall.

I'm paying attention, woman. Don't try to distract me with the situation at hand. It won't work. He yanked on my reins, Chavali. He. Yanked. On. My. Reins. He's lucky he wasn't wearing spurs or I'd have launched you both for distance, emergency or no emergency. I don't care how Colby feels— His ears twitched.

In the distance, Chavali heard a muffled explosion. She gripped Denton's shoulder, preventing her from rushing off. If Warren decided to blow up part of the palace, he had to intend it at least partially to provide cover for him to come down here.

Within seconds, a man rounded the corner in a hooded cloak, sword drawn and hurrying up the hall. He threw glances behind his shoulder as if expecting pursuit.

Chavali recognized the cloak, the physique, and the chin. When she went to see Clara, this had been the man leaving. He'd worn the same clothes, which struck her as odd. Even men who relied upon a costume for theatrical villainy usually changed their clothes. Granted, that had been a week ago, but why go to the trouble to mask one's identity only to risk identification by using the same costume?

The man stopped several feet away and pushed his hood back, revealing himself as Prince Warren. He frowned and peered around, turning in a full circle as he stepped closer to the vault door. Finally, he stopped and laughed.

"They didn't even bother guarding it," he muttered. "Idiots." Shaking his head, he dipped his hand in his pocket and retrieved a heavy iron key. He shoved the key into the vault door and wrenched it around. Clunking came from inside the door. He spun the wheel set in the center until it clicked five times, then he pressed his hand to a rectangle set into the door.

When nothing happened, he cursed and twisted the base of his pinky finger. The facade of Warren dissolved, revealing Bricene in the same gown she'd worn on the dais with her mother a few minutes ago. She pressed her hand to the rectangle again and the door clacked.

Chapter 55

Chavali let her jaw fall open and stared in disbelief. This frivolous, idiot girl had fooled her. Completely. She would sooner have suspected the queen, or Ambrye herself.

Bricene hauled the door open. Denton shifted, snapping Chavali out of her stupor. Angry beyond belief, Chavali launched herself at the princess, throwing her fist across the girl's jaw. While she squealed from the pain in her hand and shook it out, Denton and Mils pounced on Bricene, who'd stumbled to the side. Karias blocked any hope of escape.

"I had no idea punching someone hurt so much," Chavali grunted.

Mils pressed a knee to Bricene's back. "Gauntlets. I'm telling you, armor is rarely a bad idea."

Denton tied the girl's wrists. "That was a pretty good illusion."

"Unhand me!" Bricene shrieked.

Mils pressed harder with his knee. "You know what, your highness? You got a lot of people killed. Some of them were friends of mine."

"You're just the Watch," Bricene spat. "That's your job."

He scowled and smacked her head into the stone floor. "Whoops. Slipped. You saw that, right?"

"I saw it, yes," Chavali said. She crouched beside Bricene and laid her hand on the girl's bare shoulder.

Animals. Filthy, stupid animals. Her thoughts ran sluggish and groggy, making this a perfect time to get information.

"Bricene, did you help Reynolds with his plot to take over the city with the Bloodflies?"

That pompous ass served his purpose. Killed him to frame Warren. Thanks to Nasha. "I don't know what you're talking about," she mumbled, her thoughts clearing and speeding up faster than expected. Chavali noted she faked leaving her eyes unfocused in the hopes they'd leave her unguarded long enough to escape.

"Where is Warren?"

Bricene pictured him tied to a chair in a room. She'd intended to release him after murdering her mother and Ambrye while pretending to be him. He'd take the fall and Bricene would take the throne. "I don't know."

"Ease off," Denton said. "She's out of it."

"No, she's not. This is faked weakness. Make sure her bindings are secure." Chavali considered delving into the girl's mind on purpose, but had no desire to learn the depths of her depravity.

Bricene glared up at her and tried to spit in Chavali's face. The gob of saliva hit her skirt. "Who are you?"

"Someone who will not be fooled by you again. Tell us where is this room you have imprisoned your brother in an uncomfortable chair."

How do you know that? No one knows that. "I don't know what you're talking about."

"Bricene. Let me explain. I know you hired Velsin of the Broken Ring to steal the cat statue. I also know you killed Reynolds and blew up Finley's. For these things, I doubt very much you will be allowed to run messages, let alone anything to do with the government of North Cascain. If you wish to create some small sliver of good will, you have nothing left but the location of your brother."

"No one will believe any of you over me," Bricene growled. "A foreigner and two commoners? Ha. You might as well scream in the wind for all it'll matter. Warren did everything. It was all him."

"Good luck getting me to believe that now." Ambrye stood in the hallway with her thin blade, the skirt of her dress neatly torn at her knees. "How did she do it?" Chavali noted she had bare feet and several dots of blood on her shins.

Denton yanked the ring off Bricene's pinky finger and offered it to Ambrye. "It creates an incredibly convincing illusion of Warren."

"Now I know why he seemed so strange. It's fine, Chastity. I can get the location from her. You're free to take the statue now. We don't need it for anything else, and a deal is a deal. If you could avoid riding a horse inside the house again, I'd appreciate that."

Chavali turned and saw the illusion still active with Karias still hidden by it. For once, her illusion had worked better than expected. The horse staying quiet surprised her, but she didn't let it show. "Of course. Thank you, Inspector."

"Denton, if you and this officer could escort Bricene out, I'd appreciate that. I'm going to stay here and make sure Chastity doesn't accidentally wander off with anything she's not entitled to. Don't let her out of your custody unless it's to me."

Denton and Mils nodded and hauled Bricene to her feet, then hustled her down the hall. Chavali stepped inside the vault and found the cat statue, its box long gone, sitting on a shelf. She scanned the carved boxes, jeweled ornaments, and other valuable items with nothing more than curiosity, then stepped out with the statue. She helped Ambrye shut and lock the vault door.

"None of that was even tempting to you," Ambrye said as they walked up the hallway.

"No. I am paid well enough for my tastes." As soon as they turned a corner, Chavali let the hall illusion dissipate. Karias would find a way out.

"You know, when we first met, you feigned a dizzy spell or something of the sort. Now, when we're parting, you're trying to hide weakness. It's funny how things work out. You can lean on me if you'd like. I'll walk you out. You've certainly earned it."

Chavali took the offered arm and avoided skin contact. She had a thought to ask about what happened upstairs, but Colby would tell her. At the top of the stairs, she heard wailing and shouting. They passed elegant people lying on the floor, tied up. A few hugged their knees and rocked. Two bodies lay between the grand staircases, lying in pools of blood.

"That was a shame," Ambrye said with a sad sigh. "No one was able to stop them in time."

"You were unaffected by the Blue Death?"

"No. Denton had briefed me about the water facility. When you and Colby showed up and the crowd drowned out your scream, I guessed what must have happened and was able to stop my mother and Bricene. I should've let Bricene drink, I suppose, but then we would've been arresting Warren after this mess gets sorted out. We'll find Shance eventually. He'll have a harder time now that we know what's going on."

Chavali noticed Colby helping a man sit on a bench. Portia and Sivry also aided nobles under the effects of the drug. They'd join her as soon as they could.

"Is there a place I can sit out of the way while my friends help here? I do not wish to monopolize your time."

"Sure." Ambrye brought her to a lavish sitting room appointed with rich, dark tones.

Seeing something unexpected, Chavali stopped in the doorway.

Ambrye also stopped. "Huh. I guess I didn't remember because we normally only use this room for visiting foreign dignitaries." She escorted Chavali to the false mantel with a dragon statuette, similar in size and style to the cat under Chavali's arm. The dragon's wings were folded against its body and it held its head high and regal.

Chavali held the cat near the dragon and considered the possibilities. "Would it be possible for us to take this one too?"

Ambrye picked it up and tucked it under Chavali's other arm. "Consider it payment for the unexpected boon of saving my brother."

Clopping on the marble made them both turn to the doorway. Karias stuck his head into the room and whickered.

In response to Ambrye's dry look, Chavali shrugged. "Did you expect me to teleport him out?"

The princess laughed.

Chapter 56

Given the late hour, the group elected to stay at the inn and leave in the morning. Chavali stepped into the morning sunshine after a hearty breakfast. Both statues now rested in Karias's saddlebags. Portia and Sivry waited with her for Colby to fetch his horse, all three ready to leave.

"My Queen!" The man who'd seen her spirits as butterflies, still wearing the same dirty clothes, rushed to kneel at her feet with a strange object in his hands. "I've done it. Your scepter." He raised the bizarre creation as an offering. A mass of metal pipe, wrapped wire, broken glass, and crumpled paper, the scepter reminded Chavali of an enthusiastic but untalented child's attempt at art.

She gripped the pipe and found it heavier than her dagger. "You have completed your quest well." Placing a hand on his shoulder, she smiled. "I am pleased to add you to the ranks of my knights."

He took her hand and kissed it. His thoughts swirled, too confusing for her to follow. The poor man's wits remained addled even without the drug. "I am your eternal servant."

"I must return to my castle. Will you stay here and serve me in

Harbor City?"

"Command me, my Queen, my Guide!" He bowed his head in supplication. "I will do anything for you."

She handed the scepter to Sivry, who watched the exchange with amusement. Chavali pulled her necklace out of her dress and bent to show it to the man. "If anyone wearing this ring should ever need help, offer it. Otherwise, I command you to uphold the virtues of honesty, justice and...cleanliness."

He leaned in and kissed the ring. His hair smelled of salt, fish, and dried sweat. "I will be your Harbor City Champion, my Lady."

"Go forth and do good." She watched him bow and scamper away.

"Cleanliness?" Sivry handed the scepter back to her.

"It seemed appropriate. I think his mind was permanently damaged by the drug."

Colby and Karias joined them. They walked to the port, hired a boat, and watched Portia throw up over the bow. Hours later, under midday clouds, they returned to the Fallen tower. By common consent, Portia and Sivry headed for their rooms while Chavali and Colby went to Eldrack's office with both statues.

Eldrack sat behind his desk. Railan sat to the side with her feet up. While Chavali sat, Colby dug the cat statue out of the saddlebags slung over his shoulder and set it on the desk. Eldrack picked it up and examined it. Colby retrieved the dragon statue and handed it to Railan.

"What's this?" Eldrack set the cat aside and took the dragon.

"A birthday present," Chavali said with a smirk. "What do you get the man who has everything? A dragon, of course."

"Chavali, this is nothing to joke about."

Colby chuckled. "There's nothing at all to joke about from this mission. We have to laugh or we'll both punch you in the face."

"I see." Eldrack set the dragon beside the cat. The stone pieces clanked together. All four people in the room sprang back when the dragon pounced on the cat, somehow swallowing it whole despite being only slightly larger. The attack took no longer than a second, leaving them with a single statue of a regal dragon, its wings now flared open.

Chavali stared and had no words. This seemed a fitting end for the mission in some ways. She rubbed a hand over her mouth and took her seat again. She saw Eldrack seemed startled more than surprised, and Railan frowned.

Colby tapped the dragon with a finger and yanked his hand away, but nothing happened. He slid into his seat.

For several long moments, no one said anything. Eldrack and Railan shared a look. Railan moved the dragon to the bookshelf while Eldrack sat.

Watching them, Chavali had a strong feeling neither would answer any questions. Rather than waste time by asking and arguing, she launched into the report.

"In the course of locating the statue, we became embroiled in the abduction of Princess Ambrye, the heir to the throne of North Cascain. At first, we were the prime suspects, then we became the primary investigators. Corruption and treachery marked the entirety of our time there. You are already aware of this drug, the Blue Death. The person responsible for it escaped, so I believe we should be alert for it showing up elsewhere.

"This drug, however, was entirely tangential. The man who killed Harris is dead, along with most of his compatriots who attacked the caravan. If you send a list of the names of the rest of the people killed on that caravan signed by Chastity, the Queen of North Cascain will see their families compensated in some fashion. The villain turned out to be the younger princess, Bricene."

In that moment, Chavali realized she'd missed the opportunity to discover how Bricene learned about the statue. In her weakness after the bizarre clash with her clan at the water facility, she'd forgotten about it. She curled her lip. "We did not discover how she learned of the statue in the first place, but know she had detailed information that could only have come from within the Fallen."

Eldrack laced his fingers on top of his desk, his mouth set in a stony, stern line. "That would've been very useful to know."

"Yes," Chavali said, "as it seems Harris was killed because of it."

Colby tapped his fingers on his thigh, spots of blood still staining his leathers. "Why did you send Harris for a mission like that, anyway?"

Eldrack glanced at Railan.

Railan shrugged and pointed at the dragon statue. "Offhand, I'd say the dragon has devoured and the cat is out of play."

Eldrack nodded and looked to Colby. "This should maybe be for Chavali's ears only."

Colby scowled. "There are too many secrets here."

"That may be, but it concerns her power. If it involved Karias, I'd ask her to leave instead."

His scowl fading, Colby sighed. "I'll see you later. Make sure you eat." He left the room.

"He's awfully concerned about you," Railan mused.

"Do not change the subject," Chavali snapped.

Eldrack cleared his throat. "When people are revived here, there's a transition period. It can last anywhere from a week to a year. Everyone is different. During this time, the body is technically alive, but the mind isn't ready to accept its return yet. Though you don't remember it, you were awake for months before you truly woke. You walked around, ate, even did some light exercise.

"We've been doing this long enough now to recognize the signs that the mind is returning. At that point, we strapped you down so you wouldn't panic on first waking. All of this works the same for everyone. In your particular case, there was a distinct difference. Starting exactly one month after you were revived, you began telling us prophecies.

"I admit we didn't know what to make of it at first. Kelly wrote everything down. The first few almost seemed to be designed to prove what they were. Simple, easy to verify, and not disastrous to let happen. Once Railan and I figured out what was going on, which probably took longer than it should have, we paid close attention and elected to follow them to the best of our ability.

"The very last thing you told us before you woke up was not to let you know any of this until, and I quote, the dragon has devoured and the cat is out of play."

Chavali expected a punchline, a joke, or some other indication she hadn't been used quite so egregiously. Instead, Eldrack and Railan both studied her. "This is how you knew I would return with Harris. And why you sent him with us to Ket. And, I suspect, the true reason you sent Eliot as our keeper on that circuit?"

"And the reason I sent you and Colby to Harbor City. Along with a host of other things. If you want to read the prophecies for yourself, you can. They're not in the archives. They won't be until well after you die. This is too sensitive to have in the open, even among the Fallen."

At least, Chavali mused, these prophecies hadn't caused her any pain. She'd suffered no headaches from them. If they saved lives, caught killers, or prevented disasters, then she only had to reconcile with the fact she had no memory of them. His last statement, though, brought Chavali back to the mission.

"Bricene knew which caravan, which route, and when. She had an accurate description of the cat and the box. I cannot say she knew it would be Harris or what he looked like, but she knew the plan. There is a traitor in the Fallen, and the Wasting is not taking them. They are passing information, and that information got Harris killed. I saw his death. I questioned the man who did it, and he was brutal. Harris was awake the whole time. And to the end, he gave that man nothing. Harris was tortured to death and he still told them nothing." Remembering it made her eyes itch and her hands shake.

"I'm sorry you had to see that," Railan murmured.

Hating that her tears fell in Eldrack's office, Chavali wiped her face. "I need to speak with Kelly."

"Yes, that's a good idea," Eldrack said. "Whenever you want to examine those prophecies, just ask."

Chavali stood and fled. Kelly would help her with this. That was her job. She'd ease the memory and find a way to help unlock the chest Harris's stolen memories had been shoved into. Tonight, Chavali would bury herself in clan. She'd drink Penny's tea and eat whatever Biholtz made for dessert. She would hold her three children close and sleep. Tomorrow, she would find something fun to do with her clan and forget about torture, murder, and madness.

Epilogue

Robin held his head and wished he could cut it off until the ache behind his eyes passed. That infernal drug had taken a heavy toll on him, opening his gifts so wide he heard too much and saw impossible things. He even thought he saw Chavali, of all people, walking in the palace with Ambrye. The big man helping him had been real, but Chavali had obviously been a hallucination. Like the large white horse and dancing squirrels in the halls.

He obediently swallowed minty tea in the warm cup pressed to his lips. The near-scalding liquid soothed his throat and would hopefully ease his shivering. Two hours ago, some healer came in and pronounced him in withdrawal. According to her, he'd suffered through the worst of it already. In his current condition, that offered little comfort.

"Good thing you came back for the celebration." Lauryn draped a warm cloth over his forehead. Her graying hair hung loose and she seemed to have developed wrinkles since he last saw her.

"My timing was impeccable, as always." He let her force more tea on him and smiled at her. "Am I allowed to know what happened, or is it a state secret?"

"I don't know many of the details yet. With so many dignitaries laid low by that despicable drug and several dead, everyone has their hands full trying to avoid diplomatic incidents. Ambrye will get to the bottom of it eventually. For now, all I know is Bricene was using illusion magic to frame Warren for a plot against both Ambrye and myself." She sighed and straightened the velvet blanket across his chest. "Ambrye said she'd deal with Bricene as soon as everyone is through the worst of the drug's aftereffects. I'm still in shock my daughter abducted her own sister and corrupted an inspector."

Robin couldn't help but be pleased with Ambrye. The girl had lived up to her reputation and foiled the assassination plot he'd put into motion without him leaving even a single clue. Bricene had, no doubt, bungled it all on her own by doing something stupid. When he reported back on the mission, they'd accept his explanation. He touched Lauryn's cheek. This enchanting woman, ten years his senior, was worth any punishment they chose to inflict on him for his failure. "I'm sorry I wasn't here for you."

Lauryn took his hand and kissed his fingers. "I'm sorry you were caught up in this Blue Death nonsense."

"It'll pass." He sighed and wished he could stop all this. What he wouldn't give to steal Lauryn away and do nothing but care for her. But he'd been called to serve the Creator. She had her own calling and duty. In another life, perhaps, nothing would stand between them. In this one, fate had played a cruel joke on them both.

"Hopefully, soon. Are you warm enough?" She fussed with the blanket again.

"I'm fine. You should go." He smiled at her. "It's not proper for the queen to spend all her time tending to common Shappan garbage when her guests are suffering."

She snorted. "You're neither common nor garbage."

He tugged her close and kissed her. If she ever found out he'd been sent here to kill her, she'd probably castrate him. For now, he needed to get her out of the room so he could shamble to the basement and deal with Bricene. As soon as Ambrye had a chance, she'd interrogate Bricene and learn everything. He had to prevent that at all costs. Nasha couldn't be allowed to learn anything either.

Lauryn pulled away and sighed. "You're right. I need to go see to my guests and make sure they know I care and feel responsible. Try to rest, Robin."

"As you wish, majesty." He treasured her doting smile.

She adjusted her hair in the mirror on her bedroom wall and straightened her dress. "I'll be back later." She blew him a kiss and left him alone.

He waited until he heard the outer door of the queen's chambers open and shut. When he held up his hand, it barely shook. Tossing the covers aside, he saw he'd been dressed in his pajamas. For this task, he needed proper clothing. He stood with the aid of the wall and staggered to the closet. The enormous room held racks and shelves of gowns, jewelry, and shoes. He ignored all that in favor of the small section with his own clothing.

The act of walking took enough effort to make him pant by the time he reached his back corner. He dressed himself without haste, choosing dark pants and a soft blue vest and jacket to match his eyes.

Bricene needed to believe he had escaped the Blue Death fiasco unscathed.

On the way out, his steps slow and careful, he checked himself in the mirror and saw a tired man staring back at him. He could work with weariness. When he held up his hand again, it still shook, but he could cover that. Taking as swift a pace as he could manage, he clicked open the hidden door for the secret escape passage beside the fireplace and shut it behind him.

Using the wall for support, he took the steps down as fast as he dared. He reached the servants' wing where the passage let out and paused to catch his breath before pushing the small door open and crawling through. From this room used to store extra furniture, he slipped through the hallway unnoticed until he reached the most logical place to find Bricene.

Two guards stood outside the door for a small, windowless bedroom with no other exit. The other rooms along this row had similar features, but this one stood empty most of the time, used as a holding cell for anyone of high breeding who needed to be detained. According to the head butler, it had originally been repurposed from servant's quarters for a noble son caught forcing himself on a servant girl.

Robin paused, uncertain of his abilities. Normally, he could influence two guards at once with minimal effort. In his current condition, he doubted he could handle one. His best bet lay in sticking close to the truth while he continued to recover. Ten minutes might mean a great deal to his capability.

"Gentlemen," Robin said as he approached. "I'd like to speak with her, if I may?"

"Sorry, sir. We have orders to hold her for Princess Ambrye."

"I understand. Her Majesty wished me to convey a message on her behalf, but I suppose it's not terribly important."

The guards glanced at each other. He suspected they each considered a number of facts, not the least of which being the possibility Robin could become the Queen's Consort in the future. At that point, he'd have a fair amount of power over the guards.

"Begging your pardon, sir." The guard unlocked the door for Robin and stepped aside.

"We should keep this visit between us, in case it annoys Ambrye."

The guard nodded. "Aye, sir. That sounds sensible."

Pleased the gambit worked, Robin stepped inside the small room. Bricene huddled on the straw-filled mattress in the corner, stripped down to her underclothes. They'd shaved her hair off, which surprised him. Whoever made that decision probably did it to demoralize her. He doubted the queen, an adherent of the Order of Spilled Blood, would have her prepared for execution.

"Bricene."

She raised her head, showing eyes and cheeks puffy and red from crying. When she saw him, she covered her face. "Go away."

"I'm afraid that won't happen. We had a deal, Bricene." He crossed his arms and leaned against the wall. "You failed on your part, and now here we are."

Bricene thumped her fist against the wall. "I almost had it! That wretched woman was waiting for me at the vault. Her and her damned prophecy."

Robin froze. He spent half a minute wrestling his heartbeat back to normal. "What woman was this?"

"Chastity. With the stupid feather in her skull. Who wears a pink feather on their head like that?"

After Ket, he'd thought there might be another one, a sister. To hell with his recovery. Robin crouched and wrapped his fingers around Bricene's neck. He pushed his power into her head and pawed through everything, seeking every interaction with this woman. There, he found her. Bricene had dismissed Chastity, so her memories were thin aside from the one of her capture.

Chastity wore very different clothes and had a different feel than Chavali. That infernal woman had been arrogant and flamboyant, and incapable of harming anyone but herself with a weapon. This woman seemed much more competent and dangerous, and she had friends. The big man who'd helped Robin last night knew her.

Chavali had a twin sister, raised separately or off by herself when he'd found the clan. And somehow, she always turned up to meddle in his plans. Now he knew she had allies.

He released Bricene and covered his mouth to avoid saying anything stupid or showing weakness. Bricene curled into a smaller ball, holding her head and bawling. His intrusion had been neither smooth nor careful. Now Bricene knew what he could do. With him unfit to wipe her memory for now, she needed to die and not leave a corpse to be questioned by Nasha. He could dispose of her inside that secret passage for now and deal with the corpse when he had full use of his faculties.

Seizing on the plan, he let Bricene wail in the corner while he focused and found the minds of the two guards outside the room. He tapped into each mind and pushed them into a waking sleep. They'd notice nothing for the next fifteen minutes. The effort left him shaking and panting. Panic kept him going.

"Shut up," he snapped. "Get on your feet and I'll get you out of here, but you have to keep your mouth shut. Do you understand me?"

Bricene hiccuped and nodded. She scrambled to her feet and covered her mouth. Without further prompting, she followed him out of the room, past the two stupefied guards, and into the secret passage.

He pointed to the floor inside the passage. "If you aren't here when I get back, I will hunt you down and kill you slowly. Do you understand? There's nowhere you can hide from me."

She gulped, eyes wide with horror, and nodded. "I w-won't m-move," she whispered.

Assured her fear would keep her riveted in place, he slipped back into the cell and waited for the guards to emerge from their comas. As soon as they did, he walked out and shut the door, forcing himself to keep his head high and hiding how his hands shook again. "Thank you, gentlemen. I appreciate your discretion, as does the queen."

"Yes sir," the guard responded. "She squealed a bit, sir?"

"Didn't take the message well, I'm afraid. Best to leave her be for a while, I expect." He walked away without a backward glance and found Bricene where he'd left her.

The girl stared up at him, terror holding her in place. "What did you do to me?"

"Nothing important." He shut the door and shooed her up the stairs. At the halfway point, he felt ready to handle her again and gripped her shoulders from behind, provoking a gasp from her. "Bricene, what would you do if Ambrye found you?"

"Say nothing." Her breathless whisper spoke of the threat he'd already made and anticipation of worse to come.

He breathed into her ear. "Do you think that will work?"

"Yes. I can fool her. I swear it. I've done it before and I can do it again."

As he slid his hands up her shoulders to her neck, he reflected on the shape, which reminded him of her mother. In the darkness, he could almost imagine her as Lauryn. But Bricene's skin was too smooth and her muscles too weak. Lauryn had lived a full life. She'd raised children and shepherded a nation. These things left subtle marks, and he loved Lauryn all the more for them. Bricene's death would wound her, but no worse than betrayal already had.

She gulped, bringing him back to the problem at hand. Had he been thinking, he would have brought a knife. Instead, he squeezed her neck with both hands, digging his fingers into her windpipe. Bricene gasped and flailed, strong enough to knock him to the floor. He smashed her head against the wall, knocking her senseless, then resumed choking her to death.

When she stopped breathing, he held on as long as he could to be sure. He checked her pulse and her mouth and nose. Satisfied the job was done, he left her lying on the stairs and returned to Lauryn's bedchamber. Once he'd redressed in his pajamas, he slipped into bed, sipped at his tea, and drifted to sleep.

About the Authors

Lee French lives in Olympia, WA with two kids, two bicycles, and too much stuff. She is an avid gamer and member of the Myth-Weavers online RPG community, where she is known for her fondness for Angry Ninja Squirrels of Doom. In addition to spending too much time there, she also trains year-round for the one-week of glorious madness that is RAGBRAI, has a nice flower garden with one dragon and absolutely no lawn gnomes, and tries in vain every year to grow vegetables that don't get devoured by neighborhood wildlife.

She is an active member of the Northwest Independent Writers Association and the Olympia Area Writers Coop, as well as being one of two Municipal Liaisons for the NaNoWriMo Olympia region and a founding member of Clockwork Dragon Books.

Erik Kort abides in the glorious Pacific Northwest, otherwise known as Mirkwood-Without-The-Giant-Spiders, though the normal spiders often grow too numerous for his comfort. He is defended from all eight-legged threats by his brave and overly tolerant wife, and is mocked by his obligatory writer's cat. When not writing, Erik comforts the elderly, guides youths through vast wildernesses, and smuggles more books into his library of increasingly alarming size.

Thank you for reading! If you enjoyed this book, please consider posting a review wherever you buy your books.

www.tangledskypress.com

www.ingramcontent.com/pod-product-compliance
Lightning Source LLC
Chambersburg PA
CBHW070620260626
47161CB00007B/2517